Hooks Can Be Deceiving

Also available by Betty Hechtman

Crochet Mysteries

On the Hook

Hooking for Trouble

Seams Like Murder

Knot Guilty

For Better or Worsted

If Hooks Could Kill

Behind the Seams

You Better Knot Die

A Stitch in Crime

By Hook or By Crook

Dead Men Don't Crochet

Hooked on Murder

Yarn Retreat Mysteries

A Tangled Yarn

Gone With the Wool

Wound Up in Murder

Silence of the Lamb's Wool

Yarn to Go

Hooks Can Be Deceiving

A CROCHET MYSTERY

Betty Hechtman

CROOKED LANE
NEW YORK

This is a work of fiction. All of the names, characters, organizations, places and events portrayed in this novel are either products of the author's imagination or are used fictitiously. Any resemblance to real or actual events, locales, or persons, living or dead, is entirely coincidental.

PUBLISHER'S NOTE: The recipes contained in this book are to be followed exactly as written. The publisher is not responsible for your specific health or allergy needs that may require medical supervision. The publisher is not responsible for any adverse reaction to the recipes contained in this book.

Published in the United States by Crooked Lane Books, an imprint of The Quick Brown Fox & Company LLC.

Crooked Lane Books and its logo are trademarks of The Quick Brown Fox & Company LLC.

Library of Congress Catalog-in-Publication data available upon request.

ISBN (hardcover): 978-1-68331-884-2
ISBN (ePub): 978-1-68331-885-9
ISBN (ePDF): 978-1-68331-886-6

Cover illustration by Jesse Reisch
Book design by Jennifer Canzone

Printed in the United States.

www.crookedlanebooks.com

Crooked Lane Books
34 West 27th St., 10th Floor
New York, NY 10001

First Edition: December 2018

10 9 8 7 6 5 4 3 2 1

Acknowledgments

I had a lot of fun writing this book. I am grateful for the invaluable help from my editor, Faith Black Ross. Jenny Chen is the best. It was her idea to add the cat to the cover in honor of my late great cat Rocky, who was appears in the book as Mr. Kitty.

The art department at Crooked Lane keeps topping themselves with beautiful covers for my books.

Jessica Faust continues to help me navigate the world of publishing. I am eternally grateful to her for the Crochet Series coming to be.

My knit and crochet group offers me friendship, lots of conversation, yarn help, support, and fun on Thursday mornings. I'd be lost without: Rene Biederman, Diane Carver, Terry Cohen, Sonia Flaum, Lily Gillis, Winnie Hinson, Reva Mallon, Elayne Moschin, Charlotte Newman, Diana Shiroyan, Vicki Stotsman, Paul Tesler, and Anne Thomeson. Linda Hopkins will always be with us in spirit.

Roberta Martia remains my staunchest cheerleader. There are so many people who have helped me on my literary journey. My writers' group has long ago disbanded and the members scattered, some to the Great Beyond, but I will never stop being grateful to Joan Jones, Linda Bruhns, Jan Gonder, and Jack Warford for all their support, encouragement, and help with commas.

Jakey has brought a whole new dimension to my life. I wonder what he'll think when he gets a little older and finds out his grandmother writes murder mysteries.

And thanks to the rest of my family, Burl, Max, and Sam, for keeping life interesting.

Chapter One

Exciting news is supposed to be good, right? Then why did I feel such trepidation when Mrs. Shedd called us into her office?

Adele Abrams, or Adele Abrams Humphries as she wanted to be called now that she'd married Eric Humphries, didn't share my concern and pushed ahead of me to get into the office of Shedd & Royal Books and More, where we both worked. I followed with my fingers crossed that this bad feeling would seem silly as soon as I heard whatever the news was.

Despite her telling me that I could call her Pamela, I couldn't bring myself to call the woman standing in front of me anything but Mrs. Shedd, which was even more laughable now that she had married her partner in the bookstore, Joshua Royal, and officially her name wasn't even Mrs. Shedd anymore. She had briefly considered going by Pamela Shedd Royal but quickly decided that it would make things more confusing and so continued on with just one last name.

I pulled the door shut behind me and looked at my two

bosses with their back-to-back desks. Mrs. Shedd was sixty-something with a methodical manner and silky blonde hair that didn't have a single gray strand. Joshua Royal was about the same age but wore it differently. There were plenty of gray streaks in his shaggy dark hair, but he always seemed up for an adventure.

"Well," I said, ready to face whatever it was.

"Pamela will tell you all about it," Mr. Royal said, smiling as he gave her the floor.

Mrs. Shedd seemed barely able to contain herself. "It's so wonderful. A dream come true as a way to promote the bookstore and get paid a nice chunk of change too," she said. She was always on the lookout for ways to draw in customers. She took in her breath and sat a little taller. "We've been contacted by the Craftee Channel," she began. "They're starting a new program called *Creating With Crochet*, and they want to film the premiere show here in our yarn department. It's all happening very quickly—they want to tape the show here two weeks from this Friday. They had another venue, but something happened and it fell through. We absolutely don't want that to happen here." She turned her attention to me. "Molly, you'll be their contact."

And that's when I knew I was right about the trouble.

Adele's head snapped to attention. "Why is Pink the contact? It should be me." She looked at our bosses. "You do remember I did a guest shot on one of Craftee's shows, *What's Up With Crafts*." Mrs. Shedd put her hand to her forehead and looked to Mr. Royal as Adele went on. "Everybody said I was a standout, and I'm sure they'll want me back for another appearance." Adele turned to me. "And when it comes to crochet, I'm the real expert." She gestured toward her outfit. She was wearing a crocheted tunic in spring green with a ring of pink flowers around the neckline. The same shade of pink was picked up in her beanie. It seemed as though she was going to go on about being more worthy than me, but she suddenly stopped and stared at Mrs. Shedd. "Who's hosting the show?"

"They didn't say," my boss said. She tried to turn her attention back to me, but Adele started muttering to herself something about *that must be it*. Then she shared her thoughts with the rest of us.

"I'm sure they just haven't contacted me yet," Adele said. "Though it does seem rather risky on their part. I mean, for them to assume that I'm available and all." The three of us suddenly avoided looking at her, but that didn't stop her from looking at me. "Pink, did you forget to give me a message?"

I assured her I had not kept any messages from her. Was she really that clueless to think the show wouldn't have locked down a host before now? I might have thought it, but I wasn't about to tell her. Nor would I object to her calling me by my last name instead of Molly as the rest of the world did. I was sure Adele didn't even remember why she'd started doing it, but I did.

After the death of my husband Charlie, as I was trying to start a new chapter in my life, I'd gotten a job at the bookstore. There was no way I could have known at the time, but I got the job as event coordinator that Adele had expected to get. Calling me Pink had been her way of registering her annoyance. Adele had been given the kids' department as a consolation, which hadn't been much of a prize to Adele. She didn't like kids, but it turned out that they really liked all her drama and outrageous outfits. I'd even heard some of them calling her Queen Adele.

By now I'd moved up to become assistant manager and was also in charge of the yarn department. I know it seems weird that a bookstore would sell yarn, but it really grew out of the fact that the Tarzana Hookers met regularly at the bookstore. That's Hookers as in crochet. There was lots of space, and bookstores being on shaky ground these days, Mrs. Shedd was always on the lookout for a new revenue stream, so when a nearby yarn store closed, she'd bought out their stock and the yarn department was born.

Adele was far more proficient at crochet than I was and really more qualified to be in charge of the yarn department—except for one thing. Actually, one rather major thing. Adele had a problem with knitting and people who knit. It was all connected to a nasty stepmother and stepsisters who knitted and taunted Adele about her crochet habit. Even mention the word *knit* and she'd put on a storm-cloud face and give a speech on the superiority of crochet. As I said, Mrs. Shedd was looking for new revenue streams, and she certainly wouldn't want to exclude a whole branch of yarn arts just because Adele didn't like them. Crochet was my preferred craft as well, but I had no problem including knitting books and tools in the department. So it had been given to me. I knew the basics of knitting and made sure there were knitted swatches on the bins of all the yarns we carried.

I think Mrs. Shedd was used to Adele's shenanigans by now. She ignored the hosting nonsense and went back to talking to me. "They want the Hookers to be in it and some drop-in people from the bookstore. I don't know all the craft terms, but the woman I spoke to said something about a 'Make-and-Take.'" My boss looked at me to see if I understood.

"Sure, I know what she means," I said. "They'll have an easy project that's quick enough to make in one sitting and probably have some customers drop in."

"I don't know why you'd want Molly putting that together?" Adele asked, interrupting. Mrs. Shedd looked at her new husband.

Mr. Royal took over. "Adele, this isn't about the creative side of things as much as logistics. I'm sure you'll have a chance to make suggestions."

Pamela Shedd patted Adele's hand, trying to calm her. She had lots of experience dealing with Adele. "It's better to leave it up to Molly. I know how much effort you put into the children's department. We wouldn't want to divide your focus. Story time has become one of our premier draws. It seems like every day someone is telling me how much their children look forward to your productions."

Adele blinked her eyes in surprise. "Really? You think of them as my productions? Well, of course they are. I do put my all into them."

"And I'm sure you probably have some things to do putting together your next story time." Mrs. Shedd looked toward the door. "We wouldn't want to keep you from your important work."

Adele fell for it and got up quickly, saying something about a story-time throne she was creating. Just before she went out the door, she caught my eye. "We can talk about the show later."

Mrs. Shedd let out a sigh when Adele was gone, while Mr. Royal wore an indulgent smile. "She's a handful, but no one does story time like she does."

They seemed to think the problem with Adele was over. I knew better.

* * *

With the meeting done, I went back to the information cubicle that served as my quasi-office. It was set in line with the entrance toward the front of the store. I took a few minutes to process what had just happened. So the Tarzana Hookers were going to get their fifteen minutes of fame.

It was common around here to see film crews using a house or street for a shoot, but this time the location was going to be right here in the bookstore. I wondered if I'd need to have them explain why the group was called the Tarzana Hookers. The Hooker part was obvious, but since, I was sure, it was a national show, not everybody would know that Tarzana was a community in the San Fernando Valley, which had once all been part of a ranch owned by Edgar Rice Burroughs. He'd named the area after his star character, and the ranch had been broken up and subdivided but had kept a certain feeling that was different from the neighboring communities of Encino and Woodland Hills. I liked to think it had a more independent spirit.

I couldn't wait to tell the rest of the Hookers. As the afternoon began to fade, I went back to the yarn department to prepare for our gathering. The group had started meeting for what we called happy hour. Some people sipped wine and nibbled on snacks, but for us it was all about hooks and yarn.

The yarn department was at the back corner of the store. We had a permanent table and chairs on hand for our meetings and also for anyone passing through who wanted to sit for a while and work on a project or try out some new yarn. The back wall was covered in cubbies filled with yarn, and it made for a colorful backdrop. I picked up some stray strands of golden-yellow worsted weight from the table and straightened all the chairs.

"Getting everything shipshape for us?" CeeCee Collins teased when she arrived a little before five. She had kept her midlength brown hair in a similar style over the years, which somehow made it seem like she hadn't changed. She still had the same merry smile and a tinkling sort of laugh.

Up until recently, she'd always been referred to as a veteran actress, which translated to someone people recognized but whose career was over. But then CeeCee had gotten a supporting role in the movie about the vampire who crocheted. Now she was known as an Academy Award nominee thanks to the honor she'd gotten for that role. She was slightly self-absorbed, but none of it had really gone to her head. If anybody recognized her and wanted a photo with her or an autograph, she always obliged. And despite what Adele thought, CeeCee was the real leader of the Hookers.

"You know me. Clean up before the group and clean up after."

My plan was to tell the group about the TV show when they were all together, but I considered giving CeeCee a heads-up on our shot to stardom. I was about to say something when some more people arrived for happy hour. We had a core group that had been together for a long time, and then we had drop-ins.

It seemed to always go the same way. We'd see them hanging around the perimeter of the yarn department and invite them to join us. Sometimes they knew how to crochet, sometimes not, and someone, usually Adele, would give them a lesson. They'd come regularly for a couple of weeks and say how much they loved the group, then disappear, never to be heard from again. The two that had just arrived at the table had actually been coming for three weeks now, which could mean they were going to be a new part of our core group.

I nodded a greeting as they pulled out two chairs. We didn't have assigned seats, but it seemed that people always sat in the same place anyway.

CeeCee gave me a nudge and we traded glances, then both looked at the pale-blue scarf one of the women had taken out. Even from a distance it was obvious that the stitches were uneven and the sides wobbly, as if she had lost and gained stitches as she went along.

"Dear, I know she's trying, but really? Is there anything we can do?"

I shook my head. "It seems more about the experience of being here than making a great scarf."

These two had seemed more or less like our other new recruits at the beginning. They'd hung around the edges of the yarn department, watching us. We didn't just crochet but talked and had a good time, too. We'd invited them to join us, but the one who seemed to be the spokesperson had shaken her head at the suggestion, and they'd backed away. A few more days passed and the two women had finally come up to the table.

"My name is Connie Richards," the one who seemed to do the talking had said, "and she's Marianne Freeman." Connie had looked around the table as if trying to figure out who to direct her comments to. As the bookstore representative, I'd raised my hand in greeting.

"Your group seems really nice, and we were wondering about joining. I don't crochet, but she knows a little," Connie had said. Before I could assure her it wasn't a problem, Adele had popped out of her seat and offered a lesson and some help picking yarn.

The two women had conferred for a moment, and Connie had said something about having to get the okay from Errol.

Whoever Errol was had apparently agreed to let them come back, because they showed up the next day ready to officially join us, and we put them on our roster. Adele gave them a lesson and helped set them up with hooks and yarn. Adele was of the belief that once you knew the basic stitches, it was best to make something instead of just endless swatches. She was the one who found the worsted-weight blue yarn and size J hook for Marianne.

Connie had chosen to make squares for an ongoing project of ours. We would accumulate everyone's squares, and periodically we'd have a get-together and sew some into a blanket, which was then donated to a local shelter. CeeCee had written up the directions for Connie and made a cardboard piece to show the correct size for the square.

From then on, the women had come regularly. Connie talked a little, but it was never personal. Sometimes she'd tell a joke or repeat something she'd read online. I guessed she was in her late twenties, and she was always dressed in jeans and a loose top.

Marianne would greet the group and say good-bye, but that was about all she said. She seemed older than Connie, probably close to forty. She was a pretty woman with wavy dark hair that framed her face, but there was something odd about her expression. She kept narrowing her eyes as if she was trying to focus. And she always carried a bottle of sparkling water, which she drank from continually. I had the feeling that she was wealthy. She dressed rather plainly, but the cut of her clothes made me think they were expensive. And she carried the kind of designer purse where even the knockoffs cost a fortune.

At first we'd wondered about their relationship. They didn't seem like sisters or really friends, either for that matter. Though none of us ever said anything to the others, I was pretty sure we all thought Marianne was struggling with some sort of problem. Then, because they were so quiet, we let them be and any conjecture ended. Nobody said a word about Marianne's wobbly-sided scarf, either.

Actually, it was more that the rest of the Hookers let them be. I kept trying to draw the pair out. It was the busybody in me.

Connie had taken out her hook and a skein of multicolored wool yarn. "I'm starting a new square," she said when I stopped next to her. Marianne was already at work on the scarf and didn't look up until I touched her hand and asked how she was doing.

She appeared startled and then grabbed my hand in some kind of death clutch. It seemed to be her usual reaction, and I was used to it by now. I knew that after a moment she'd realize what she was doing. She muttered, "I'm sorry," and released her grip before looking up at me and managing a small smile. "This is the high point of my day," she said, and though her tone was flat, I felt she really meant it.

"There you are," Dinah Lyons said, coming up to me. She had an aura of exciting energy, wore her short salt-and-pepper hair in a spiky do, favored long scarves wrapped around her neck, and was my best friend. She pulled me into a warm hug and whispered something about us needing to talk that sounded like trouble. But when she released me, she was all smiles as she put her tote down on the table and greeted CeeCee, Connie, and Marianne.

I would have liked to ask Dinah what the problem was,

but she was busy already looking at the square Connie was working on. Even without any details, I was betting it had to do with her newly married state. She and her new husband, Commander Blaine, were both in their fifties, and adjusting to each other's ways hadn't been easy. Like Mrs. Shedd, Dinah had gone through a whole issue about whether to change her name. Dinah taught freshman English at the local community college, and everyone knew her as Mrs. Lyons. Even though *Lyons* had come from her skunky first husband, Jeremy, she was hesitant to drop it or add *Blaine* to it.

The rest of the Hookers filtered in. We certainly weren't a cookie-cutter group. The only thing we all had in common was crochet—well, and the fact that we all liked to get together. Rhoda came in with Elise. They looked as different as night and day. Rhoda Klein had a thick New York accent despite having lived in the Los Angeles area for over twenty years. Her dark hair was cut short in a style that required nothing more than a comb. She stuck with comfortable clothes, and though I never actually saw the waistband of her pants, I was sure they were elastic. She didn't know the meaning of the word *subtle* and always went directly to the point. She'd been the one to ask all the questions about Connie and Marianne's relationship when the two women had first joined us.

Elise Belmont had a windblown, ethereal appearance and a birdlike voice. But it was all a ruse. She had an iron core and a determined personality. She'd gone through a passion for vampires and then moved on to real estate. She had a way of finding an angle to turn a profit. When she'd been into vampires, she'd developed kits to crochet scarves and other accessories in vampire style. Now that she was selling houses with her husband, she'd started placing small colorful afghans in every house they listed, making sure everyone looking at the house knew the afghan was for sale.

She took her usual spot at the table and already had her hook flying through the afghan she was working on before she greeted everyone.

Sheila Altman came in next, from work. She was our youngest member and worked at the lifestyle store down the street. She'd had bouts with anxiety, which our group's friendship and crochet had helped. Though she still had moments when she seemed to be falling apart, she was handling her life much better these days. She made a point of greeting Marianne but seemed uneasy. Sheila never said anything, but I guessed that seeing how difficult it was for Marianne to function frightened her. As if Sheila could see herself in the same spot.

Eduardo came in last. All that was left of his career as a cover model and then spokesperson were his good looks. No more billowy shirts and leather pants; now he wore well-tailored sport jackets and slacks with a collarless shirt. He owned a high-end drug and sundries store in Encino called The Apothecary, and he took off an hour to join us most evenings. He touched Marianne on the shoulder as he passed her and said hello. She flinched and her eyes registered surprise, though it seemed like it was in slow motion. It was the most emotion I'd ever seen her express.

"Now that you're all here, I have something to tell you," I said, taking the floor.

"Wait for me, Pink," Adele said, rushing to the chair at the opposite end of the table from CeeCee.

I gave her a moment to take her seat, and then, in typical Adele style, she upstaged me and told them about the show taping at the bookstore before I could get a word in. She was pretty short on details and then said, "There's probably going to be more exciting news about me to share in the next day or so. I probably shouldn't jinx it, but I suppose I could give you a hint—"

"And they want all the Hookers to be part of the show," I said, cutting in. It was useless to wait for Adele to take a breath, so the only choice was to interrupt. "They want us to host a Make-and-Take event. Isn't that exciting?" I glanced around at the group, and they all nodded. Only Marianne's nod was a beat behind the others.

Adele stood up abruptly. "Sorry I can't stay, but Cutchykins is picking me up." Cutchykins was her pet name for her husband, Eric. She grabbed her things and started to rush to the front of the store.

We all watched her progress and saw her stop suddenly. "Uh-oh," Rhoda said. "It looks like Cutchykins isn't alone." Eric had come into the store with his mother right behind.

"You know, if she stopped calling her Mother Humphries, maybe they'd get along better," Rhoda said.

"Dear, I don't think it's what she calls her mother-in-law

that's the problem," CeeCee said. "The woman doesn't see Adele as the right woman for her son and never misses a chance to tell him so. And the three of them all living in that townhouse." CeeCee put up her hands as we watched the three of them leave the store.

The group seemed quieter without Adele, and everyone went back to working on the projects they'd brought along. I took out the beginnings of the small afghan I was making for my mother using Elise's pattern.

"What's with this yarn?" Connie said in an annoyed voice. She held up the square she was making and showed us all how the strand of yarn she was working with had pulled free from the rest of the skein.

"Give it to me," Rhoda said. As soon as she had the skein in her hands, she tugged at the strand coming off the ball, and after a couple of inches, it broke off as well. "It's defective. You just pull and it frays."

I got up and checked another skein of the same kind of yarn. I pulled out a length, and when I gave it a tug, it came apart, too. "I'll get it out of here," I said, starting to collect matching balls of yarn in a box. When I left the area to take the yarn to the back room, I noticed a man standing at the edge of the yarn department watching the group. I didn't think anything of it, but when he was still there when I returned, I went up to him.

"Can I help you with something?" I said with a wary look.

"I didn't mean to come across like a stalker," he said,

picking up on my reaction. "Michael Kostner." He held out his hand. He was tall and had a pleasant face with stubble that seemed intentional.

"Were you looking for some yarn?" I asked. His face opened into a smile.

"What an ego," he said, rolling his eyes at himself. "To expect that you would know who I am. I'm a producer at the Craftee Channel. *Creating With Crochet* is my current project. I'm local, and I thought I'd stop in and see what the crochet group looked like in action."

I invited him to come closer and introduced him to the group.

"That's crocheted?" he said, sounding incredulous as he looked at the red mohair flower Rhoda was just fastening off.

"I'm going to attach it to this wrap," Rhoda said, laying the flower on the white mohair shawl.

"Impressive," he said, nodding, before he turned his attention to Elise. She wasted no time in telling him that she was in real estate, and I thought she was going to give him her card, but thankfully she just showed him the multicolored afghan she was adding the last row of black edging to. "They're like my trademark," she said. "Every house I list has one on display on the end of a couch. I like to think of them as arm candy. Get it? They're pretty and on the arm of the couch." She chuckled at her own cleverness and didn't seem to notice that no one else joined in.

Sheila was sitting next to Elise and glanced up shyly when Michael's attention moved to her. She was never one to talk herself up. Eduardo stepped in and explained how Sheila mixed shades of blues, greens, and lavender in the different pieces she made. "We think her shawls and scarves have the look of an Impressionist painting, like Monet." Michael leaned closer to get a better view of the scarf Sheila was working on and nodded in agreement.

"You all seem so accomplished," he said as he moved down the table in the direction of our two newest members.

Connie seemed upset as she stared at Rhoda's red flower and then looked down at her half-done square with the frayed strand of yarn hanging off of it. She glanced up at Michael and muttered, "Now I get it." Next to her, Marianne was trying to fold her scarf so the wobbly edges didn't show. I wondered if I should step in and explain that they were just learning.

Thankfully, CeeCee rushed in and distracted Michael so that he glanced over the pair and focused on our actor–slash–crochet leader instead.

"Molly just told us about the program, and we're all very excited to be a part of it," CeeCee said.

Michael beamed at her. "It's always a plus to have a celebrity in the mix. You'll certainly add an exciting touch to the show."

I stepped in and introduced myself, explaining that I was to be the contact for the bookstore.

"Nice to meet you, Molly Pink. My people will be in touch." He glanced around the table for a last time. "I don't want to keep you from your work. Hook on, ladies and gentleman," he said with a twinkle in his eye.

Chapter Two

"Good save," I said to CeeCee. Happy hour had ended and everyone had scattered but the two of us. I hadn't even gotten a chance to find out what it was that Dinah had wanted to talk about before she rushed off.

CeeCee finished the row she was working on and began to fold up the rose-colored scarf she was making. She glanced at where Marianne had been sitting. "I don't know what's going on with her, but I do know that she seems to be trying so hard with that scarf that I couldn't bear the thought of the man from the Craftee Channel giving her a disapproving glance." CeeCee held up her hook and waved it around with a smile. "We Hookers have to look out for each other, dear."

When she left, I cleared the yarn scraps from the table and straightened all the chairs. I stepped back and looked at the yarn department as a whole and tried to imagine how it would look on TV. Then I spent the rest of the evening helping a few customers find books and arranging things in the information booth.

It took me just a few minutes to drive home, and I left the car in the driveway. The Greenmobile, as I called it, was a blue-green 190E Mercedes. Rather than calling it *old*, I preferred *vintage* or *classic*. There was no screen to display the traffic or a clicker to unlock the car. It was strictly put-the-key-in-the-door-and-open-it. No buttons to push to start the ignition either, just the same key.

I could already see my welcoming committee through the glass of my kitchen door as I walked across the stone patio, illuminated by the floodlights along the back of the house. Cosmo, the black mutt, had first position, with Felix, the gray terrier mix, pushing in from the side. The two cats were hanging on the other side of Cosmo, probably planning how they were going to escape when I opened the door. Blondie was nowhere to be seen. I knew she was probably across the house, sitting in her chair. I really should have named the strawberry-blonde terrier mix Greta because she preferred to be alone.

The two dogs started wiggling and yipping as I put my key in the lock. As soon as the door was open a crack, they slipped out and began running around the yard. I rushed inside and pulled the door shut as the black-and-white cat and his purplish-gray cat companion tried to make their move.

"No way," I said, looking down at them. "It's daytime only *and* when I'm out there with you so I can see what you're up to." I tried to make it up to them by offering them each a cat treat. I never knew quite what I was going to come home to. My younger son, Samuel, had moved in and out several times and was on an "in" phase for now. He'd left a note on the kitchen counter saying he'd fed all the animals and taken Blondie for her walk.

I glanced around the living room as I walked through, and everything was in its usual place. That would sound like a given to most people, but most people don't have a mother who's the lead singer of the She La Las. She was enjoying a resurgence in her career and used my living room as a rehearsal hall.

I continued through the den and on to the master suite. A short hall led to a seating area near the closets and bathroom. I went down the two steps to the bedroom, and as expected, Blondie was sitting in the old orange chair with her head resting on the arm. She looked at me as I came in but didn't lift her head.

"Are you sure you're a terrier mix?" I said. She had the looks, with the wiry strawberry-blonde fur, but not the disposition. I'd adopted her right after Charlie died. She'd been a little standoffish when I'd seen her at the shelter, but I'd thought it would all change when I brought her home. It hadn't, and then looking over the paperwork that had come with her, I'd determined she'd been adopted once before and returned. "This is your forever home, no matter what," I had told her.

I didn't go up to her and stroke her head. She didn't like to be petted. She didn't like to cuddle either. She didn't care about food or dog toys. The only thing she got excited about was her nightly walk, and she'd already had that. I coaxed her out of the chair and got her to come across the house and go outside.

When all the dogs had come inside, I threw together a hasty dinner for myself and took it into the den to eat in front of the TV. Since we were going to be on the Craftee Channel, I wanted to see what their programming was like. I had seen Adele's guest appearance on one of their yarn shows, but I'd watched only the few minutes she was on camera.

I found the station, and the program on was called *Glitterati* with a subtitle of "Fun With Glitter." As I watched, I developed a whole new appreciation for the sparkling particles. I was curious about the setting and spent a lot of time trying to look beyond the two women hovering over a table. It seemed to be a set and felt very flat. Shooting in the yarn department would come across as richer and more exciting—or at least, I certainly hoped it would. Mrs. Shedd was over-the-top enthused about the taping and was depending on me to pull it off. There was no reason to be nervous about it. All I really had to do was help the Craftee people with the arrangements, like when I was putting on an author event. I let out a sigh of relief and turned off the TV. It had been quite a day.

* * *

The bookstore was extra quiet when I went in the next morning. Adele always took Tuesdays off, so there was no story time with a gaggle of kids and their escorts hanging around waiting to be checked in. And of course, no Adele to stir things up.

I didn't even have to worry about setting up for happy hour, since the Hookers didn't meet on Tuesdays. I took my break in the yarn department and spent some time working on the afghan I was making for my mother. I was using Elise's pattern, which was really all about the colors. My parents had lived in Santa Fe for a while, and my mother had fallen in love with all shades of turquoise stones. I was making the coverlet in shades of green and blue that reminded me of the stones and separating the color blocks with rows of black.

I was just finishing up my coffee when Mrs. Shedd rushed into the yarn department, holding the phone to her ear. "I'll give you over to Molly Pink. I'm sure she can take care of all your requests. She's the one handling everything for the shoot." My boss put her hand over the phone and frantically began to whisper, "It's someone named Ellen, and she says they need us to set up some things. I'll let her explain."

Before I could react, Mrs. Shedd had pushed the phone on me and was on her way out of the yarn department. I had a sinking feeling that "set up some things" was going to turn out to be an understatement.

"I'm sorry this is so last minute," Ellen began. "We had everything arranged, and then the location we had dropped the ball." There was an annoyed tone to her voice when she said the last part. "Mrs. Shedd assured us that wouldn't happen with you and that you would handle all of our requests."

"What exactly are we talking about?" I asked.

"One of our sponsors is a craft supply company, and we'd like you to use their products in the Make-and-Take project."

"Sure. I assume you'll be giving us the details of the project and get us the supplies," I said, and I heard the woman make an uncomfortable sound.

"Actually, our understanding is that you are responsible for the project and the instructions. Of course, our sponsor will arrange for the supplies. I'm sure you'll be able to arrange to have some customers make the project when we tape. We'll expect your group to provide assistance. We'll need written instructions to put on our website. And another of our sponsors—National Mills Flour—would like a recipe from one of your people using their flour. We'll have a plate of whatever it is on the table during the show." She stopped just long enough to take a breath.

"It sounds like you want us to do everything. What's left for your people to do?" I said it as if I was being facetious, but really it did sound like it was all falling on us.

"You notice that I didn't say anything about writing anything for the show. We'll have all the copy explaining the benefits of having people drop in to do crafts, and we'll be adding an insert with the history of crochet."

I looked around the bookstore and caught sight of Mrs. Shedd as she scooted into her office. What had she gotten me into?

"Then we're good?" Ellen asked. I answered with a weak yes, and she continued.

"Some of our people will be coming by to look at the area. It would be good if you could give them a demonstration of the project then," she said. "I think that's it. We'll be in touch." And before I could say anything, she hung up. I made sure the line was clear and punched in CeeCee's number. When I told her what was going on, she promised to come up with the project, much to my relief. I spent the rest of any free time I had designing signs that we could put around the bookstore and in the window to get people in the store for the Make-and-Take.

At six, I found Mr. Royal and told him I was taking off. "Wish me luck," he said. "I'm taking over open-mike night for the poetry group."

"I forgot they got moved to tonight. Do you want me to stay?" I asked. As event coordinator, I was usually there for groups we had and book signings.

"I think I can handle a bunch of emotional poets," he said with a smile. I had no doubt that he could. Joshua Royal had been everywhere and done all kinds of interesting things during the time he'd been just a silent partner in the bookstore. So silent that when I had first started working there, I hadn't thought he actually existed. He pulled out a piece of paper from his pocket. "I even wrote a little ditty myself. I call it 'Working the Rides at Tivoli.'"

"Knock 'em dead, break a leg, or whatever is appropriate to a successful poetry reading," I said, laughing.

I grabbed my jacket and headed out the door. I stopped when I got to the sidewalk and saw that the curb was empty. Mason had said he'd pick me up around six, and it was just a little after. Even though it was April, the air was chilly now that it was getting dark. I shivered and zipped up my jacket as I watched the traffic go by.

A black Mercedes SUV pulled up to the curb with a squeak, and the passenger window lowered. "Sunshine, your ride is here," Mason called. He called me Sunshine since he said I brightened up his day.

Mason Fields was my significant other. I didn't really like the title, but then, how else could I describe him—my man of the moment? I had struggled with the whole concept of middle-age relationships. What did you call them? Saying we were dating sounded silly. We were just two people who were spending a lot of time together. Mason was divorced and not interested in getting married again. I was on the same page. I'd married Charlie when I was very young and had never really lived on my own. When he died, it had seemed like the time for me to figure out who I was, other than a wife and a mother. And now my life was so busy, I liked having my freedom.

We had both agreed that our relationship had no destination in mind. It was nice to know someone was there who liked to spend time with me, but at the same time made no demands.

"What do you feel like?" he asked when I got in the car. I saw that he was still in his work clothes—a beautifully tailored suit with a silky-soft dress shirt. He leaned over and gave me a hello kiss. "Something far away and exotic?"

"How about someplace close and easy," I said.

His broad face broke into a grin and, as a joke, he drove

alongside the curb for half a block before stopping in front of a Thai place we both liked.

"That works for me," I said as I got out of the car.

"Sorry about last night," Mason said as we walked into the restaurant. "Dinner with clients." Mason was a few inches taller than me and had a solid build. His dark hair was shot through with just enough gray to make him appear experienced and distinguished. No matter how he combed it, a lock always fell free across his forehead, which I thought made him somehow appear earnest and hardworking.

"No problem," I said. "Remember, we both have our own lives." I sniffed the air and smelled curry and spices and jasmine rice, and my stomach reminded me I was starving.

We took a table in the back and ordered soup, pad Thai, chicken satay, jasmine rice, and yellow curry. Once the order was in, Mason leaned on his arm and looked at me. "What's going on with you?" he said.

"Why don't you tell me about your day first," I said.

"It was just the same old, same old for me," he said.

"Really? The same old, same old?" Mason was an attorney whose clients were mostly celebrities who had gotten themselves into trouble. He had a corner office with a view of the ocean on a high floor of a building in Century City. He had said once how every case was different and a challenge. He put up his hands in capitulation with a sigh and urged me to take the floor.

"Okay then. I do have some exciting news," I said. "The Hookers are going to be famous. That is, if I can pull everything together." I told him about the show taping at the bookstore and the list of demands I'd gotten and even Adele's fantasy that she was going to be the host.

"I knew your news was more interesting than mine," he teased.

The soup arrived in a metal doughnut-shaped receptacle with a flame underneath. I was about to start serving it when I noticed a couple entering the restaurant. I didn't recognize the man, and it took me a moment to place the woman, since I was seeing her in different surroundings.

"What's going on?" Mason asked when I stayed frozen in position with the ladle full of soup in one hand and a bowl in the other. He looked over his shoulder to see what had grabbed my attention.

"It's just somebody I know," I said. "Her name is Marianne and she's a Hooker."

Even though Mason was very familiar with the name of our group, his eyes still widened and he grinned before taking the ladle and bowl out of my hands and starting to serve the soup.

"There's something about her—none of us can put a finger on it. She's quiet most of the time, and she comes with another younger woman." Mason had put a bowl of soup down in front of me, but I was still looking at Marianne. "I ought to go over and say hello." I got up and walked to the front of the restaurant. I don't know why I felt I needed to greet her, but I had the impression she didn't have a lot of social contact and that our yarn group was like some kind of life preserver for her.

She sensed my presence when I stopped next to her table and looked up. Her face seemed to light up, and she grabbed my wrist in her death grasp. "Molly, so you like Thai food, too." She glanced across the table at her companion. "Molly works at Shedd & Royal and she's in the crochet group." She released my wrist and muttered an apology.

"It's pretty exciting news that we're all going to be on TV," I said.

"TV? You're going to be on TV?" the man said. He gave Marianne a critical glance. "Do you really think that's such a smart idea?"

Her shoulders dropped, and she looked at him as if he'd just popped her birthday balloon.

As my eye grazed over the table, I noticed a pill container next to Marianne's water glass. The man tried to be surreptitious as he moved to close the lid and remove it, but all he did was spill the selection of pills all over the table.

"Errol, it's okay. I can take them later."

"No, it isn't," the man grumbled, and with an annoyed shake of his head, began to gather up the pills. He closed the lid and pushed the container closer to her. I looked at Errol and tried to figure out their relationship. The only thing I knew for sure was that he was the one Connie had had to check with about Marianne joining the group.

I checked his hand and found a wedding ring. Marianne's ring finger was bare. When I looked at him again, I saw the resemblance between the two. "Are you Marianne's brother?" I asked.

He nodded and held out his hand. "I'm Errol Freeman."

His expression was wary as he looked at me intently. "And my sister is doing okay in your yarn group?"

I gave him an enthusiastic yes, never making mention of her wobbly-sided scarf. He suddenly turned impatient and waved the server over as he announced that they were ready to order.

Marianne seemed to pick up on her brother's rudeness and apologized for it. "He has a lot of responsibilities," she said. "And I'm one of them." She managed to smile at me. Errol grunted in response and then gave their order to the server. I got the message that our visit was over. I reached for her hand and gave it a reassuring squeeze. "See you tomorrow night."

"I'll be there," she said.

* * *

"You look puzzled," Mason said when I slid back into my seat.

"I just wonder what's going on. You should have seen the pile of pills she had to take. The guy with her is her brother, and he seemed to be in a hurry. What happened to Connie, the woman who comes to happy hour with her?"

Mason smiled at me. "Everything is a mystery to you." He pushed the bowl closer to me. "Eat your soup before it gets cold." He glanced in Marianne's direction. "Maybe you should just leave it alone," he said. Then he reconsidered what he'd said. "That's not going to happen, is it?"

I looked up at him with a guilty smile.

He stared down at his soup and suddenly seemed a little glum.

He was usually full of fun, and I wondered at the serious expression. "What's the matter, Mason? Is something bothering you?"

He paused for a moment and then looked at me directly. "Do you really want to know?"

"Of course," I said. "That's why I asked about your day."

"I know you think everything just rolls off of me, and people in general think lawyers are just about winning. But I started to think about *what* I'm winning. I've been looking at the clients I represent and thinking, is this what I want my legacy to be? I've always joked about getting naughty celebrities off for silly things like driving into a stop sign. But I'm beginning to think of them more as sleazy celebrities and facing that they drove into the stop sign because they were drunk. Do I really want it on my conscience that, through my skill, I've gotten people off who actually did what they were accused of? And what if they do whatever it was again? It could be considered my fault." Then he looked at me with a rueful smile. "Sorry. I guess it's just middle-age angst." He sat up straighter. "I promise to be all fun for the rest of dinner and beyond."

"How shallow do you think I am?" I said. "Do you really believe that as soon as you're not a barrel of laughs, I'm out the door?"

He grinned. "I hope not."

Chapter Three

Cosmo was on one side of me when I awoke Wednesday morning. The small black dog was in his usual position, lying on his back with his short feet in the air. Felix preferred to burrow under the covers and cuddle next to my legs. Mr. Kitty slept on a pillow behind my head, and Cat had found an empty space in the crook of my arm and claimed it. I laughed as I pulled free of my menagerie and thought of Mason's reason for wanting me to spend the night at his place. He'd said he hated to think of me sleeping alone. Ha!

The troops followed me across the house. The sun was streaming in the two big kitchen windows that took up almost the whole wall. The yard was greened up from the winter rains, and the pansies I'd planted in the flower bed outside the window added some color to the mostly succulents that had taken over the raised area. I made myself some coffee and opened the door for all of my furry dependents to go outside. The cats were so used to me stopping them that they looked at me with a question.

"You can go out now," I said. I gestured with my arm to reinforce the point, and they walked out the door. I grabbed my coffee and followed them outside. It was a little chilly for breakfast in the yard, but the velour robe I had on made it feel just fine.

I kept an eye on the cats. Any sign they were going to jump into the neighbor's yard, and I'd grab them. And if Cat decided to do some hunting, I'd grab her before the execution.

I'd forgotten that I had the cordless in my pocket, and when it began to ring, I jumped.

I checked the screen and saw that it was Dinah. "Well, hello, Ms. Tease," I said in a joking voice. "You whisper that you have a problem, and then I never hear from you what it is."

"Sorry. I got distracted both by the problem, which I will tell you about, and by my students, who have found new ways to drive me crazy." Dinah taught freshman English at Beasley Community College. She was old-school, and it was a constant battle trying to get her students to write an essay without putting in emojis. They were so used to using a keyboard that they didn't know how to handwrite and could barely print legibly.

"What is it this time?" I asked.

"It probably wouldn't bother me so much if I didn't have the other problem. One of them made a video of her reading her essay and wouldn't turn in a print version."

"What's the other problem, the one that's really distracting you?" I asked.

She dropped her voice and then laughed at herself, explaining that she was on campus and far away from the perpetrators of the problem. "Commander's daughter Cassandra made a surprise visit. Well, a surprise to me. He knew she was coming and didn't tell me. She's staying with us—for three weeks."

"I'm guessing it isn't just the length of her stay that's the problem," I said.

"I'll just say this for now. If looks could kill, I'd be a corpse." I heard voices around Dinah, and she suddenly said she had to go. "We'll talk later," she said, and then was gone.

"Mom," Samuel said in an exasperated tone, running outside in his pajamas and grabbing Cat as she was about to lunge at a squirrel. "You're supposed to be watching them." The purplish-gray cat squirmed in his arms in protest as he took her inside. I found Mr. Kitty lounging in a sunny spot and picked up the big black-and-white cat.

By now I was running behind and had to hurry to get ready for work. I didn't even have a chance to find out what was going on with my son.

I'd left my car in the parking lot and had just turned the corner onto Ventura Boulevard when I noticed a crowd of people hanging by the entrance to Shedd & Royal. When I got to the fringe of the group, I asked a woman in jogging clothes what was going on.

"I don't know. I saw a crowd and thought something exciting must be happening. So far, it just seems like a lot of standing around." She took a last look and started to sprint away.

I pushed my way into the heart of the clump of people. I gathered from the abundance of camera equipment and their slightly scroungy appearance that they were paparazzi. I grabbed a guy with a wild head of black hair and a graphic T-shirt that had an image of some rock musician and asked him what was going on.

"Nothing right now," he said in an annoying smart-aleck tone.

"You're all here for something. You know I'm the assistant manager of the bookstore, and I could make you move, claiming you're blocking the exit."

"Assistant manager, huh," he said, giving me an assessing look. "You probably have the power to let me come inside. I could sure use a cup of something super-caffeinated."

"Tell me what's up and I'll think it over," I said.

Just then, a huge black Escalade pulled up to the curb. The driver's door opened and a woman got out and walked around the SUV to the curb. Seeming oblivious to the gathered crowd, she opened the back door and helped a girl and boy out. They looked to be around three and weren't as oblivious to the crowd as their mother—or at least that's who I assumed she was. The kids both waved and smiled until the woman turned. "Can't I have privacy anywhere?" she said in an annoyed tone.

My paparazzi buddy snorted. "Sure, honey, we buy that you're annoyed to see us." He turned to me. "The so-called tip that she was going to be here and had some big news probably came from her publicist, or maybe even from Rory directly."

I looked at the woman again and tried to place her. Her auburn hair was cut short and tousled, and she was dressed in what I'd call mom clothes—leggings with a long tunic and cloth slip-on shoes. The photographers grabbed some shots of her, and she stopped acting annoyed and began to play to the crowd. When she yelled out "Dance Break!" and started to gyrate, I suddenly knew who she was. Rory Graham had played a teen in an ensemble cast on a TV drama. She had been well into her twenties when the show ended, and nothing had clicked for her after that until she turned herself into a personality and created her signature Dance Break. I hadn't really followed her career, but it seemed to me that she had made the rounds of game shows that had celebrity panels, along with doing a couple of reality shows with her husband, showing off what an adoring couple they were. She was a master of keeping herself in the public eye. I hadn't realized she was a Tarzanian until now.

When she stopped dancing, she acted as if she was reacting to a question from the crowd, though I hadn't heard anybody say anything.

"I'm here to bring my little ones to story time," she said.

The guy next to me rolled his eyes and then called out to her that he'd heard she had some big announcement about her career.

She stopped and turned so they could get a good shot of her. "Yes, I'm going to be hosting my own show on the Craftee Channel. *Creating With Crochet*. In fact, we'll be filming the premiere episode here at Shedd & Royal Books and More."

I hoped no one was looking, because my mouth had fallen open, and I looked around to see if Adele was anywhere within earshot. Well, there went her fantasy of hosting.

One of the paparazzi opened the door for her, and Rory walked inside holding hands with her kids. The guy next to me turned to me. "Can I follow her inside?"

"You can get that coffee you wanted, but no photos." I went in and rushed after her, but before I could catch up with her, she was already at the entrance to the kids' department.

For once I was glad that Adele had a whole setup of membership cards and lists for checking in the kids and that Rory was too busy dealing with it to have a chance to bring up her latest career move or call out for one of her Dance Breaks. I don't think Adele even recognized her.

Most of the parents went to the café while the kids were with Adele, but Rory walked to the middle of the main area of the bookstore and glanced around. I followed her, and she turned abruptly, almost bumping into me. "Do you work here?" she asked, then didn't wait for an answer. "I'm sure you know who I am. I understand you have a yarn department and you have a group that does something with yarn." She left it hanging for my response.

"You must mean the Tarzana Hookers. Yes, we have what we call a happy-hour gathering from five to six most weekday evenings." I gestured toward the back of the store.

"Oh, goodie," she said, then she leaned against one of

the display tables. "I noticed that you said *we.* Does that mean you're part of the group?" she asked, and I nodded.

"I have kind of a situation," she said, dropping her voice. "I'm going to be hosting a yarn show. In fact, the premiere episode is going to film here. I might have, well, . . . overrepresented my skills just a bit," she said, biting her lip.

"How much did you overrepresent them?" I asked. "What exactly do you know?"

"I know that you use yarn and pointy things," she said, speaking even lower. "I was hoping that your group could give me a speed course on how to make scarves and things. So I could appear on top of things, you know, when I do the show."

I wanted to put my face in my hands, thinking of how Adele would react to knowing that not only was Rory getting the hosting job, but she wanted *us* to teach *her* how to crochet. But I couldn't say no. How could they tape the first show with a host who didn't know how to crochet? Finally, I took a deep breath and suggested she come back at five.

Now the problem was how to break the news to Adele.

* * *

"Why are you pacing?" Dinah said when she came into the yarn department that night. I hadn't realized that was what I was doing, but now that my friend brought it up, I looked down and saw that I was walking back and forth by the long dark wood table where we all would be gathering.

"It's about Adele," I said, and Dinah laughed.

"Isn't it always about Adele? What now?"

I recounted my meeting with Rory and the situation, and Dinah sighed as she took out a ball of pale blue-green yarn and a large crochet hook. As we talked, she made a slip knot and began to make a long chain of stitches.

"Get ready for fireworks." I had stopped pacing now and was leaning against one of the chairs.

"Fireworks?" Rhoda repeated as she joined us. "What's going on?"

I told both of them about Rory getting the job hosting *Creating With Crochet*. They didn't understand the problem until I explained that Adele thought the job was going to be hers.

"I get it now," Rhoda said.

Before I could explain there was more to the problem, Sheila and CeeCee came up to the table. Rhoda rushed to tell them her version of what she'd heard, which seemed to center on Adele throwing a hissy fit, though the reason why seemed to have gotten lost. I waited until Elise and Eduardo arrived before I told the whole group the story, rushing before Adele made an appearance.

"Here comes Rory now," Elise said, giving us all a concerned look as she pointed toward the entrance of the store. Rory had just come in and was passing the children's department as Adele came out of it, and they headed to the yarn department together.

"Oh, dear," CeeCee said, "somebody better do something." Making it clear the someone was me.

I got out of my chair and rushed to join the two women,

ready to intercede, but with no idea what I was going to do. I put on a bright smile and prepared for damage control. "I see you two have met," I said brightly.

"I was just telling Miss Adele that I came to join your group," Rory said.

"She goes by Queen Adele for story time," I corrected. It was just a small point, but one less thing for Adele to be upset about. "And when it comes to crochet, Adele is the queen as well. We all think she's a wonder. She made that jacket."

Rory turned to give Adele an appraising glance. The jacket was spectacular, as was everything Adele made. I was never sure if that was spectacular in a good way, though. Maybe *showy* was a better word. The actual jacket was all black, and she had crocheted sunflowers and attached them to it.

I was trying to come up with a gentle way to break the news to Adele so she wouldn't make a scene, but before I could say anything, Rory dropped the bomb on her.

"Maybe you can show me how to make those flowers. It would be great if I could whip some up as I'm talking to the camera." She seemed to pick up that Adele didn't know what she was talking about. "I'm the host of *Creating With Crochet*," she said in cheery voice before turning to me. "And thank you so much in advance for the lessons." She let out a little giggle as she leaned closer to us. "It'll be our little secret that I kind of oversold my skills to get the show."

I grabbed Adele's arm and whispered in her ear not to make a scene. Rory walked on ahead as we neared the yarn department and began to introduce herself around, though she kept saying she probably didn't need to since she was sure they all knew who she was.

I managed to keep Adele from exploding by reminding her they were doing the premiere show in our yarn department and saying that surely when the powers that be saw how fabulous she was, they'd want her to be a regular on the show.

"You mean like a sidekick?" she said, brightening.

"Absolutely," I agreed. Anything to keep the peace. "Once Rory sees what a great crocheter you are, she'll want you at her side to take the heat off of her."

Adele went full steam ahead and made sure that Rory sat next to her. Before any of us could suggest it, she offered to teach Rory how to crochet. "We'll be yarn sisters," Adele said, grabbing a size J hook and some worsted-weight yarn.

"Good job," Dinah said, leaning next to me when I sat down. "I don't know what you said, but it worked."

CeeCee looked around the table. "Should we get started?"

Our core group was all there, but Marianne and Connie were still missing. I mentioned seeing Marianne the evening before and how she'd said she'd be there.

"Who knows with that pair. I think we all thought they were a little strange," Rhoda said.

"Maybe they're just late," I offered.

"I want to show you what I came up with for the Make-and-Take," CeeCee said. "I suppose we could give them a little longer to show up."

The group proceeded to work on their own projects, while Adele and Rory stayed huddled together at the opposite end of the table. Finally, I looked at my watch and saw that half the time was already gone.

"I don't think they're coming," I said.

"And look what I found under the table," Sheila said. She held up a pale-blue scarf in progress, and we all recognized the wobbly edge. "She must have dropped it last time she was here."

Rory looked up as Sheila held the partial scarf, and I saw her wrinkle her nose. "That doesn't look very good," Rory said.

Her criticism triggered something in me, and I felt the need to defend Marianne. "Crocheting isn't just about the finished project. For some people, the act of doing it is very therapeutic."

"Absolutely," Sheila said. She explained to the actress how the rhythmic quality of it had gotten her through a lot of anxiety attacks. She even showed off the ball of string and hook she carried in her pocket for emergencies. "If I start to feel panicky, I just take this out."

Rory had pulled out a piece of paper and was scribbling something down. "That's something I should know for the show," she said.

"Don't worry," Adele said in a cloyingly sweet voice. "I know all about crochet and its benefits. You can always ask me anything you need to know. You probably saw me on *What's Up With Crafts* when I was the guest. Us pros need to stick together."

Rory seemed to shrug off what Adele said, but I rolled my eyes, wondering if I'd made a mistake in giving Adele the idea of being Rory's sidekick. It had been foolish of me not to realize that Adele would take the idea too seriously.

"Let's make use of the time we have left," CeeCee said. She stood up and let her gaze move around the whole group. "As you all know, *Creating With Crochet* is going to tape their premier episode here, and we're going to be hosting a Make-and-Take. Molly said they expect us to come up with the project." She nodded toward me as she spoke. "I brought in something I thought we could use." She produced a circle of stitches with a pompom on the end. A silver ring was attached to the stitches. "It's a key chain," she said, and then passed it around.

Rory took it last, examined it, and wrinkled her nose. "A key chain, really?" she said. "Who would want to make that?"

CeeCee seemed deflated and asked the rest of the group for their thoughts. Now that Rory had said it, they all kind of agreed that the key chain had no magic.

"Maybe if we came up for a catchy name for it," Elise said. She was very into marketing. "I've decided to call the afghans I'm making Color Squares. It sounds a lot more sophisticated than calling them what they really are—big granny squares.

"What else could you call it but a key chain?" Rhoda said.

Everyone started tossing around suggestions that kept getting more and more ridiculous. *A key escort, really?*

Meanwhile, I couldn't help but keep glancing toward the door for the missing pair of Hookers.

"Let's be honest," Rhoda said at last. "We don't like the key chain."

CeeCee seemed a little miffed, but she finally agreed that maybe it wasn't very exciting and promised to find a better project. I hated to pressure her, but I reminded her that we didn't have a lot of time.

"I already have something else in mind. I'll bring it in tomorrow," CeeCee said.

When the group broke up, Dinah stayed at the table with me. "Whatever you said to Adele certainly kept her from exploding. She's practically joined at the hip with Rory." We watched Adele walk Rory to the front of the store arm in arm.

I looked at Marianne's scarf. "I think I'll drop this off at her house," I said.

"Are you being considerate or nosy?" my friend asked, and I laughed.

"Maybe both."

"I'd go with you, but Commander planned a family dinner at Cassandra's favorite restaurant." She squeezed my hand. "Promise me you'll come over later. We can go in my lady cave and crochet and eat cookies."

Chapter Four

When I got ready to leave Shedd & Royal, I checked the roster we kept of the Hookers. Adele had wanted to make it all complicated like she had with story time, with all of her membership cards and check-in lists, but I'd nixed that idea. We simply had a list of addresses and phone numbers. I tried Marianne's phone number first, but it went right to voicemail. Then I decided to just take the scarf to her house.

Tarzana was different from other San Fernando Valley communities. It had once all been a ranch and, when it was developed, had been sold off piecemeal. There were some streets with tract houses, but a lot of the area had been built up one house at a time. Because much of the community was draped across the base of the Santa Monica Mountains, there were a lot of strange little streets that meandered off the main one. I'd never heard of the street Marianne lived on, and it was only because I checked a map that I found it. Even still, as I drove along Wells Drive, I passed the turnoff once. The second time around, I saw the sign for the private road that went up a barren-looking hill.

The road ended in a cul-de-sac, and I drove through an open gate into a paved area in front of a sprawling house. I couldn't really make out the style in the dark, other than that it was a single story and I was pretty sure it was white stucco. Though I was less interested in what the house looked like than in the cars parked out front. Floodlights along the front of the property illuminated a pair of police cars. I was still getting used to their new vehicles. The old cruisers had seemed sleek and like they could roar through the streets with ease. The new ones were SUVs that somehow reminded me of high-top sneakers. They seemed cumbersome and like they must bounce the cops around a lot when they were involved in a pursuit.

I got an ominous feeling when I saw the black Crown Victoria, which meant a detective was there along with the uniforms. I got out of my car and went to the door with my heart thudding. It was open, but a uniform blocked my entry with a curt, "You can't go in there."

I was too stunned to think it through and just bluntly asked what happened. The cop looked at me as if I'd just asked the most ridiculous question and then told me he didn't have that information. Did he really think I was going to buy that? He seemed intent on not letting me in, but not as concerned about getting me to leave. I hung by the open door, leaning this way and that, trying to get a view inside. When I leaned so far to one side that I almost fell backward, I was able to see past the entrance hall into the living room. A tall, dark-haired man dressed in a suit was standing in front of the couch with his back toward me. I didn't need to see his face to recognize Homicide Detective Barry Greenberg. He was my ex, though I never knew quite what to say after that. Ex-boyfriend didn't work for me. He was in his fifties and our relationship had hardly been the dinner-and-a-movie type. I'd given up trying to find the right title for him so just left it at ex.

There was a woman standing next to him. I got only a side view of her, but I recognized her as one of his fellow detectives. Her name was Heather Gilmore, but to me she was simply Detective Heather. Not that I ever referred to her that way directly. I always said that if there were a Barbie doll homicide detective, she'd look like Detective Heather. She was impeccably dressed in a dark suit, and her long, champagne-blonde hair was upswept. I couldn't see her face, but I was sure her lipstick was fresh. Instinctively, I patted my hair and realized that, unlike her, I showed signs of being at the end of a long day.

I ignored any feeling stirred by seeing Barry and focused on the fact that his presence there could only mean one thing. All I wanted to know was who had died.

It felt like my heart was in my throat. I was going to try some of my investigative tricks on the uniform to see if I could shake loose some information, but then Barry shifted his position and I finally got a view of the couch. My breath came out in a rush of relief as I saw Marianne sitting on the sofa with a bewildered expression. Her brother was standing behind the couch with another man I didn't recognize.

I looked down at the wobbly scarf and yarn in my hand. I didn't know what was going on, but the poor woman looked like she could really use a dose of crochet. I got the cop's attention and showed him Marianne's work in progress and explained that I'd brought it for her.

"She really needs it now," I said. I gave him a short speech on the curative qualities of crochet and then urged him to look at her. "If ever there was a time she needed her crochet, it's now."

As I said it, the metal hook came loose from her work and hit the ground with a loud ping. Barry suddenly looked in the direction of the door. He had his blank cop face on, but when he saw it was me, there was some sort of flicker in his eyes.

He came to the door and stepped around the uniform, took my arm, and pulled me away from the open door.

"What are you doing here?" he asked in a stern voice.

I explained that I'd brought the crochet project Marianne had left at the bookstore. Then I looked him in the eye. "So who's dead?"

He was caught off guard by my direct question, but he recovered fast. "I won't confirm or deny anything." Then he told me I had to leave. He stood watching me until I went to my car.

I was still shaken up when I pulled my up in front of Dinah's. Before I could walk into the small yard, the door opened and a dark-haired woman came out and walked down the steps. She had the same shape as Commander Blaine, but her expression had none of his warmth. I watched her walk to the street and get into what I assumed was an Uber.

I gave it a few moments, then knocked at the door. By Dinah's unhappy expression, I was pretty sure she thought Commander's daughter had come back. When she realized it was me, she grabbed me in a bear hug. "Am I glad to see you."

She brought me inside, and we crossed through the small living room. Commander Blaine was headed down the short hall toward the bedrooms. He turned and flashed a warm smile when he saw me.

"Have fun with your girl time," he said.

Dinah pulled open the sliding glass doors that at one time had led outside and now opened into an added-on den. Dinah had never used it much when she lived in the house alone, but since marrying Commander and discovering that they had very different body clocks, she'd turned it into her lady cave and late-night haven.

Though *late night* was a relative term. To Commander Blaine, it had already stretched into that time zone, though it was barely after eight o'clock. As the heavy sliding door clicked shut, my friend let out her breath and turned to me. "What an evening." Then she caught sight of my face. "What happened? You look stunned."

We both flopped onto the chartreuse couch and, before she even made tea or got the cookies, I told her about my stop at Marianne's house.

"I know just where you mean, but I thought there was nothing on top of that hill," Dinah said. "Did Barry tell you what happened?"

I rolled my eyes. "Are you kidding? He just hustled me out of there."

"What about Marianne? How was she?"

"I only got a glimpse of her, and she looked the way she always does when she comes to happy hour, only more so."

When I asked about Dinah's evening, she waved it off as nothing compared to mine and went to make tea and get cookies. We often played what we called the Sherlock Holmes game, which amounted to seeing what we could deduce about something. Without even mentioning it, we began a game of deduction as we drank our tea. We started with the obvious.

"It was definitely some kind of crime scene," I said, remembering that I'd seen some yellow tape stretched along the side of the house.

"The fact that Barry was there and he's a homicide detective makes it pretty certain that someone died. Since you saw Marianne, we know it wasn't her."

"Whatever happened must have happened outside." I mentioned the location of the yellow tape.

"And since you didn't see Connie and the two seemed inseparable, it seems likely that it might have been her," Dinah said.

"And I think we know now why they were no-shows at happy hour," I said with a sigh. I drank some of the orange pekoe tea and let it work its soothing magic. The warm drink seemed to fill my insides with a peaceful feeling, and I began to relax.

Dinah topped off my cup and paused to think. "None of us said much about the two, and they certainly didn't say much about themselves."

"But I bet if we think about it, we know more than we realize," I said. "Like, even before I saw the big house, I figured she was well off." I brought up the designer purse I'd seen Marianne carrying and admitted that I'd checked out the price online. "It was crazy. Who pays a thousand dollars for a purse?"

"Obviously, Marianne," Dinah said with a smile. She guessed Marianne was around forty. Then I mentioned seeing her in the restaurant with her brother. "So we know she has a brother. I never noticed a wedding band, so I'm guessing she's not currently married. And she was obviously medicated. She always had a look about her eyes as if it was a struggle for her to stay focused."

"That's absolutely true," I said. "I saw the drugs." I mentioned the pill container on the table and that her brother seemed to want to hide them and she didn't seem to want to take them.

"My two cents is that the drugs were for something emotional instead of physical," Dinah said, and I agreed. Then we both admitted to feeling bad that we'd taken the easy way out and just let her sit there during the gatherings instead of making more of an effort to talk to her.

"Her brother was odd when I mentioned the Hookers were going to be on TV. It seemed like he didn't want her to be part of it. But then, I don't think he wants her to be part of the Hookers at all. He wasn't very friendly."

"Did she mention Connie?" Dinah asked.

"No, and I thought about asking about her, but it felt kind of odd, since we don't know what their relationship is, so I didn't say anything." I thought it over for a moment. "What do we know about Connie? I noticed her purse, too. I'd seen one like it at Costco, and it didn't cost a thousand dollars," I said with a chuckle. "They dressed differently as well. Marianne's clothes were kind of plain but looked expensive, and Connie's didn't. So, it seems safe to assume the two women weren't on the same financial level. There was an age difference, too. I suppose they could be friends, even though Connie seemed like she's only in her late twenties." I pictured the two women and thought of something else. "I don't know if you noticed, but Connie handled everything, like giving their information, paying for the yarn and hooks. If you put it all together, it means only one thing."

"I think I know," my friend said. "Connie works for Marianne."

"Exactly the conclusion I came too." I reached for a cookie and felt something vibrate on my wrist. My Apple Watch was set to vibrate when emails or texts came in and was supposed to get my attention. It didn't work most of the time, as I was usually too busy to notice. But when the vibration continued, it finally registered that it was a call, and I looked at my wrist.

"It's Mason," I said, rummaging in my purse for my phone.

"Are you okay?" he asked, sounding a little frantic. "I've been calling everywhere. This is the third time I tried your cell. Remember, you were going to call me when you got home and we were going to make plans?"

I apologized and then quickly told him about my trip to Marianne's and that I'd gone to Dinah's afterward. He seemed hurt that I'd gone to my friend's instead of calling him. He suggested we get together so I could tell him everything in person, but all that adrenaline rushing through my veins had worn me out.

"How about a rain check for tomorrow," I said. He balked but finally agreed.

"What happened to casual dating?" Dinah said when I got off the phone. "I remember when he said he was just interested in fun with no ties."

"Human nature. I keep a distance and he wants to be closer. I bet he'd be a lot different if I suddenly got clingy and demanding," I said with a chuckle. I finished my tea and got up to leave.

Dinah followed me to the door. "So, what are you going to do?" she asked.

I was puzzled for a moment. "You mean about Marianne? I guess nothing. For once, just mind my own business."

Without even looking at her, I could tell Dinah was rolling her eyes as she said, "Sure."

Chapter Five

The greeting committee was waiting by my kitchen door when I got home. As soon as the door was open, Cosmo and Felix rushed out into the yard, but I made sure to block Mr. Kitty and Cat. The two dogs began to run around the perimeter of the yard while I went around turning on the lights. Samuel was off somewhere, though he'd left a note saying he'd fed them all and walked Blondie.

The strawberry-blond terrier mix was the only one who was truly mine. The rest of them had come in piecemeal. Cosmo, the black mutt who looked like a mop, had been adopted by Barry Greenberg and his son. We'd been a couple at the time and, due to Barry's crazy schedule and Jeffrey being a kid who might not always remember he had a dog who needed care, Cosmo had lived at my house from the start. When we broke up, Cosmo had stayed, though the Greenbergs had visitation rights. I'm pretty sure Cosmo knew who really took care of him, but he always played up to them when they came over. Though it was mostly Jeffrey who'd come to visit since the breakup, and as I said, he was a kid, so it wasn't exactly on a regular schedule.

My son Samuel was in his midtwenties and unsettled. He worked as a barista by day, but his real love was music. He had landed a regular gig at a local restaurant, and he worked as the musical director for my mother's group, the She La Las. When he'd moved back the first time, he'd brought the two cats. They'd started out with other names but now were known as Cat and Mr. Kitty. I was always at a loss for how to describe Cat's coloring. It seemed sort of purplish gray, with some faint calico markings. She was a foodie and loved getting table scraps.

Mr. Kitty was a cuddler and seemed more like a dog than Blondie. The black-and-white cat even came when he was called.

Felix had been the last addition. Samuel had moved out and in with his girlfriend, and they'd found the scruffy gray terrier mix somewhere. The relationship hadn't lasted and Samuel had moved back in, bringing Felix with him. Felix lived up to his breed and was feisty. I'd thought Blonde might pick up some hints from him, but she never had.

I went through the house to coax Blondie out of the chair and brought her to join the others.

I watched the two other dogs play while Blondie wandered around the yard on her own.

I was grateful for the row of mostly redwood trees that grew along the back fence, blocking most of the view of the two-story monster house that had recently been built on the property behind me. The whole area had been part of an orange grove at one time, and there were four trees left from it, though they were beginning to show their age.

I loved my yard and spent a lot of time sitting at the umbrella table, enjoying what felt like my own little park. I didn't care what my other son, Peter, said; I wasn't looking to downsize.

I brought all the animals in and then looked around my kitchen, realizing that I'd never had dinner, unless you counted the cookies at Dinah's. I was starting to think about what I could make when the phone rang.

I grabbed it without looking at the screen to see who was calling, though I was pretty sure I knew who it was. Was there any chance that I'd show up at a crime scene and Barry wouldn't have a few questions?

"Detective Greenberg," he said in his cop voice. You would think that after all we'd been through, he'd just say *Barry*, but he had a whole protocol when it was official business, including a phone call before coming to the door. I'd given up fighting it and accepted that I still felt a flutter when he called.

"I suppose you want to talk to me," I said before he had a chance to say it. "And I'm guessing it's now. And you're probably in front of my house."

"Yes," he said, sounding annoyed that I'd said it all before he did.

"Okay," I said. "I'll open the door."

I realized he must have been calling from my front porch because he was standing right in front of the door when I opened it. He was neatly dressed in a dark suit and dress shirt. His tie was still pulled tight, but there was the beginning of stubble on his stubborn jaw and shadows under his eyes. Who knew when his day had started, and it still wasn't over. I knew I wasn't supposed to care, since we were broken up, and he couldn't deal with the idea of us being friends, but I couldn't help feeling concerned.

"I'm sorry it's so late," he said, which surprised me. Barry had tunnel vision when he was working and lost all track of time. I was stunned that he even realized it was late.

The dogs had followed me in and stayed with me as I went to the front door. Felix gave Barry a few barks and then a sniff. Cosmo went right up to him and put his paws on Barry's leg, letting him know he expected a treat.

"Is it okay if I give them something?" he asked. He was so sure of the answer, he barely paused before going to find the treat jar.

I followed him into the kitchen, and it reminded me that I'd been about to pull together something for my dinner. I guessed that Barry probably hadn't eaten either. When he was working on a case, he turned off his feelings, whether they be hunger, tiredness, or probably any residual feeling he had for me. However, any reference to food cut right through his resolve.

"I was just going to eat something. How about you? Are you hungry?" It was a silly question. I'd never known him to say no.

I watched his benign cop face begin to come undone. "Now that you mention it, food would be good."

"How about you conduct your official police business while I make something," I said.

I watched his expression change to frustration. "No, you are not going to do it this time. I'm the one in charge here. I'll decide when I start the interview." He seemed flustered. "I haven't even asked you anything yet, and already you're trying to turn the tables."

This wasn't the first time he'd shown up to question me about a case he was working on. It always turned into a dueling match of who was going to get the most information from the other. He usually managed to give out the least information, but then I usually managed not to give him much in the way of answers either.

"How about some eggs?" Then I looked at him with a sly smile. "Oh, no, did I make that sound like a question?"

He rolled his eyes. "Molly, it's been a long day. Anything would be fantastic."

I pulled out the eggs, butter, and odds and ends from the vegetable drawer along with some slices of Swiss cheese. I made omelets, fried up some leftover potatoes with onions, and toasted some pretzel bagels. Barry watched it all and by now was so lost to his hunger, he had a hard time grilling me. Actually, all he asked was how I knew Marianne. The smell of the toasting bagels was getting to me too. Maybe that's why I went easy on him and just answered with the basics.

"She joined the Tarzana Hookers about three weeks ago and has been coming to our happy-hour gatherings regularly."

"I can't believe it. You gave me a straight answer," he said.

"In gratitude, then, maybe you can tell me what happened. Who died?"

He shook his head. "I should have known it was too easy." It seemed like he said it more for effect than anything else.

He helped me take the food into the dining room, and we sat down across from each other. The junior detective set my son Peter had given me as a birthday present sat on one of the shelves on the row of bookcases that lined the room. I saw Barry look at the set, and I waited for a comment, but he said nothing.

Something was up. I expected him to at least roll his eyes at the gift, or say something jokey about me using it to solve crimes—probably with an admonishment about not getting involved with the situation at Marianne's.

But then he began to eat without saying anything other than to comment on how good the food was. It began to make me very nervous. Particularly since he seemed to have something on his mind.

"It's Connie Richards who died, isn't it?" I said.

He looked at me with his even cop expression that gave away nothing. Even so, I went on. "What exactly was her relationship to Marianne?"

Barry put his fork down and then blew out his breath. "I'm going to say some things, but first you have to promise that it goes no further. You can't go telling the Hookers or Mason." He made a slight snarl when he said Mason's name.

I suddenly sat up straighter. He was going to tell me something. "Okay," I said, "My lips will be sealed."

I did that stupid thing of pretending to lock them and throw away the key. He didn't smile.

He seemed to be struggling with himself. "I can't believe I'm doing this," he muttered, before looking at me directly. "Heather is the lead detective on this case, and she's made up her mind on what she believes happened." His shoulders dropped as if in some kind of capitulation. "But it doesn't feel right to me. Your Hooker friend is already lawyered up, so she's not going to talk to us." He looked into my eyes. "But I think you can get her to talk to you." He didn't say anything after that as it sunk in what he was asking.

"Really, you're asking for my help?"

"Yes." He suddenly looked stern. "But this isn't you just going off on your own and investigating. You'll have to tell me everything you find out as soon as you find it out, and I'll put together the pieces. Okay?"

I was so accustomed to him telling me to stay *out* of things, it was taking some serious getting used to now that he wanted to me to get *into* them. But in the past, I'd put together the pieces myself, and this time he just wanted the information.

"I don't know if I just want to hand everything over to you," I said.

"You'd be doing a good thing. Helping to get at the truth," he said. He took a moment to think. "And how about this. We can talk over what you find out."

"Okay, deal," I said. "So tell me what you know."

"I don't know if that's a good idea. I don't want to

muddy the waters. I think you should start out with a blank page. The first thing you have to do is get her confidence."

I was speechless. Barry was asking for my help.

"Remember, no one can know that you're working with me," he said. "And absolutely nothing to Heather." He shook his head with concern at the thought of his partner finding out he was questioning her ability.

"Not even Dinah?" I said, and he shot me a stern look.

"No one means no one," he said.

He started mumbling to himself, questioning if he was making a big mistake. I interrupted his mutterings and told him it would all be fine.

"So, then I call and report what I find out?" I was about to ask him how often I should fill him in.

"No, no phone calls. It has to all be in person." He glanced around my house. "I'll come here. It's probably best if I do it late like this."

"So, I'll be working for you, huh? Do I at least get a junior police badge?" I joked, and he cracked a smile.

Chapter Six

The next morning, I took my coffee out onto the patio and let the cats get some outside time while all three dogs wandered around the yard. The air had a sweet smell from the last of the orange blossoms and the hyacinths that had just started to bloom. The night chill was gone and the air felt soft against my skin. I was still in disbelief that Barry had actually asked me to help him. But that didn't mean I'd wasted any time getting started. I'd already checked all the online news sources trying to find a story about what had happened, since Barry wouldn't give me even the barest details. I found a small item that showed up on the *Tarzana Patch* that didn't list any names but did give a location on the private street, and since Marianne's house was the only one on the street, it had to be about what had happened at her place. The piece said a woman who worked as a companion had been found dead on the lawn, apparently electrocuted under suspicious circumstances, and the police were investigating.

"And I am, too," I said as I put my cell phone on the glass

table. It seemed like a safe guess that the nameless woman was Connie Richards, and I was pretty sure I'd figured out what it was that Detective Heather was so sure about. She must have decided that Marianne had killed Connie or was somehow responsible. I was glad that Barry didn't agree.

"Okay, first order of business is to forge a relationship with Marianne," I said to Mr. Kitty, who'd had enough wandering and had jumped into my lap. "It's going to be a challenge. She barely said more than hello when she came to happy hour." The black-and-white cat didn't seem very concerned.

I picked up my cell phone and clicked on her number, thinking that at least I had an opening. I could offer to bring over her crochet project on my way to work.

After a few rings, I expected her voicemail to kick in, but then I heard her say hello.

"Hi, it's Molly from the bookstore," I said in my friendliest voice. I mentioned that I'd found the scarf she was making and could bring it by, acting as if I had no idea that anything had happened at her place.

"That would be very nice," she said in the same flat tone she always had, and we agreed on the time. It was so strange. Her words suggested that she was happy at the prospect, but her monotone voice sounded like she didn't care.

It was much easier finding Marianne's house the second time, both because it was daylight and because I now knew where the turn for the private road was. How funny that I'd driven by there countless times and never realized there was a house on top of that barren-looking hill. As I drove up the private street this time, I noticed that the wild plants that grew on the hillside were beginning to turn golden now that the winter rains had ended.

I reached the end of the cul-de-sac and went through the gate, which was ajar as it had been the previous night. I hadn't been able to see the lay of the land in the dark. Now I saw there was a large paved area, which at the moment contained a white van and a Subaru. The house was a one-story white stucco ranch style with a terra-cotta roof. It was definitely old and had classic arched windows on the front and a tiled walkway that led to the entrance.

I parked behind the Subaru and made a point of walking past where the white van was parked. When I peeked around the front of it, I saw the yellow tape blocking the entry to an open area, which for now was covered with a tent. I was sure the tent and the van were both part of the police investigation. It seemed pretty quiet, and for a moment I thought about peeking in, but my good sense kicked in before I made a move.

I continued on to the door and rang the bell. A woman in a gray uniform answered and seemed wary as she looked at me. I held up the crochet work and explained why I was there, which didn't seem to help.

"I'm not supposed to let anyone in," the woman said.

"I spoke to Marianne on the phone," I said, holding my ground. "Go ask her. She's expecting me." I gave my name, but the woman wouldn't leave the door.

I was afraid we were stuck in a standoff, but then Marianne appeared behind her. "What's going on, Hilda?" she asked of the uniformed woman.

"I was instructed not to let anyone in," the woman said, keeping her eye on me as if I might try to sneak in.

"It's okay to let Molly in," Marianne said.

"But your brother said—" the uniformed woman began before Marianne interrupted.

"This is my house, and I said it's okay to let her in." I was surprised at the strength in Marianne's tone, but she seemed to pay a price for it, because as the uniformed woman finally stepped out of the way and I went in, I noticed that Marianne was leaning against the wall.

Hilda stepped closer and offered Marianne her arm while admonishing her. "Don't get yourself all worked up, or I'll have to give you another injection."

Marianne pulled away from the woman and found her balance. "No, no more injections." She turned to me. "Let's go in the den."

* * *

"Do you think that's such a good idea?" Hilda asked. "Your brother asked me to keep you out of there. He thought it might be disturbing."

"Fine, then we'll go into the living room," Marianne said, and she led the way to a comfortable-looking room that I noticed was an eclectic mixture of styles. A ball-shaped lamp with a paper shade hung over the seating area, and an old grandfather clock sat against the wall. Marianne offered me a seat on a buttery-soft leather couch and sat down next to me.

I wondered why the den would be disturbing to Marianne, but there wasn't an opening to bring it up.

"Could you bring us some sparkling water?" Marianne said to the woman as I put my tote bag on the coffee table in front of us.

"I'm not supposed to leave you alone," Hilda said, but Marianne told her to get the drinks. The woman looked at me. "Don't say anything to upset her while I'm gone." Reluctantly, she left the room.

"My brother found her from some service and left her a bunch of ridiculous instructions. I would have been fine by myself," Marianne said, shaking her head mechanically. "Errol doesn't think I can manage on my own. He worries about me driving, doing anything, like making coffee, or even eating a sandwich. It's the meds. They mess with everything, and sometimes I do have days where I can barely move."

I wondered if I should bring up Connie now that we had a moment alone, but before I could think it through, the uniformed woman had returned with a tray holding two bottles of lemon-flavored sparkling water and two glasses with ice. She set it down on the coffee table and started to fuss with the caps, but Marianne shooed her away and said, "Why don't you take a break?"

The woman held her ground and repeated that she'd been told not to leave Marianne alone.

"I'll be fine," Marianne said to the woman. But when Hilda suggested discussing the situation with her brother,

Marianne told her she could stay. "I'm not going to trouble Errol any more after all that he's done."

The woman took a seat in the corner and tried to pretend not to be watching us.

Marianne took the top off her water and began to drink right from the bottle. "I drink and drink and my mouth is still dry."

"This is nice," I said. "We've never really had a chance to talk before."

She put the bottle on the table. "It's hard for me in a group." She attempted to smile.

If it weren't for the drugs keeping her expression so flat, she'd have been a pretty woman. Her dark wavy hair softened the square shape of her face. It seemed to me that her clothing choice was out of sync with her age. The adjective that best described her clothing was "simple to put on." The black pants probably had an elastic waistband, and the long royal-blue shirt she wore over it fit loosely. She noticed me checking out her outfit.

"Not very stylish, is it? But at least it's something I can manage myself." She held up her hands and moved her fingers awkwardly. "They don't work like they're supposed to. That's why the scarf looks the way it does. I try and try, but my fingers won't obey."

I handed her the scarf, and she eagerly started to crochet. I watched her struggle and wished there was a way to help her. I had liked Marianne right away and felt terrible that she was living her life in such a fog. I wondered what the problem was.

I pulled out the project I always carried with me and

began to crochet with her. It was a nice moment, but the uniformed woman looked at her watch and intervened.

"It's time for your meds," Hilda said, dropping her voice as if she was trying to keep me from hearing.

"We can do it later," Marianne said.

The woman had already produced a little cup with a number of pills and was making her way across the room. "You have to take them now," she said.

Marianne hung her head and tried to protest, but the woman prevailed, and Marianne swallowed the cocktail of drugs. Hilda finally returned to her seat.

Marianne leaned back with a thud, and her shoulders dropped almost instantly. Her facial features seemed to droop. "Sorry, they're kicking in. It makes it hard for me to feel anything." She made an effort to face me. "It's probably hard for you to believe, but people used to think I was funny. I was really good at telling jokes." There was a dreamy sound to her voice. She held on to the crochet project. "Thank you for bringing it by. I really liked being in the group."

"You should come back," I said.

"I'll have to see what I can do." Her words were getting slurry. "Not sure what Hilda's duties cover."

Our time together was clearly ending, and I hadn't even brought up the tent in the yard. It was now or never.

"What about Connie?" I blurted out.

Marianne looked at Hilda and then at me. "Can't talk now," she said in a woozy voice. The next thing I knew, Hilda was showing me the door.

My first day on duty, and I'd struck out.

Chapter Seven

"I'm glad you're here," Mrs. Shedd said as I came into the bookstore after leaving Marianne's. "Someone from the Craftee Channel called and said to let you know they'd be coming by on Monday and needed to see the Make-and-Take project. And"—my boss indicated a formal-looking woman sitting in one of the easy chairs spread around the bookstore—"she's here to see you about the upcoming author event."

It took a moment, and then it all came back to me. With the show taping to deal with and then the business with Marianne, I had forgotten about the signing we had coming up. A local author writing under the name Missy Z had contacted me some months back just as her self-published book, *The Hot Zone*, was coming out and wanted to arrange a signing at Shedd & Royal. To be honest, I hadn't expected her book to draw much of a crowd, so I had offered her a chance to take part in an event we put on every few months for local authors to talk about their books.

But something had happened between then and now

that had changed everything. It had started when a columnist for *The Huffington Post* wrote a piece about books that had the same titles but very different content. She had a lot of fun comparing *The Hot Zone*, which was about Ebola and scientists garbed in protective gear, with Missy Z's book, an erotic romantic comedy about an unlikely couple who got stuck alone on an island for a month. He was a stuffy sex therapist and she a woman who'd been dumped by her boyfriend and was down on men.

The perky host of a national morning talk show then picked up on the column and ended up reading Missy Z's book. The host raved about it, saying that it made her both blush and laugh. The book suddenly took off, and we offered Missy Z her own event. As I said, things had changed, and Missy Z's representative had called me the previous week and said she'd be coming in to talk over the arrangements.

"You're Frances Allen, the publicity person for Missy Z, I take it?" I said, holding out my hand to the woman. I'd dealt with publicity people before, but it was usually on the phone and concerning things like whether the author wanted ice in their water. I sat down in the chair adjacent to her and asked what I could do for her.

"Missy Z hired me to handle her appearances now that her book has become a best seller. I'm afraid she has some very specific demands," she began. I felt very underdressed in my khaki pants and sweater next to the publicity woman's black pantsuit and heels.

"Could you show me where her signing is going to take place?" the woman asked, and I led her to our regular event area. For now, it was empty, but I told her we would set up chairs, and I stepped to the front of it and showed her where the author usually stood and talked to the crowd.

"And we have a table and a chair for the actual signing."

"That all seems fine, but she wrote the book under a pseudonym and is adamant about keeping her identity unknown."

I nodded in agreement, and she continued. "There must be a staging area set up for her with complete privacy. She'll arrive alone and anonymously and will slip into the backstage area, where she will put on her covering. She'd like the lights in the whole bookstore lowered during her appearance. It will be up to the bookstore employees to keep the signing line moving. When the signing is over, she will return to the backstage area, remove her disguise, and blend in with the crowd to leave." She looked to me for my approval.

I pointed to an open area near where we'd put the table and chair. "I'm sure we can rig up some sort of private area for her. You can tell her where it will be," I said. We went over a few other minor details, and when everything was settled, we walked toward the front of the store together. She continued on to the door, and I headed to the information booth.

I felt a hand on my arm just as I got inside the cubicle. "Am I glad to see you," I said as I looked up and saw Dinah.

"The feeling is mutual," my friend said as she reached over and gave me a hug. "I thought we could get some coffee. I couldn't drink mine at home." I thought she was going to explain, but she got distracted by the cover of a book sitting on the information booth counter. "You're reading this?"

I laughed and told her it was just a mock-up of *The Hot Zone*. The cover had a photo that appeared to have been blacked out and had the word CENSORED written in yellow across it. All that was visible were the heads of a man and woman seemingly lost in ecstasy.

"I just met with a publicity person about the book signing." I showed Dinah that the inside was empty, explaining that it was a new edition and we wouldn't have the actual books until the event. "I don't think Mrs. Shedd even realizes what kind of book it is. She just knows that it's become a best seller." I told Dinah the story line and read her the cover copy:

> *There's a sizzle in the tropics when a mismatched couple work out their differences by finding exotic erotic ways to pleasure each other. No details spared.*

"Whew, sounds pretty hot," Dinah said. "What's the author like?" She pointed out the name below the title.

"I don't know. I haven't met Missy Z and will probably never get to know her. She's doing the signing in a disguise and is insisting on complete anonymity. Mrs. Shedd is sure we'll sell a boatload of copies, so all the fuss will be worth it." I let out a sigh. "And if that wasn't enough, Mrs. Shedd said someone from the Craftee Channel called to let me know they'll be coming by and would like to see the Make-and-Take project."

"I get it. And we don't even have the project figured out yet. It definitely sounds like coffee time to me." Dinah waited for me to exit the information desk. It was nice having our two new hires. All I had to do was tell them I'd be in the café if they needed me.

Bob, our barista, started making our order as soon as we got near the counter. "Ladies," he said pushing a red eye toward me and a café au lait toward Dinah. "Any treats?" He made a broad gesture toward the glass counter. Along with making great coffee drinks, he baked fresh cookie bars. I'd skipped breakfast, and the Linzer bars looked fantastic.

"This is definitely a cookie bar day," Dinah said, ordering two for each of us. We carried our goodies to a table by the window where we could talk without being overheard.

Dinah took a sip of her half coffee/half milk and held the cup up in a toast to Bob. "Perfect as usual," she called out before turning back to me. "So what happened after you left my place? Barry came over, didn't he?"

"Well, yeah," I said. He hadn't forbidden me to mention that he'd come over, just the part about why.

"He doesn't think you're a suspect, does he?"

"No. But he wanted to know what I was doing at Marianne's." I drank some of my red eye and took a bite of the cookie bar hungrily, glad that Dinah had ordered two for each of us.

"Did he tell you what happened, or did you have one of your usual dueling matches where you both ask each other questions and try not to give out any information?"

"No. He just refused to tell me anything."

"But I bet you fed him," she said, shaking her head with a laugh that sent the spikes in her salt-and-pepper hair rocking. "I don't care what you say, you still have feelings for him."

"When we broke up, he said he couldn't do the friend thing, but that doesn't mean I can't. I'm feeding him as a friend." I really wished I could tell her the whole story and add *co-investigator* to *friend*. That's how I was describing it, even if Barry never would.

Dinah rolled her eyes. No matter what I said, she kept insisting there were still something going on between Barry and me.

"I admit, I always feel a tug when I see him, but there's no point. It would never work out. He's married to his job, and he has to be in charge all the time. I can't deal with the way he controls all his emotions."

"Yes, but when the dam breaks and all those feelings pour out"—Dinah pretended to fan herself—"now that would make some steamy novel. Maybe you should talk to Missy Z about it."

I wanted to get the conversation off of Barry and told Dinah about the online news story I'd seen. "There were no names given, but I bet it was Connie," I said.

"How creepy that she was electrocuted," Dinah said with a shiver. "I wonder how that happened."

"I don't know—well, except I think I saw where it happened." I described the white van and the tent over the open area at Marianne's and then explained that I'd gone back there before coming to the bookstore.

"So the story didn't say if it was murder, just suspicious circumstances?" Dinah said. "What do you think?"

"Okay, Dr. Watson," I said with a smile. "I don't know enough about the circumstances yet. But I do know that we were right when we figured that Connie worked for Marianne, and we know her title now—companion. Whatever that means." I thought of Hilda, who was obviously Connie's replacement, though she seemed more like a warden. "I'm going to tell you about my visit and see what we can figure out." I went on to describe my whole time there while Dinah listened with rapt attention.

We discussed it afterward and came to a number of conclusions: Marianne had more spunk than we'd realized. She seemed to be more self-aware than we'd thought. She didn't like having a companion, and she certainly didn't like taking her medicine.

"You know, if somebody killed Connie, the most obvious suspect is Marianne," Dinah said.

"It's too soon to say that. We don't know all the details." I thought of what Barry had said about Detective Heather jumping to that conclusion. "Let's talk about something else, like why you couldn't have your coffee at home," I said.

"Okay, fine. Dr. Watson just closed up shop." She took a deep breath. "It seems rather petty now, but I couldn't have my coffee or do anything at my house thanks to Cassandra. Did I mention that she's a yoga teacher? She invited some of her old friends over and was giving an impromptu class in my living room. I tried stepping over all the bodies sprawled on yoga mats to get to the kitchen but ended up grabbing my stuff and going out the front door instead."

"Poor you," I said.

Dinah let out a sigh and drained her cup. "Maybe it's not so bad. The coffee is better here, anyway. Now, I'm off to face my students."

* * *

It felt like déjà vu when Mrs. Shedd snagged me as soon as I headed back into the bookstore. "Is everything okay with Missy Z's event?" She said it a little fast, which made her sound a little frantic. I assured her I had it under control.

"Good, but what about the crochet project for the taping? It's all set up, right?" Before I could say anything reassuring, she continued, "This is such an opportunity for the bookstore. The Craftee people didn't say anything exactly, but I'm sure if they're happy using us as a location, they'll tape more of the shows here. It isn't about the money they'd pay us. It's the exposure for the bookstore." Her voice trilled as she began to describe the excitement of seeing our shop on TV. "Please, Molly, do whatever you can to make the taping a success." She did something she'd never done before—she reached out and hugged me, and I thought I saw tears welling in her eyes.

All I could think was, *Thank heavens she doesn't know we don't have the Make-and-Take project yet.* I waited until she went back to her office, then rushed back to the yarn department and started pulling out crochet books, looking for anything marked *quick*.

At four thirty I was still at the table, only now it was littered with hooks and half-finished projects and a lot of open books.

"Back from the student wars for a dose of crochet. I'm early, which shows how much I need it," Dinah said, arriving at the table. She looked over the mess as she put down her tote bag. "What's going on?"

"Mrs. Shedd is pinning so much on the success of this taping. I just can't let her down. I was trying to find a project for the Make-and-Take." I showed her a pattern for a tiny crocheted bag meant to hold a sachet. "What do you think of this?"

She shook her head. "Sorry, but there's no magic." She pulled out her chair and sat down. "Don't worry, I'm sure CeeCee will come up with something."

I saw our resident celebrity Hooker coming. She went right to the head of the table and set a large green Whole Foods bag on the table before coming over to us. "What are you doing, dear?" she asked, looking over my shoulder at the book.

Before I could answer, she figured it out and let out a tinkle of her laughter. "No worries. I have it covered. I found the perfect project." When I tried to get her to show me, her eyes crinkled as she smiled. "I'll do the big reveal when everyone is here."

By five o'clock, almost the whole group was there and they'd taken out their individual projects to work on. It was easy to see who was missing, since everyone seemed to have a regular seat. Only Adele had moved around the corner from the foot of the table, making sure we all knew her old place was reserved for Rory.

"She told me that I'm her crochet companion," Adele said.

"What does that mean?" Rhoda said, taking the seat next to Sheila.

"Doesn't *companion* usually mean having someone with you all the time to look after you? Kind of like a babysitter for an adult who has some kind of issues," Dinah said, and then looked at me. I knew she was thinking about Connie.

"It sounds like something for Hollywood types and rich people," Rhoda said. She glanced down at the potholder she was working on, realized she'd missed a stitch, and began to rip out the row.

"I like the title," Adele said defiantly. "I'll be there to guide her hand and catch her if she starts to mess up her stitches. And then, since I've been on the Craftee Channel already and anybody can see I'm a real pro in front of the camera, I bet the show people'll want me to be her sidekick."

"How did we get from talking about what a companion does to talking about your career?" Elise asked as she finished the first round of another of her small afghans. She had a birdlike voice that stood out from the others. It was funny how Rhoda really looked like who she was—solid with her feet on the ground—but Elise's appearance was deceptive. She had sort of an ethereal air, and it seemed like a good gust of wind could knock her over, but inside she was nothing like that. When she got into something, whether it was vampires or real estate, she had an iron core. She looked around the table. "Anybody know anyone who wants to sell their house?" She asked that almost every night and then followed up with offering new services, including staging a house so it had its best potential to sell.

"Not to rush you or anything," I said to CeeCee, "but could you show us what you brought in for us to consider for the Make-and-Take? Which, by the way, the Craftee people are coming by to see on Monday."

"Of course, dear," CeeCee said, and began to unload some supplies from the tote bag. She put a sandwich-size plastic bag containing some small wooden beads on the table. "When you see it, I think you'll agree that I've found an ideal project for the Make-and-Take. It has the magic that was missing from the key chain, and I even came up with an appealing name." She gave me a smile and a nod of reassurance.

Eduardo came in and slid into a seat just as she finished pulling out her supplies. He nodded a greeting to the group and let out a sigh. "Just the break I need before going back to the Apothecary," he said. It had to be a very different life than the one he'd had when he was a cover model and commercial spokesperson. Instead of intense days during photo shoots or filming, he was now doing something that kept going day after day. And since the upscale drug and sundries store belonged to him, the buck stopped with him, too.

"I'll show you the supplies first." CeeCee spoke to the group and then turned to me. "You said they all had to be from the show's sponsor." She offered me the labels that went with the length of cording and some small wooden beads in the plastic bag, and everyone stopped working and turned to her.

"We're not all here. Wait for Rory," Adele said.

"*Tsk.*" CeeCee rolled her eyes. "I don't consider her actually one of the Hookers. She's just seizing on yarn to further her career. If they were doing a show on how to be your own plumber, she'd be wielding a plunger and wearing coveralls."

As CeeCee was talking, Marianne slipped up to the table and took her seat. She took out her scarf and begin examining it intently, looking for where she'd left off.

"You came back, Marianne," CeeCee said in a welcoming voice. Though there was a hint of a question in the way she said it as we all focused on the empty seat next to her.

"Where's your fr—" Rhoda began to say, but I gave her a sharp shake of my head to stop her. "I mean, it's so nice you're here." Rhoda smiled at Marianne.

CeeCee was about to get back to revealing her Make-and-Take project when there was a flutter of excitement at the front of the store as Rory roared in. She didn't walk but seemed to almost twirl, stopping several times to have a Dance Break with an unsuspecting customer. In no time, she was surrounded by shoppers. She signed a few autographs and then came back to join us.

Even though CeeCee was a bit self-absorbed—but then, what actor wasn't?—she was also incredibly warm and caring, and her reaction to Rory was uncharacteristic. It almost looked like she snarled when Rory reached the table.

"Sorry I'm late," Rory said, addressing the whole group. Her voice was loud, and I noticed a few customers in the vicinity turning her way. Adele waved her over to the empty seat next to her, and Rory plopped down. "Now fill me in on what I missed."

There was a little furrow in CeeCee's eyebrows, a sure sign she was perturbed, but then she brought out her usual merry smile. "To get back to the Make-and-Take project." She held out a long circle of stitches with some beads at the end. I wasn't going to say anything, but it really didn't look like much. That is, until she wound it around her wrist, and suddenly it became a really attractive bracelet.

"We could call it the Gratitude Circle and say that it's meant to remind the wearer of all the good things in their life." She was in the process of taking it off so she could pass it around the table when there was a new disturbance. I sensed someone marching into the yarn department sending out an angry vibe. Errol Freeman reached the table and put his hand on his sister's shoulder. "I figured this was where you went." He looked at the empty seat next to her. "Hilda called me and said you left. Are you crazy?"

She gave him a pained look and then turned to the rest of us. "Sorry, I have to go." He seemed impatient as she gathered up her things and he hustled her out of there.

"What was that about?" CeeCee asked. She seemed to be directing her question at no one in particular.

"Molly knows," Dinah said, and all eyes turned to me.

My answer brought them all to a halt. "Connie is dead."

There was dead silence for a moment, and then they all started talking, wanting to know what had happened. As soon as I mentioned the article I'd seen, most of them nodded with recognition.

"That was about Connie?" Rhoda said. "It was awfully short on details. Just that a woman had been electrocuted in Tarzana."

Rory kept looking around at everyone and seemed upset when no one was looking back at her. She actually stood up, called out "Dance Break," and did her signature move to try to get their attention back. But when it comes to a choice between details of a mysterious dead body and a celebrity doing a silly dance move, the body always wins.

I think the group was disappointed I didn't have more details, and they began to talk about Marianne's abrupt departure. Rhoda was the one who put two and two together. "Connie was a companion, like what you were talking about before, and the man who showed up was concerned because Marianne needs to have someone with her."

After that, the time flew by, and suddenly it was six and the Hookers were getting ready to scatter. CeeCee did manage to get a vote on the bracelet before everyone left. It was a unanimous yes.

At least one problem was solved.

Chapter Eight

For once, I didn't have time to hang around either. I barely had time to pick up the yarns scraps, make sure all the chairs were pushed in, and watch Rory dance her way out the front door before I had to grab my things and go.

Mason had made the plans as soon as his law firm had bought a table at the Make a Miracle Foundation fundraiser. These charity dinners were as much about business as they were social. When Charlie was alive, we'd gone to things like this often. Though usually he was doing the PR for the event, so it was more like work.

Tonight was going to be the first time since Mason and I had gotten back together that we were going to a big social event. I didn't think anyone really cared, but he looked at it as an announcement that we were a couple.

The program was always pretty much the same for these things. There'd be a lot of schmoozing as the crowd checked out the items at the silent auction. Most of them were entertainment business related, like walk-on roles on a popular sitcom, signed scripts, jewelry designed by a celebrity, and some regular stuff donated by famous people.

There'd be dinner, followed by a celebrity host doing a pitch for the charity, followed by some entertainment, followed by a live auction for fabulous trips, expensive jewelry, and designer purses that cost absurd amounts of money. The evening would end with dessert, dancing, drinking, and the results of the silent auction.

I gave the animals everything they needed as soon as I got home and then went to get ready for my so-called debut. The handle to the bathroom door had been replaced, but after getting locked in there previously when it had fallen off, I wasn't taking any chances and left the door wide open. I was home alone anyway, so it didn't matter. I'd already planned what I was going to wear, so my turnaround time was pretty quick. My dress was simple, almost like a slip, in a soft shade of peach that was flattering on just about everyone. I did my makeup and caught a glimpse of myself in the mirror. I'd always thought of my hair and eyes as being brown with no fancy description attached, but now, as the light caught my shoulder-length hair, I saw the gold and red highlights. And as I looked at my eyes, I thought they could be considered loden green, which was a whole lot more exciting than just brown. I laughed at my own vanity and left the bathroom.

I heard the dogs start a ruckus and then between barks heard the doorbell ring. "You're really taking this date thing seriously," I said as I pulled open the front door. Mason had gone all out and was wearing a tuxedo. I was surprised that he wasn't holding a corsage in a box as well.

"You look great," he said, adding a wolf whistle.

"You could have just called and I would have come out," I said.

"I'm not some teenager honking for you," he said with a grin. "That's one of my strong points. I offer the full gentleman treatment."

He waited while I grabbed my wrap and purse. Then he took my arm, and we walked across the front yard to his Mercedes SUV in the driveway.

He opened the passenger door for me and helped me in before going around to the driver's side. I saw him look back toward the street. A black Crown Victoria had just pulled to the curb.

"That looks like Barry," Mason said. He turned to me. "What's he doing here?"

For a moment I had that deer-in-headlights feeling as I wondered what to say. It was obvious Barry had come by for a report of what I'd found out. I certainly couldn't tell Mason.

Mason paused at the open car door. "Maybe I should go talk to him. Find out what he wants."

"No. Don't do that," I said. Then the perfect solution came to mind. "He just came by to see his dog." I started to get in the car. "We can go. He has a key."

Mason gave the car a dirty look. "That's still going on? Maybe it's time to resolve it one way or the other. He takes the dog or gives it up."

I didn't want to tell Mason that I couldn't do that to Barry or his son. Their visits were sporadic, but they both cared about Cosmo. And for Barry, it seemed the only time he really let go was when he was playing fetch with the dogs. Of course, I hadn't seen him doing it that much lately. In fact, their visits had all been when I wasn't home. I mentioned the last fact to Mason, and it seemed to calm him down.

He finally got in the SUV and backed down the driveway. By the time we'd gotten on the 101, he was back to his usual upbeat self. "So, tell me, anything new?" He asked offhandedly. I knew he was going to be shocked when I told him what had happened since I'd last talked to him, leaving the Barry part out, of course.

He listened with rapt attention as I told him the about the article and my second trip to Marianne's house.

"You should have called me," he said.

"It seemed like it could wait," I said. "It's not like I'm a suspect or anything." I couldn't say that my first thought had been to talk to Dinah and that I was now working with Barry.

I still found it a little funny that someone who had once been so committed to not being committed was getting so possessive. I told him the rest of the story as we drove up the hill on the 405.

"Well, there isn't really a reason for you to get involved," he said.

"Oh, you know me. I can't help starting to wonder what happened and who did what to who," I said with a laugh. "Once you've gotten a taste of snooping around, it seems like a natural reaction anytime you come close to a crime. Besides, I like Marianne, and I'm afraid the cops might think she did it."

"How about you put it on the back burner and we just have fun tonight," Mason said as he pulled in front of the Century City Hotel and the valets opened the car doors.

The main ballroom was set up with a sea of round tables, a stage and dance floor, and a bar and schmoozing area adjacent to an arrangement of long tables with the silent and live auction merchandise. We located our table, which I was surprised to find in the primo area at the very front, and then went to join the crowd at the bar. Mason had his hand against the small of my back, partly to direct me and partly as a sign to all concerned that I was with him. He seemed to know everybody, and they all stopped to greet him. I always forgot what a powerful attorney he was, but seeing how people deferred to him made it abundantly clear. He made it a point to introduce me to everyone. We had never been able to come up with terms for our relationship, so he simply said, "This is Molly," but the way he said made it clear that it was more than a casual relationship.

I remembered that when Charlie's PR firm had worked on events like this it was important to get celebrities to show up. Whoever had organized this event seemed to have succeeded and I recognized a number of well-known entertainers.

Mason was all smiles as he worked the crowd, but then he leaned in close. "It is so much more bearable going to this now that you're here." I knew it was all just business to him and most of the people there.

"Well, it's the bookstore lady," a male voice said. When I turned, I was face-to-face with Michael Kostner. It made sense that he would be there. He fit right in with the rest of the crowd. "You clean up nice," he said in a joking voice; then he saw who I was with, and I heard a little "oh" escape his lips.

I could tell that, in that second, I had jumped up a whole lot of notches in position in his mind. He seemed to know Mason, and they exchanged some small talk before he turned back to me.

"My people were supposed to reach out to you. I hope everything is going smoothly." I nodded and mentioned I'd gotten word they would be stopping by. He seemed pleased. "You know, it was my idea to use the bookstore. I thought the vibe of the place would add a whole dimension to the program."

Michael had a natural charm, and I found myself smiling as he explained that he was new to this kind of programing and wanted to make it appealing to more than a niche audience.

I felt Mason's hand on my back as he gave me a nudge toward our seats. "Good seeing you, Michael," Mason said as a way of ending things.

Mason introduced me to everyone at our table. I gathered they all worked in the law firm in one position or another. They all smiled politely, but I couldn't really tell if I met with their approval.

Dinner was forgettable. The food at these things always sounded good on the printed menu at each plate, but was usually tasteless and hard to chew. As soon as the dinner plates were cleared, the program began. I half listened to all the wonderful plans the charity had for the money raised, which was a pitch to get everyone to make generous bids on the silent-auction items before it closed. It was bad form to just sit there, so Mason and I went to make the rounds but quickly got separated.

"We meet again," Michael said. He glanced around. He looked at the silk scarf I'd picked up to examine. "Is that the one they used in *St. Louis P.D.* to kill the opera singer?"

"One and the same," I said, pointing to the written description on the bidding sheet.

"Now that's a real collector's item," he joked. I laughed and put the scarf down and prepared to move on, but he pulled me aside and seemed more serious. "You're probably a good person to ask," he said. "I heard that Rory Graham is hanging out with your crochet group. She sold us on what an expert she is with yarn and crochet. You've probably seen her in action. She really is an expert, right?"

I shuddered. Rory had admitted that she might have oversold her skills, which I had taken to mean that she'd told them she knew how to crochet. But claiming to be an expert was a whole other thing. I wasn't sure if Adele had gotten past having Rory practice doing chain stitches so they weren't all loopy looking. What was I going to say? I hated to lie, but I couldn't out Rory. Besides, I had confidence in Adele's teaching abilities. "She's a real wiz. You should have seen her offering to help everyone."

He gave me a puzzled look, and I realized I was laying

it on too thick. Nobody who knew Rory would buy that she was so into helping anyone but herself. But then he continued. "It's very important that we come across as authentic. I'm sure someone told you that we want some baked goods on the table made with our sponsor's flour, and we need everyone to eat them was gusto."

I told him I was already on it and understood there should be a recipe on the website. "It doesn't have to come from Rory, does it?" I asked, and he shook his head.

"No, and she doesn't have to claim to have baked it either, just eat a cookie and say it's great." I heard music starting and saw people moving to the dance floor.

"I'm glad you reassured me about Rory's skills," he said finally. "I don't know what we'd do if it turned out she wasn't what she'd said she was. It would be a shame to have to postpone or cancel everything because we found out that she couldn't perform."

I was relieved when Mason snagged me and said they were playing our song. *Really? We had a song?*

On the way home, I told Mason the truth about Rory.

"Oh, no," he said. "Maybe you should have told him the truth. It will be a mess if she can't deliver what she promised."

"You seemed to know Michael pretty well," I said.

"He was a client." We'd gotten on the freeway and were heading toward the dark mountain section of the Sepulveda Pass.

"What naughty thing did he do?" I said in a teasing tone.

"It turns out, nothing," Mason said. "I helped him at a rough time. Just met him once and didn't even charge for my services."

"Good, then he likes you. Promise you'll help me if things hit the fan with Rory. Mrs. Shedd would be crushed if they didn't do the show at the bookstore."

Mason patted my hand. "It's one of the benefits of being my woman—free legal help."

"Your woman?" I said. "Please tell me you didn't say that to any of the people we saw tonight."

Mason sneaked a glance at me. "Of course not. I was just teasing you. You're more like my gal." This time we both laughed.

"You were the belle of the ball." We'd reached the end of the looming mountains and begun the steep descent into the San Fernando Valley. The lights spread before us in a twinkling panorama. "How about a nightcap at my place and cappuccinos and croissants for breakfast?"

"I don't know," I started. "I wouldn't have my car or clothes for the morning. I don't know if Samuel's coming home after his gig and can take care of the animals. And I have to go in early and deal with the whole Rory situation."

I heard Mason chuckle. "I'm talking romance and you're all about logistics."

"Sorry," I said. "I guess I'm guilty of being too responsible."

Chapter Nine

Mason pulled into my driveway and cut the motor. "If you won't come to the mountain, the mountain could come to you," he said, touching my arm tenderly.

"No," I said a little too abruptly. In the back of my mind, I was thinking that if Barry had come by earlier, there was a good chance he'd at least call later. If I didn't answer the phone, Mason would wonder why, and if I did, he'd want to know who called. The worst imaginary scenario had Mason actual answering the phone. There was no anonymity anymore. Even if Barry hung up, all it took was pushing a few buttons on the phone and you could see who called.

I caught myself and softened my tone. "It's just been a very long day, and there's so much going on at the bookstore."

He let out a disappointed sigh. "You shouldn't work so hard. But then, I should talk." His mouth curved into a grin. "And I'm sure Spike would thank you. He doesn't like it when I stay out all night." He turned toward me and stroked my hair. "How about a rain check for this weekend?"

"Perfect." I opened the door to get out.

He insisted on walking me to the door. As we walked on the stone path across the front yard, I kept stealing a look at the street, worried that Barry might suddenly drive up.

"Well, then, I guess it's good-night," Mason said when I'd unlocked the front door. "This is kind of exciting, kissing good-night at the door."

He took me in his arms and outdid himself showing me what I was missing. It almost worked, but then I pushed the door open with my foot and said good-night.

I let out my breath in relief when I shut the door. I'd managed to keep Barry and Mason apart. I looked down the hall and saw that the door to Samuel's room was open and the lights were off, which meant he wasn't home. I'd barely walked in the kitchen to open the door and let Cosmo and Felix out for a run when the phone rang.

"Greenberg," he said when I'd barely gotten out a hello. "Is it okay to come in?"

I couldn't help but laugh at his insistence on being so official. "You could just say it was Barry."

"I guess I could, but that makes it seem social, and this is all official police business."

"Official? Really? Then your superiors know you're using me as a source for information."

I heard him make some uncomfortable noises. "How about we talk about it when I come in?"

I agreed, and when I opened the front door, he was standing on my porch, holding a box. I looked out past him to the street and saw that the curb was empty. "You parked down the street?"

"Yes," he said without elaborating, so I did it for him.

"If this is so official, why try to hide that you're coming here?" I teased.

He blew out his breath in consternation. "Okay, you're right. It's not really official police business. Are you happy?"

"Yes." Before I could say more, the two dogs had pushed the kitchen door open and come inside. They ran to greet Barry while I rushed to shut the door before the cats figured out it was open.

Barry came into the kitchen with the two dogs in tow. "Is it okay to give them something?"

"Sure," I said. In the light, I got a good look at what he was carrying. A pizza box. He saw me looking at it.

"You're always feeding me. I thought it was the least I could do." He set it on the counter and gave the dogs a treat.

The smell of the pizza wafted across the kitchen, and this time it was my stomach that gurgled in response to the scent.

He glanced at my outfit. "But then, I suppose you've already eaten." He seemed surprised when he checked his watch. "I didn't realize it was past eleven." He looked at my dress again. "You must have been out somewhere fancy with Mason."

"It was one of those charity events. And I'm sure you've heard the term *rubber chicken*." I opened the box and looked at the large cheese pizza. "I didn't realize it, but I'm starving."

"Welcome to the club."

I was about to pull out some plates, but I asked for a short delay. I was starting to feel chilled in the thin dress. Now that it was spring, the days were warm, but the nights had a cold edge. He offered to set things up while I changed.

I came back a few minutes later feeling much more comfortable in leggings and a long sleeve T-shirt. Barry had set everything up on the coffee table in the living room and was sitting on one of the twin couches. I got some sparkling water for us and sat across from him. I served him a slice before putting one on my plate and then began struggling to cut it with a knife and fork while I balanced the plate on my knees. He had left his plate on the coffee table and simply picked up his piece and took a bite before setting it back down. "Well, we might as well get down to it."

I stopped trying to cut my piece and looked up at him. Something had been on my mind. "I was wondering. Since you said that Heather is so sure what happened, why no arrest?"

Barry's brow furrowed and his dark eyes flashed. "I thought we weren't going to do that."

"Weren't going to do what?" I asked.

"There you go again. You know what I'm talking about. I'm supposed to ask the questions and you're just supposed to give me information."

"You're being a little pigheaded," I said. "I just thought it would help me to understand more if I knew why no one had been arrested, since Heather already decided what happened."

Barry took another bite of his pizza and chewed it thoughtfully. I knew he was stalling. When he set down the slice, he seemed a little uncomfortable.

"Is it because it could be accidental?" I asked.

"It's really not your concern," he said.

"How'd Connie get electrocuted?" I asked, and he looked up.

"Did Marianne Freeman tell you that's what happened?"

I told him about the online story and that I had figured out it was about Connie Richards even though it didn't mention her name. "The story mentioned the street, and Marianne's house is the only one on it." I asked him again how Connie had gotten electrocuted.

"That's what I'm hoping you can help us find out."

"But what was the means? You must know that," I persisted.

Barry made a face. "You just can't help it, can you? You have to keep making everything a question."

I shrugged. "I learned it from you when we were together."

"It's too bad I was such a good teacher." He finally cracked a smile. He looked at me with the knife and fork. "Why not make it easy on yourself." He demonstrated by picking up his piece again and taking a bite.

Maybe he was right. I put down the silverware and followed suit. It was certainly a lot easier. When I'd demolished most of the piece, he nodded at me.

"So are you ready to tell me what you've found out?"

I smiled and simply said, "Yes."

But telling him that I liked Marianne and how sad it had been when she said she used to be funny wasn't what he wanted to hear. He perked up a little when I mentioned that she'd come back to the Hookers group on her own but her brother had shown up and insisted she leave. "I did get the impression that she doesn't like taking all the meds. She had a temporary helper who had to insist that she take them."

"She must have been upset about what happened. What did she say about the victim?"

"That's the problem. She didn't seem able to feel much of anything. I think the drugs keep her in kind of a stupor. Do you know why she's on them?" I asked, then winced, thinking he was going to make a fuss about another question.

"Heather was following up on that," he said, seeming not to notice that I had asked another question.

"I'll have to find that out on my own."

"I'm really hoping you can find out more about Connie Richards. Marianne was close with her. She must know something about her life." He paused and stared at me directly. "I didn't say this before, but I don't want you to go sneaking around or anything. Nothing that would put you in danger, and absolutely don't do anything illegal. I was hoping you could just pick up things in conversation. It's good that she wants to come to your group. It gives you access."

"I'm not so sure her brother is sold on it. I'm not sure if he was upset because she came alone or if he didn't like her coming to the group at all."

"See what you can do," Barry said.

I smiled at Barry. "And you said you couldn't do the friend thing when we broke up. Look at us, eating pizza and talking about your case like a couple of buds."

"I wouldn't quite call it that, but I do appreciate your help."

We'd eaten our fill of pizza, but it seemed like it needed some kind of finish. I offered him some tea and cookies.

"I knew I forgot something. Dessert. And something hot would be good," he said.

I went into the kitchen and made two mugs of green tea and put some oatmeal cookies on a plate. But when I walked into the living room, Barry was slumped on the couch asleep.

I considered what to do. I figured I should probably wake him, but he seemed so peaceful. So I got a blanket and draped it over him and took my tea in the kitchen.

I checked on him when I came through the living room on my way to bed. He hadn't stirred, and Cosmo was cuddled next to him.

I was glad to finally fall into bed myself. It had been a long day for everybody.

Chapter Ten

The phone cut into my dreams, and it took a number of rings to clear the fog enough for me to reach over and grab the cordless. Mason's cheerful voice startled me.

"We didn't have our sleepover, but I did promise you breakfast. I'm in the driveway with cappuccinos and rolls from the French bakery."

I started to smile at his thoughtfulness, but then I remembered Barry was on the couch and freaked. I looked around the room frantically, as if some answer would pop up. Meanwhile, Mason was asking if he should come in the front or kitchen door.

"Front door," I said. "But could you give me a minute to pull myself together?"

"You don't have to fuss for me. It isn't like I haven't seen you looking bleary-eyed."

"No, no, this is worse," I said, getting up as I spoke. "We're talking smeared mascara, hair askew. If you saw me now, you'd probably want to rethink our whole relationship." By now I was in the living room. Barry was still asleep, and I had to give him a nudge to wake him up. He looked up at me with a puzzled smile, and then reality began to kick in as he sat forward.

"Yes, Mason, it's so thoughtful that you brought over breakfast. Just give me a few minutes to freshen up, and then you can come in the front door." I was doing my best to keep my voice natural, but I was afraid it sounded forced.

Barry nodded with recognition, and I led him to the kitchen door. He was a detective, so I was sure he'd figure out that he needed to give it a few minutes for Mason to come in before he went down the driveway. He mouthed a *thank you* and went out the door.

I hadn't looked in the mirror, and I hoped that I didn't look as bad as I'd described, since there was no time to fix it before I opened the door for Mason.

"Good morning, Sunshine," he said brightly as he came in the door. He looked over my face. "I don't know what you did, but you look great to me. We can have breakfast in the living room." He walked right to the couch and sat in the spot Barry had vacated. His gaze stopped on the pizza box on the table.

"You had a pizza party?" he asked with a puzzled look.

"Me? A party? No way," I said. It wasn't a lie. It hadn't been a party—more of a meeting. I was relieved when Mason drew his own conclusions.

"It must have been Samuel. You ought to make him clean up after himself."

Mason was dressed for work, and we drank our cappuccinos and ate the rolls and then he was on his way to the door.

I picked everything up after he left and put it in the

trash. I looked down the hall to Samuel's room. The door was shut now, which meant he'd come home during the night and was still asleep. I felt a little twinge of guilt that I'd let him take the rap for the pizza box.

The chill of the morning had softened, and the angle of the sun was moving back up in the sky as a reminder that winter was past. The light jacket I'd tossed over my work clothes was enough. As I crossed the stone patio, I looked out at the yard. The last of the orange blossoms clung to the trees, but most of the petals were sprinkled on the ground now. I caught the scent of a lavender hyacinth flower that had appeared in the middle of the flower bed.

I was ready to face my day.

* * *

The first order of business was dealing with Adele. And as soon as I walked in the bookstore, I went looking for her in the kids' department. She was settled at one of the small round tables with a cup of coffee and a stack of books. When she saw me, she held up three of them fanned in her hand. "Which one do you think I should do next?"

I didn't have much time to study them, other than to see that the one in the middle had a picture of somebody in a cape. Adele always dressed for story time, and she favored the dramatic. Before I could point to it, Adele had chosen it herself.

"I'm assuming you came in here for a reason," she said.

"It's about Rory. I have to know. How's it going with her lessons?"

Adele got a smug smile. “She’s going to need me to be at her side.”

“You don’t understand,” I said. “She passed herself off as an expert. She has to be able to hold her own with a hook. If they find out she misrepresented herself, they could pull the plug on the show until they find someone else. Mrs. Shedd would be crushed if that happened.”

“It wouldn’t be a problem. I could step in,” Adele said.

“No, you couldn’t. They want a name. Somebody who will draw viewers.”

Adele seemed stunned at this news, and I saw her lip quiver.

“I know that you’re a great teacher, so use all your skills to bring her up to speed. Okay?”

Adele was caught between the compliment to her teaching ability and the fact that she wasn’t a name. But then it began to sink in that it would be her fault if the show fell apart. She suddenly stood up taller and did a fake salute. “General Adele on the case. Rory won’t be faking it.”

I asked that Adele keep all of this to herself. As I walked away, I heard her say that she was really going to be Rory’s crochet companion now. I hadn’t even dealt with my concern that CeeCee still needed to try out the Make-and Take bracelet, and we needed a recipe.

Rachel, one of our new hires, waved me over as I walked toward the information cubicle. She was holding out the phone and gestured that the call was for me.

I was surprised to hear Marianne on the other end of

the line. "I'm sorry about my brother," she said. "I'm afraid he overreacted. I really want to come to the group. I hope I'm still welcome."

I immediately thought about what Barry had said about talking to her, and her coming to the group would definitely give me an opportunity. "Of course you're welcome, but it seemed like your brother was concerned about you coming alone."

"I have it worked out. For tonight, at least," she said.

"Then I'll see you later." It was certainly going to be an interesting happy hour.

* * *

Adele was already at the back table, looking toward the bookstore entrance anticipating Rory's arrival, when I came into the yarn department that afternoon. Dinah came in behind me, gave me a hug, and whispered that we had to talk, before she sat down. I'd tried to call her earlier but only gotten her voicemail. I knew she wanted details about the event with Mason. I wasn't sure how I could tell her the rest while keeping Barry's secret a secret.

CeeCee took her spot at the head of the table. "I brought some more samples of bracelets for the Make-and-Take," she said as she began to unload her tote bag. "I hope the group gets to try making them tonight." She laid four different versions on the table. The design was the same—a large loop meant to be wound around the wrist—but the materials were different. She'd used different kinds of cording—one even seemed to be made out of a heavy weight of crochet thread. And they all had beads hanging off the ends. "Then we can pick a favorite to use."

Sheila, Rhoda, and Elise came in with Eduardo and went to their usual spots. The empty seat next to Adele was beginning to make me nervous. What if Rory thought she'd already picked up enough to bluff her way through?

But then there was a ruckus at the front of the store. I wondered if Rory ever arrived anywhere without making a stir. She called out "Dance Break!" and began to gyrate near the cashier stand. She kept going until everyone in the line had noticed her and had given her high fives as she walked past them. With a final wave, she came back to join us.

Her Dance Breaks seemed to energize her. She was all perky as she greeted the group as a whole. She seemed to be ignoring Adele, who was patting the spot next to her. I could tell Adele was getting steamed. I only hoped that she would manage to keep it together and coax Rory rather than demand.

I had made sure there would be enough chairs for Marianne as well. She had just said she'd worked it out but hadn't been clear if she was coming alone or with someone.

Rory finally calmed down and took her seat. Adele was on her right away. I saw that my fellow Hooker was trying to see what Rory had learned from their couple of lessons. Adele's eyes bugged out, and I guessed it wasn't good.

My encounter with the producer from the Craftee Channel the night before had reminded me about the baked goods we needed for the taping. I grabbed the floor and explained the situation. "I was hoping someone has a favorite recipe for cookies or cake." I looked over the group expectantly.

"I could give you my easy coffee cake recipe," Rhoda said.

I gave my instant approval. I'd tasted it and it was delicious. I was about to see if she'd agree to make it for the taping when I felt a hand on my shoulder. I looked up and Marianne was standing behind me. And she wasn't alone. The woman with her was wiry with dark hair. She looked at the group around the table and seemed a little nervous.

I was about to suggest we introduce ourselves, but as her eye moved from CeeCee to Rory, she let out an excited squeal and turned to Marianne. "You didn't tell me CeeCee Collins and Rory Graham were in the group."

Marianne was subdued as usual, though she did manage a small smile. Was this woman's Connie's replacement? She certainly wasn't the silent type.

"CeeCee, you seem like an old friend. I used to watch *The CeeCee Collins Show* when I was a little girl," she gushed. CeeCee smiled back at her, but there was just a little twinge of displeasure in her eyes. She had said once that it made her feel old as time when people said things like that. Next, the woman went up to Rory and pointed at her as she squealed "Dance Break!" and mimicked Rory's moves. Rory was out of her seat so fast to join in that her hook bounced off the table and hit the floor.

Marianne took it all in with a placid face, and I suggested they all sit down. Dinah, ever my best friend, stepped in to help.

"I'm Dinah Lyons," she said, extending her hand to the woman. "And you are?"

The woman gave Marianne a sideways glance. I was trying to figure out what it meant. Was she deferring to Marianne to see if it was okay to introduce herself, or was she miffed that Marianne hadn't introduced her at the start?

Marianne seemed to have lapsed into a momentary haze, but then she appeared to rejoin us. I'd noticed it before, and I assumed it was connected to whatever meds she was on. "This is Kelly Freeman, my sister-in-law."

Kelly seemed edgy, and her timing was off in the opposite way from Marianne. She punctuated everything with a nervous laugh and seemed to talk too fast. "I just came for tonight." She dropped her voice. "Marianne needs someone with her until we can find a replacement." She fluttered her eyes. "My husband doesn't want to tell them what happened to the last woman, but you can't keep that to yourself. As soon as they hear . . . well, they're out the door." She glanced toward Marianne again.

Rhoda was never one to be subtle, and she came out and asked what we had all wanted to know but been too polite to ask. "So what exactly happened to her?"

"I don't know. I don't know that anybody does. Somehow she got electrocuted. It has to have been some kind of freak accident."

"You can bet Molly will find out what happened and who did it if it wasn't an accident," Rhoda said. "She's our own local independent investigator."

Suddenly, all eyes were on me. I muttered something

self-effacing, though I really wanted to ask Kelly for more details on the so-called freak accident. But now Kelly seemed to regret she'd said anything and apologized for keeping the group from their work.

Most of the group had taken out their projects when they sat down and were already busy with their hooks and yarn. Marianne took out her scarf and began to move her hook slowly and deliberately through the stitches. She couldn't seem to get a rhythm going, and the previous row was so tight she was having a hard time getting her hook into the next stitch. Just as I was thinking that it couldn't be very relaxing for her, Sheila got up and came around the table and handed her a smaller-size hook.

"Been there, done that," Sheila said, looking at the tight stitches. "Use this hook, but make sure that you make really loose stitches. Then you can go back to the bigger hook on the next row." Sheila stayed while Marianne tried the smaller hook, making sure she kept each stitch loose.

Kelly seemed even more ill at ease as she glanced around the table and saw that everyone but her was occupied with yarn in some way. "My coming with Marianne was very last minute, or I would have thought to bring my knitting."

The word hung in the air, and Rhoda, CeeCee, Elise, Sheila, Dinah, and Eduardo all looked at each other and then at Adele. She was practically glued to Rory, and I thought she hadn't heard. But it seemed that Adele had a sixth sense when it came to anything to do with knitting. She turned to Kelly and gave her a disparaging scowl and then directed her attention to Rory. "Let this be a teaching moment for you."

Adele stood up defiantly as she glanced around at all of us and zeroed in on Kelly. "Crochet, how do I love thee? Let me count the ways. Number one, you don't have to agonize if you make a mistake. There's no trying to figure out how to pick up a dropped stitch. You just rip and redo.

"Number two, you only need one tool. No pointy needles making holes in your tote bag.

"Number three, you work one stitch at a time unless you're working Tunisian Crochet. So no stitches slipping off your hook and disappearing.

"Number four, you can make amazing things you couldn't possibly knit. Has anybody ever heard of a knitted granny square?" Adele opened her mouth, no doubt getting to number five, but CeeCee stepped in.

"We get the message, Adele. You love crochet," CeeCee said. "But we're supposed to be an inclusive group. We all love crochet, but it isn't right to discriminate." She turned back to Kelly. "It's perfectly fine that you're a knitter."

I heard Adele snort.

Marianne pushed her chair back and excused herself to go to the restroom. Kelly got up to follow her, but Marianne told her to sit. "I'm not helpless," she said, trying to put as much force into her words as she could.

As soon as she was gone, Kelly began talking quickly, her words falling over each other. "It's very nice that you let her come. It certainly means a lot to her. Errol bows to her every whim. I thought she ought to stay home until she had a new helper. But he said she made such a fuss about coming tonight and asked me if I'd go with her. He thought it would look odd having a man here."

Eduardo let out a yelp. "Watch out what you say," he said with a smile. "There's nothing for him to be embarrassed about. Crochet is for everybody."

Kelly apologized and said it had come out wrong.

"I think it's nice that he's so concerned for her," Rhoda said. The way she ended her statement, it almost sounded like a question. I was sure she was hoping to pump Kelly about the reason Marianne was on such heavy meds.

Kelly didn't pick up on the bait. "You can say that again. And it's not like he's the older one. She is."

I mentioned that I'd run into Errol and Marianne at a restaurant.

"He always does that when her companion has the night off." She seemed to shudder. "That was when it happened."

"You mean when Connie died?" Rhoda said.

Kelly nodded her head decisively. "Marianne would be so much better off if she agreed to sell that place and go to an assisted-living facility. Then there wouldn't be all this trouble of finding someone."

Rory hadn't seemed to be following the conversation and appeared confused. "When you said companion, what kind of companion did you mean?"

"I didn't know there were different kinds." Kelly seemed surprised.

"I had a twenty-four/seven food companion once," Rory said.

"Because you were anorexic or something?" Elise asked.

"No, it was all about keeping me—" Rory abruptly stopped midsentence and picked up a new thread. "The reality show I was doing then paid for her. It was the one that was supposed to show the real me—mother, wife, and celebrity." She was playing with her hook as she spoke. "Did you say that her last companion died?"

Kelly nodded and said, "Poor Connie."

Rory cocked her head and I thought she was going to say something, but if she did, it got lost as Marianne made her way back to the table. Kelly put her finger to her lips. "Don't repeat anything I said." Before Marianne had a chance to sit down, Kelly was on her feet. "We've been here long enough. I have to get home and take care of the kids."

After they left, CeeCee showed off the different versions of the bracelet and passed them around and we took a vote. The one done in a medium-weight cording with some small wooden beads won. I made sure I had a sample of it along with the instructions. The Hookers didn't meet over the weekend, and I wanted to be sure to have something to show the Craftee people when they came on Monday.

"I was hoping you'd all get a chance to make one," CeeCee said. "I suppose there's always next time."

As the group broke up, I glanced at Rory and Adele. They were still huddled together, and Adele seemed to be demonstrating something. My fingers were crossed that Rory was paying attention, or we were all in trouble.

Chapter Eleven

"Marianne left her work again," Dinah said, picking it up from under the table. "That sister-in-law of hers hustled her out of here so fast, I'm surprised she didn't leave behind a shoe." Dinah was taking her time packing up, and I was clearing up the scraps of yarn and pushing in the chairs.

"You're stalling, aren't you?" I said. "What's going on?"

"I have to go home and face Commander and his daughter at dinner." Dinah sighed. "It's more than the yoga classes—there was another one this morning. She keeps acting like I'm the other woman. I know it's hard for her to deal with her mother being gone, but he has a right to make a new life for himself."

"I get it. She feels he's being disloyal to her mother. Thankfully, both of my sons are past that stage. Now I think they look at Mason as taking me off their hands," I said with a grin. "Maybe when Commander's daughter gets used to the idea that he's remarried, it will be better."

Dinah rolled her eyes. "I thought she hadn't come to

the wedding because of some sort of conflict in her schedule, but now I think he didn't want her to come because he knew what her reaction would be. It's no picnic having her stay with us."

"You could hang out at my place," I said, but she shook her head.

"I have to go home eventually." She let out a heavy sigh. "I might as well face it now. And maybe I can win her over with my fabulous personality," she joked, striking a pose. She let go of the pose and pushed all of her yarn and hooks into her tote bag before getting up from the table.

"Good luck," I said, giving her a reassuring hug. "And remember, you can always come over, or at least hide out in your lady cave."

When she'd left, I began to pack up for the day. The last thing I did was grab Marianne's scarf. Now that I'd been there, finding my way to her house was easy even in the dark. I was still surprised that I had never realized before that there was a house on that hill. But the topography in this part of the Valley was filled with surprises. There were finger-shaped slopes with houses at the top that were visible from a distance, but it was a mystery where the street leading to them was. A ravine ran down from Corbin Canyon that was dark and mysterious. I imagined that the houses built along the two sides of it must have coyotes running through their backyards all the time. That was the personality of the area, a mixture of neat houses and wild areas.

I drove through the open gate onto the property and parked my car behind a dark sedan. A large arched window spilled light onto the area in front of the house. I got out of the car and found my way to the front door. A wall sconce gave off a warm glow that lit up the tiled entryway. I noticed the door was ajar.

I considered ringing the doorbell or knocking but decided to walk in and call out a greeting. I heard the sound of voices coming from the living room. As I got a little closer, I recognized the sound of an argument. I'm afraid my nosiness kicked in, and I flattened myself against the wall and edged closer until I could make out the words.

"If you would just be realistic," a man's voice said. "Living here in your situation doesn't work." I moved a little closer and saw that the voice belonged to Marianne's brother. He was standing, and she was sitting on the couch.

"I don't want to leave and go live in some assisted-living arrangement. I can take care of myself."

"Only with my help. Like now. I had to leave as soon as Kelly got home to watch the kids and come here because the companion I was finally able to hire isn't here yet. I did my best to downplay that the past one died here, but what if the new one reconsiders? She might not even show up. The lawyer seems to be keeping the police at bay, but the case is still open." I had plastered myself against the wall next to a tall bookcase, anxious to hear more. There was the sound of some fumbling. "At least take your meds," Errol said.

"Let me wait a little longer. They make me feel awful."

"See, you can't take care of yourself. If someone wasn't here to make sure you take the drugs, you wouldn't do it. And we know what happens then."

I heard movement coming from the room and decided it was time to slip back outside. I backtracked and got to the door. I made sure the door was shut, then pulled out my cell phone. I could hear a phone begin to ring inside, and finally Marianne answered.

I explained that I was outside and had her scarf. A moment later, Errol appeared at the door. I was afraid he was just going to grab the scarf and send me on my way, but he invited me in.

As I followed him down the hall I'd just been hiding in, he said something about Marianne not getting much company. She seemed pleased to see me and immediately invited me to sit down. I noticed a container with an assortment of pills on the coffee table in front of her as I went to put down the scarf. Errol's cell phone started to ring, and he answered with a slump of his shoulders as if he was anticipating bad news.

He walked away to keep his conversation private, and Marianne gestured to a chair. I'd just sat down when Errol returned, slipping his phone back in his pocket. "That was Janine. She said she'll be here within the hour."

He looked so much like his sister. They both had wavy hair that was either black or the darkest shade of brown. Their features were similar as well, but Marianne's seemed flattened out somehow, whereas Errol's gaze was sharp and the set of his mouth more controlled.

I guessed Janine must be the new hire taking Connie's place. Marianne took a moment to collect her thoughts. "Then you can leave. I'll be fine until she gets here."

He looked at the drugs on the table. "Only if you do what you're supposed to."

Marianne capitulated and began to swallow the cocktail of pills. He watched her and then turned to me. "Do you suppose you could stay until Janine arrives?" He didn't give any details about why Marianne needed someone there. I wasn't sure if he didn't want to tell me or if he thought I already knew.

"Sure," I said. "My dance card is empty tonight." I was trying to keep things light, but neither of them smiled. Errol took the empty pill container and glass of water.

"Feel free to help yourself to anything in the kitchen," he said to me.

Marianne's expression darkened. "I can take care of my guest," she said.

I could tell she was trying to be forceful, but her voice came out flat. Errol took a moment to look around, as if he was trying to make sure he hadn't forgotten anything.

"You'll be sure to stay here until Janine gets here?" He peered at me until I gave him a confirmation. Finally he pulled on his jacket and went to the door.

"He means well, but I wish he'd stop treating me like I'm an invalid." She started to get up from the couch and then slipped back. It took a second attempt for her to succeed at standing. "That's not me. It's the drugs." She started to walk out of the room and urged me to follow. "The least I can do is offer you some coffee or something."

Her intentions were the best, and I watched as she fumbled with the coffee pot and paper filter. It was hard for me to watch her struggle without offering to step in, but it seemed important to her to do it herself.

We sat down at a small table in an eating area off the kitchen. A sliding glass door led outside. From my vantage point, it looked like a black hole with some lights coming from a building in the distance. Marianne had seated herself so her back was to the view. It seemed intentional, and I realized the black hole was probably the yard. Did she connect it with what had happened to Connie?

The coffee was more like brown water, but I told her it was good. She sighed and then managed a smile. She offered me food, saying there was a full supply of frozen things she could put in the microwave, but I said the coffee was fine.

I didn't want to upset her, but I really wanted to find out everything I could. It wasn't just about helping Barry anymore. I was genuinely curious. There was no polite way to ask her why she was on the drugs, or more important, what her brother had meant when he talked about what would happen if she didn't take them. So, I chose another topic. I asked her if the police had finished their investigation.

Marianne had made a cup of herbal tea for herself. I recognized the distinctive scent of chamomile. She didn't answer right away. I couldn't tell if it was because it was hard for her to collect her thoughts or because she was considering what she should say. "Yes, I believe they have whatever they need," she said finally. There was nowhere to go with her comment, so I changed the subject.

"It seems like a big place for you, but then I should talk. People say the same about my house," I said.

She made a movement with her mouth. "Sorry, but my mouth is so dry." She drank some of the tea and swallowed a few times. "I always think drinking something will help, but it doesn't." Her gaze scanned the pleasant room. "This is my family home. It's where I grew up, and when my parents died, I was left in charge. Errol has wanted to sell it from day one. But I don't see the point. I like living here."

I was wondering about the expense of it all and trying to think of a way to bring up the subject, but Marianne did it on her own. "We were both left trust funds. It was better when I was working, but mine covers the expenses of this place. Now he's trying the angle that I can't take care of myself and should be living somewhere with twenty-four-hour care. Connie's accident gave him new ammunition. I knew we'd find somebody to take her place." I could tell by the way her tongue seemed to stick that her dry mouth was making it hard for her to speak. But she seemed determined and drank some more tea, clearly hoping it would help.

"It's really not a bad job. I don't require as much care as Errol thinks. The woman before Connie was working on a book. It's more about them being available rather than hovering over me."

"Then you were happy with Connie?" I asked, and she shrugged. "But I suppose you really got to know her."

"We weren't friends, really. It was a very lopsided relationship. Her job was to care about me. My end of the bargain was to pay her. That makes me sound pretty awful," she said. "I did try to ask about her life, but she said something about keeping a professional distance. I had a feeling that she didn't want to make it seem as if we were friends because she thought I might use it to manipulate her."

Although she didn't say it, from the two times I'd seen Marianne fuss with her brother about taking her meds, I thought it had to do with that.

"So it's pretty much a round-the-clock job," I said.

"It's really about someone being here. My driving is a little shaky, and sometimes I need help doing things. The job comes with room and board," she said. She turned and peered out in the darkness. "See those lights? It's a nice little guesthouse. I used to use it as an office." Marianne sounded almost wistful. "Things were a lot different then."

As I listened, it seemed to me that she was very self-aware despite the brain fog from the drugs. I almost brought up the elephant in the room and asked why she needed them. But I was going to have to work my way up to it. What struck me as I talked to her was that while she talked slowly, she clearly wasn't slow-witted. I thought back to when she'd first joined the Hookers. We'd all reacted to the way she talked and had never really included her in the group. Everyone had always greeted her but then left it at that.

"You know, I'm the one who found Connie." She said it calmly, but I was stunned. I desperately wanted to know more, but she had picked up her teacup and stopped talking. The answer seemed to be to ask her something to keep her going.

"Do the police know?" I asked, and she nodded.

"I'm the one who called 911. Then I called Errol and he

took over. He wouldn't let me say anything until he got the attorney."

I was still processing that she'd been the one to find Connie, and I asked her for details. I half expected her to clam up after what she'd said about her brother and the attorney, but if anything, she seemed anxious to talk.

"Connie always came to the house in the morning to do this and that. I was okay with it when she didn't come in that morning. I can certainly get myself up. But it got later and later and she still hadn't come. After lunchtime, I tried her cell phone, but there was no answer. I went outside and saw her car parked in the driveway. That's when I decided to go to the guesthouse and knock on the door." She turned to look at me. "There's an opening to the lawn just past the garage, and I thought I'd walk across the grass."

I didn't let on, but I knew exactly where she was talking about. It was where I'd seen the white van and the tent.

"That's when I saw her lying there."

"Did you ever find out what happened to her?"

I sensed she was thinking over what to say and willed myself to be patient and move at her speed. "It seems like it was a freak accident. Something happened to her when she stepped on the grass." She drank some more of the tea. "My brother said it was a reason to sell this place. He said it could have been me."

What? I forced myself to seem calm and asked for more details.

"Almost every night, the last thing I do before I go to bed is take a walk around the perimeter of the yard. It's my way of saying good-night to the world. It makes me feel peaceful, and then it's easy to fall asleep. Not that I really need any help with that. The pills knock me out." I noticed she had gotten a soft smile as she talked about her nightly habit. "I've been doing it since I was a kid. And now it's one of the few things I do completely on my own." She turned back toward me. "But I didn't walk that night because I turned my ankle."

I let what she'd just said sink in. And realized that it changed everything.

* * *

My mind was whirling when I got home, and my stomach was protesting the lack of dinner. Samuel had taken care of the animals before he'd gone out, so all I had to do was let the two dogs out for a few minutes. I stayed out with them and drank in the heady scent of pink jasmine flowers coming from another yard.

I greeted Blondie in her chair in my room when I went to drop off my jacket. Then it was on to dinner. Mason had a business dinner that night, so he was out of the equation. For a moment I considered calling Barry to let him know that I'd found out something important, but Barry had been clear that he had to be in control and would contact me.

I threw some leftovers in a casserole dish and stuck it in the oven. I had chosen the larger casserole dish, thinking in the back of my mind that Barry might call. But then he might not. It momentarily annoyed me that he just showed up whenever, but then I let it go. That was just how Barry rolled.

The air filled with the delicious scent of the cooking casserole. The concoction of vegetables, rice, eggs, and some cheese wouldn't make a stir on a cooking show, but it tasted good to me.

I had just finished putting the dishes in the dishwasher when Mason called to check in and give me some bad news. He profusely apologized, but our weekend plans would have to be put on hold. He had to fly up to San Francisco and do some damage control for a client.

"You could come along, though most of your time would probably be spent alone," he said. "I'll be tied up hand-holding." He let out a tired sigh.

It wasn't even a consideration, since I was working both days. I was going to tell him about my day, but I could hear him yawning and I knew he had an early flight. I wished him safe travels and we hung up. When I put down the cordless, I looked at the clock. It was already eleven. Just as I was thinking Barry wouldn't come for sure, the phone rang.

"Detective Greenberg," he said when I answered. "Er, I mean, it's Barry." His tone was confused, still part official business and part regular Barry. "Well, I'm here on business. This isn't a social call."

I felt bad that I'd hassled him about his formal greeting. I hadn't meant to cause him so much confusion. "Okay, I know who you are and why you're here. I'll open the front door." I suppose I could have told him he could use the key he had for dog care, but I thought that would confuse things even more—maybe for both of us.

He had his standard late-night look, suit with no wrinkles and more than a five o'clock shadow on his chin. He held himself erect with no hint of how long he'd been working. The dogs came running and gave him a royal welcome, and I saw him crack a smile, though he tried to hide it.

"I'm sure you're probably hungry," I said, skipping right to the point. "I have some leftover casserole. It's not going to win any cooking competitions, but I liked it."

This time he showed his smile. "That would be great."

I sent him to the dining room and heated up a portion of the mixture. I added some orange slices for garnish. I put it in front of him and then went to get some sparkling water for both of us.

"Well," he said when I finally sat down across from him. "Tell me what you know."

"You're certainly getting right down to business," I said. "But I have a few questions first." I took a sip of the orange-flavored sparkling water and watched as he stopped with his fork in the air.

"I thought we agreed. You were just going to cooperate and be my informant and tell me what you found out. It was going to be a total one-way street of information. You to me."

"But I can't understand the importance of what I know without knowing how the pieces fit. I could completely miss telling you something that is a key to everything because I didn't realize it mattered."

"I should have known," he said, shaking his head. "The

idea was that you weren't going to put together the pieces. That's my job. You are just supposed to give me the pieces that need to be put together."

I folded my arms and looked across at him. "That doesn't work for me. I can't possibly tell you the very big turning-point piece of information I have unless I know something first."

He started to put the fork down, but I urged him to go ahead and eat. He went back to working on the food. He looked down and I was sure he was trying to figure out what to say so that it wouldn't seem he was giving in.

"It's hard for me to consider your offer without knowing exactly what it is that you want to know. So what is this information that you need so badly?" He had a hint of a smile.

"I saw that smile. I think you like that I give you a hard time," I said. "It keeps you on your toes."

"Don't be silly." He'd gone back to his cop face. "The last thing I want to do is wrangle with you. So tell me what you want to know."

"The news article I read was very short on details. How did Connie Richards end up electrocuted?"

"Electricity passed through her body," he said. He had his cop face on, but I knew inside he thought he was being clever.

"But what were the circumstances?"

"Do you know that water is a conductor of electricity?" he said, and I nodded.

"The sprinklers had soaked down the yard, and—"

"And there was something that electrified the water on the ground, so that when she stepped on the soggy ground, she got electrocuted." I said excitedly.

"Right," he said, seeming annoyed that I'd finished the thought.

"What was it? Something with outdoor lighting?"

"No, if that was the case it would be a clear-cut accident," he said. Then he seemed to regret saying so much. "Oh, hell, I might as well fill in the rest of the blanks instead of playing this game. There was an old radio connected to a frayed extension cord that was plugged into a socket in the garage. The radio had been left on."

I sat up straighter. "Now I get it. The radio could have been turned on when everything was dry, but when the sprinklers came on, the lawn became a killing zone. Connie came back from her evening off and, as she walked across the lawn to the guesthouse, she was zapped. Did you ask Errol Freeman about it?"

Barry let out a heavy sigh. "Of course. I'm a real detective, remember?" I saw his gaze go to the junior detective set and then back to me. "Freeman thought the gardeners must have wanted some music while they were working and found the radio and cord in the garage. Nothing is locked in that place."

"Did you talk to the gardeners?"

Barry rolled his eyes, and I could see he was getting annoyed that I was asking more questions. "Yes, we spoke to them. They insisted they didn't know anything about the radio."

"Were the gardeners Latino? Did you see what station the radio was tuned to?"

He got where I was going and, for a flash, he looked excited, but then his expression went back to serious. "So, now you know what happened. Now it's your turn to pay the piper and give me this earth-shaking piece of information."

I took pity on him and decided to make it easy. "Okay, here it is. What about if someone besides Connie was the intended victim?"

"Wait a second, that's not giving me information. That's asking me another question. You're not playing fair."

"Sorry, you're right," I said. He seemed surprised that I'd given in. Then I told him about Marianne and her nightly walk. "It was only by chance that she skipped it that night."

Barry took a moment to digest the information. "You're right. That does change the possibilities."

"Did you say I was right?" I got up and did a dance of triumph. "Oh geez, I'm turning into Rory Graham and her Dance Breaks." I sat back down. "I'm just so floored that you said I was right about something."

He seemed concerned. "Is that what you think? That I think you're wrong about everything?" I suddenly got the feeling he wasn't talking about detective skills anymore.

"Well, yes," I said finally.

"I'm sorry. That simply isn't true." He continued looking at my face a little too long before he slipped back on his inscrutable cop expression. He pulled away from the table and picked up his plate. He quickly dropped it in the kitchen and headed to the door.

"Thanks for the food and the information. I'll be in touch." He was already out the door as I said good-night.

Chapter Twelve

"I'm here to take you away from all of this and make up a little for canceling our weekend plans at the last minute," Mason said. He was standing in front of the information booth with a big grin on his face. It was the middle of the day on Monday, and he wasn't wearing a suit. "Someplace special, where it's green as far as your eye can see."

I'd worked both days and spent my evenings using the instructions I'd gotten from CeeCee to make samples of the bracelets. I was pleased how they'd come out and was wearing one now.

"What's up? Are you playing hooky?" I said noting the jeans and Hawaiian shirt.

"Sometimes you just have to be naughty," he said, glancing around the bookstore. "It looks pretty quiet. Do you think you could take a long lunch?"

"I'm the assistant manager," I said, feeling my lips curve into a smile. "I think that gives me some clout." I told him to wait and I'd see what I could do. I found Mrs. Shedd busy working with Phyllis, one of our new hires, arranging a display table with cookbooks along with some cooking tools.

"Molly, I think we should try to have some events connected to cooking again." She didn't need to remind me why we hadn't put on any for such a long time. The inevitable setting off of the smoke detectors and arrival of the fire department had deterred our efforts. Though, as I recalled, we had still sold a lot of books.

I agreed and then reminded her of the event we had coming up later in the week that I expected to be a big draw.

"I'm sure Missy Z is going to attract a big crowd. Romance *and* an author in disguise," my boss said with a happy smile.

"And hot sex," Phyllis added.

Mrs. Shedd chuckled and blushed. "I'm sure you're right. We need to make sure we have lots of chairs." Her expression turned serious. "Did you hear from the *Creating With Crochet* people?"

"They called this morning to confirm they were coming by to look at the yarn department and check on things."

Mrs. Shedd stepped a little closer to me. "I'm depending on you to look out for the interests of the bookstore. See if you can get an idea where they're going to have the cameras so we can conveniently place some signs with our name. Wouldn't it be great if they were visible for the whole show?"

Mrs. Shedd was always looking for ways to promote the bookstore, but it wasn't just about upping the profit. She loved the place and thought it had value to the community. I heartily agreed.

I got to the point of why I'd found her, and as soon as she saw Mason standing in the front of the store, she said she was fine with me taking a little extra time. She knew that I usually worked far more hours than my allotted shift. Her only request was that I be back by the time the TV people were supposed to be there.

"Let's go," I said to Mason when I rejoined him. I'd already gotten my purse and jacket, and he took my hand and we went out the door feeling like two wild teenagers ditching school.

"So, what's the plan?" I asked as we walked to the Mercedes SUV.

"You'll see," he said as he beeped the car open. Mason was big on making everything into a surprise adventure. And I turned it into the Sherlock Holmes game as I tried to deduce the plan based on where he drove. He got on the 101 and headed east, which left the options open. As we got closer to the interchange to the 405, he didn't move to the right.

"Okay, I see you're not getting on the San Diego Freeway, so that means no beach," I said.

He just wiggled his eyebrows with an impish smile. "I think we both need something different," he said.

There was just the slightest sigh, which seemed out of character, and I realized it might not be a clue. I had always thought that everything sort of rolled off his back, but then he'd occasionally shown a vulnerable side that surprised me. Who would have thought he would react to our last breakup with sad songs, a bottle of whiskey, and a broken heart?

"What gives?" I asked.

"Instead of spending a weekend with you, I was stuck doing damage control for Billy Buxford."

I recognized the name of a well-known pop singer who threw temper tantrums and wrecked hotel rooms. The only reason Mason mentioned Billy by name was that it had been all over the media, which had shown Mason giving a statement that Billy was innocent and declaring that when he had his day in court, the truth would come out. I didn't ask Mason for details because I knew he couldn't give any, attorney-client privilege and all, but I was willing to bet money that Billy had done it.

"No more about that. This is about fun." He chuckled as he watched me studying the backdrop as the freeway cut through Sherman Oaks and then Studio City.

I caught sight of the sign for Gelson's and, in the distance, Universal Studios. I kept watching for Mason to move toward an off ramp, but he stayed in the left lane.

We zoomed down the freeway as it ran along the base of the mountains, first passing Forest Lawn with its very green grass before it morphed into Griffith Park, and I caught a view of the old trains in Travel Town.

"Give me a hint," I said. We were nearing the interchange to the 5 freeway.

"No hints," Mason said with a laugh. "So tell me what's going on with you? Anything new about the woman in your group who died? The small piece I saw said it was under investigation. Knowing you, you're probably in the middle of trying to figure out what happened."

"Well, actually, I am, but it's kind of challenge," I said, and then told him how Connie and Marianne had been silent members of the group. "I hate to say this but, before Connie died, I really didn't think much about her at all. We never knew what the relationship was between the two women. They just sat there and crocheted. I still don't really know much about Connie, but at least I do know what their relationship was." I looked over at Mason. "Connie was Marianne's companion."

I explained that Marianne seemed to need someone to look after her, though I didn't know why.

"How's the prep for the crochet show taping going?" he asked. I held up my arm to show off my wrapped bracelet and explained that at least we'd settled on a project.

He took my wrist and moved it into his line of sight and stole a look. "I like it. So that's crochet?" he asked.

I affirmed, and he asked how it was going with Rory. I made a face. "That bad, huh?" he said with a laugh.

"She is so desperate to be in the spotlight that when we were talking about Marianne having a companion, she had to say she'd had one too, only hers had something to do with food. You can bet that if it had been her companion who had died in a freaky way, she'd be doing interviews all over the place and probably trying to turn the investigation into a reality show."

Mason shook his head in disbelief. "Celebrities are their

own breed." A car cut in front of us, and he focused on trying to keep us safe. It wasn't until we'd passed the interchange with the 5 freeway that something I'd said registered with him. "You said the woman's aide died in a freaky way? What happened?"

Now it was me who was distracted. We were on the 134 now, and for some reason, the way the roadway hugged the side of the mountain made me think of the Wizard of Oz. On one side was rugged brush, and on the other was a view of the tall buildings of downtown LA peeking between the hills dotted with houses. It felt like we were traveling into another world. I forgot about Mason's question as I realized where we were going.

"You're taking me to Pasadena," I said, just as we passed the Arroyo Seco bridge with its iconic design over the dry ravine.

"Ah, but the question is where in Pasadena," Mason said as he turned off of the freeway.

As we drove past the old trees and beautiful homes, I thought of what Mason had said about taking me away somewhere where there'd be green as far as I could see, and then I knew.

"I know where we're going," I said triumphantly. "We're going to the Huntington Gardens."

"Technically, it's called The Huntington," he said, pretending that he was disappointed that I'd figure out his surprise.

Whatever the official name was, it was a wonderful place, with a mansion that had an art gallery, a library that had a Gutenberg Bible, and over a hundred acres of fabulous botanical gardens. It was a perfect place to get away from it all for a while. Once you were inside, the outside world melted away and you couldn't even see the streets that bordered it.

"I bet this is what heaven looks like," Mason said as we passed a green lawn with flower beds filled with sweet-smelling pink blossoms. "I thought we could get lunch over there." He pointed to a café with a view of the rose garden.

I liked the idea of forgetting about everything and enjoying the moment, but the only problem was that all the lawns and gardeners tending them brought me right back to thinking about Marianne. I almost choked when I saw a sign along the walkway that said *Caution When Wet*. I must have made a face and let out a sigh, because Mason appeared concerned. "We don't have to eat there. We can go somewhere else if you'd like."

"The place you chose is fine," I said. "It's just that seeing all this reminded me of what I was trying to forget about for a while." I told him where Marianne's house was situated and the size of the property. Then I told him how Connie had been electrocuted.

I described the lawn and mentioned the sprinklers and added the radio with the frayed extension cord. I had already decided that if he asked where I'd gotten the information, I could pass it off as coming from Marianne.

"Yes, that is a crazy way to die. It could have been a weird accident or a clever way to kill someone. Who found the body?" Mason asked.

"Marianne did," I said with a shudder, thinking of how horrifying it must have been. "She said that when Connie didn't show up all morning and didn't answer her cell phone, she was going to go to the guesthouse, but then she found her lying on the grass."

"And Marianne didn't get electrocuted, obviously, or even shocked," Mason said.

"You're right," I said. "She said she didn't go looking for her until the afternoon. Connie had stepped onto the watery ground the night before. By the time Marianne went out there, the ground and grass must have dried out and there wasn't any water to electrify."

"Hmm, maybe Marianne knew that," he said.

"And she set the whole thing up?" I said. "But I saw her out that night having dinner with her brother—" I stopped short as I went over something in my mind.

Barry and I had talked about the possibility of it having been an accident caused by the gardeners' desire for music. The idea was that they could have set up the radio when they were working and then forgotten about it. But Marianne could have done the same thing with a bit of a twist. She could have set up the radio in the afternoon and then left it, knowing the sprinklers would come on and soak the ground before Connie returned. I got a bad feeling in the pit of my stomach.

"But what could the motive have been?" I asked.

"You mentioned that Marianne seemed on heavy medication. I imagine it was the companion's job to make sure she took her meds." He shrugged. "I don't know Marianne, but I've had clients who were on drugs for mental health issues. They don't like them and try not to take them. Maybe it was connected with that." He turned to me for my response.

"That's it." I put my hands up in capitulation. "Back to the original plan of getting away from it all," I said as we walked into the café. "I'm sure even Sherlock Holmes took a lunch break."

Chapter Thirteen

"There she is," Mrs. Shedd said as I came in the door to Shedd & Royal. She shot me a relieved look, and I realized that lunch had taken longer than I'd realized. It's easy to forget about time and the world outside when you're surrounded by gardens. We'd enjoyed high tea with a selection of savories and sweets served in an elegant room that looked out into a sea of rosebushes. In fairness to me, though, the Craftee people had shown up earlier than we'd agreed on.

I looked over the cluster of people at Mrs. Shedd's side, and I didn't recognize the woman dressed in arty layers over leggings or the man in fancy jeans and a graphic T-shirt, but the third person was a familiar face.

"Hi, Michael," I said, greeting him before introducing myself to the pair, who turned out to be Felicity, the set designer, and Ethan, the director.

"This way," I said, walking the three of them to the back of the store. I was surprised when Mrs. Shedd stayed with the group. She had every right to tag along, but it still made me uncomfortable, like when my son Peter used to listen to me talking on the telephone and made comments about what I was saying. I almost suggested that she handle showing them around.

"This is the yarn department." It was really a silly statement, since they could obviously figure it out on their own. The three of them went into the heart of the area and began looking around. Then the two men started rearranging things.

"I'm sure Molly would like to know where the camera is going to be," Mrs. Shedd said before she turned to me and winked. The two men had already changed the angle of the table before answering her question.

"It's really cameras," Ethan said. "There'll be a stationary one facing the head of the table where Rory will be standing, and then we'll have two people with handheld ones moving around the table. We don't want the program to have the hollow look of a single camera on a cheap set. We want to make it exciting."

There was more walking around and talking about lighting needed and moving bookcases to define the area more. I was really just an observer, though I did feel a twinge when they mentioned where Rory was going to be placed.

Michael turned to me. "We want to make sure everyone gets a good look at her hooking." Then he chuckled. "Sorry, I don't know the technical term."

"We just call it crocheting," I said.

"Speaking of that, I understand you're going to show us the Make-and-Take project," Michael said. As if on cue, I held up my wrist to show it off. It looked much better when worn, so I let them all examine it on my arm.

I was relieved when they all approved and went back to looking around and taking notes and photos. Mrs. Shedd and I stood watching them like a couple of statues, and when they were done, we escorted them to the door and watched them as they headed out.

I expected Mrs. Shedd to walk away then, but she didn't move, and I saw her leaning so she could see a distance down the sidewalk at the disappearing group. I heard her let out her breath, and she straightened. "They're definitely gone now, so we can talk." Her expression darkened. "I saw you make a face when the producer mentioned where Rory was going to stand. What's going on?"

"Nothing," I said. But then I reconsidered and realized I ought to tell her the truth. "I found out that Rory isn't the expert with yarn that she told them."

Mrs. Shedd's expression cracked. "How bad is it?"

"She doesn't know how to crochet at all," I said.

Whatever good humor Mrs. Shedd was holding on to now turned to horror. "What will happen when they find out?"

"Hopefully that won't happen," I said. "I have Adele on the case. It should go better now. Adele *was* angling to be her sidekick and figured it didn't matter how well Rory crocheted, but I explained the situation, and now Adele is working with her." I rolled my eyes. "She even calls herself Rory's crochet companion."

Mrs. Shedd gave me a blank look, and I realized she had

no idea what I was talking about. "Molly, do what you have to," she said. "I know it wouldn't be our fault that Rory misrepresented herself, but we'd bear the fallout. I'm depending on the exposure we'll get. Imagine, all over the country and maybe the world, people will be seeing our little bookshop. We could become a tourist stop."

I was concerned that Mrs. Shedd was overestimating the viewership of the show. *Around the world?* But she was right about the exposure putting us on the map. Maybe we wouldn't be a tourist spot, but in our own way, the store would be a star.

"Believe me, I'm doing everything I can," I said.

Once again, Mrs. Shedd surprised me by grabbing me in a hug. "I know you'll come through, Molly." But maybe she wasn't completely convinced. That evening when the Hookers gathered for happy hour, Mrs. Shedd came into the yarn department. She wasn't a crocheter or knitter, and the whole yarn department had come about almost by accident. But she was a supporter of our charitable projects and had the store supply the yarn.

CeeCee greeted the owner as she came in, though afterward CeeCee shot me a glance with a question in her eye, obviously wondering what was up. The rest of the group had a similar reaction as they came in and found their seats. Only Rory didn't seem to think there was anything strange about Mrs. Shedd hanging by the table.

"Why don't you join us?" Rhoda said, pointing at one of the empty chairs.

Mrs. Shedd put up her hand and refused. She must have

realized how strange her standing there seemed and began to fiddle with one of the cubbies filled with yarn.

CeeCee glanced over the seat where Marianne usually sat and the empty one next to it. "Should we wait or start?"

I held up my wrist and showed off the bracelet. "The show people are happy with the project, but you all need to try making one."

Dinah looked in my direction. "Are you sure Marianne's coming?"

I shrugged and was about to suggest giving her another five minutes when Mrs. Shedd spoke up and suggested we start. She drifted down toward the far end where Rory and Adele were situated.

"If you say so," CeeCee said with her usual merry smile. "Are you sure you don't want to join us?" she asked.

We all looked at Mrs. Shedd, and it appeared to finally get through to her that her presence seemed odd and was making everyone feel uncomfortable. "Oh, no, I was just curious to see how everything was coming together. I'll just stand back here and watch."

Everyone relaxed after that, and CeeCee got things under way. That is, everyone but me. I knew there was some truth in what Mrs. Shedd said, but I was pretty sure her real mission was to spy on Rory and see how her lessons were coming along.

"Elise made up kits for us with the supplies for one bracelet," CeeCee said as our wispy-looking Hooker began to hand out sandwich-size plastic bags.

"You'll have to let me know how many to make for the

actual show," Elise said in her birdlike voice. "You'll probably want to start stocking them in the yarn department. I'll be happy to handle keeping you supplied."

Elise's vampire craft sets had made her quite the expert at kit making. I looked at the bag she handed me and noted that it had everything in it, including a length of cord, a small hook, a tiny bag with some beads, and even a small length of thin wire to use for threading the beads onto the cord.

Everybody started taking the contents out, except Rory, who looked at the bag as if it was all totally foreign to her. Finally, Adele unloaded hers for her.

Mrs. Shedd had moved closer to the table. "If Rory is the host of the show, shouldn't she be standing at the end of the table showing off how to make the bracelet?"

"We'll work it out for the actual show, but for now Adele can be my crochet double," Rory said, not missing a beat.

Adele popped out of her chair and placed the supplies on the table in front of her. CeeCee started to demonstrate how to start the project, but Adele took over. Mrs. Shedd looked at me and shook her head with a worried expression.

Just then, Marianne came in with Janine, her new companion. They slipped into their seats without trying to draw any attention. I had already met Janine, briefly anyway, when she showed up for her first night on the job. I'd been the one to stay with Marianne until she got there so Errol could leave.

Janine was tiny with sharp features and had seemed less than thrilled to be there. Upon arriving, she had gone to drop off her suitcase in her room while I stayed in the living room with Marianne.

"I wish she didn't have to stay in the house with me, but with everything going on with the yard right now, staying in the guesthouse isn't an option," Marianne had said. I had been at a loss for what to say, other than that it would probably get worked out soon. Then Janine had reappeared and I had felt like an intruder and left. I had felt sorry for both of them.

The whole group turned to look at the new arrivals. After the stir Marianne's brother had made when he came to drag her home, and then the next night all the chattering his wife had done when she accompanied Marianne to the group, Marianne's silent presence was forever gone.

Adele tried to pull everyone's attention back to her acting as Rory's crochet double, but Rhoda spoke to the just arrived pair. "Oh, you've brought someone new."

Janine seemed to ignore the comment. When Connie and Marianne had first joined the group, Connie had introduced herself and handled everything. She had always stayed next to Marianne during the hour, though they rarely spoke to each other, which I now realized had been a definite clue as to their real relationship.

Janine seemed very different. She didn't respond to Rhoda's comment or acknowledge the group. She just waited until Marianne was situated and whispered something to her employer before going off into the bookstore. I noticed she took one of the easy chairs not far away. When I looked at her again, she was staring at the screen of her phone. It was only then that I noticed that Mrs. Shedd had slipped away.

"We were all about to make one of the bracelets together," CeeCee said in a slow, deliberate way, as if she was talking to a child. I'd been guilty of the same behavior until I'd gotten to know Marianne a little. I had to remember to explain to everyone that we needed to treat Marianne as if she were the same as the rest of us. Elise handed Marianne one of the kits.

Then everything seemed to grind to a halt. Marianne kept trying to open her eyes wider as she fumbled with the contents of the small package. By the time she had arranged the coil of cording, hook, and beads in front of her, Eduardo was pushing away from the table and I saw that the hour was up.

I felt like I had to do something about Adele. She had taken too well to the idea of being a crochet double. She had to understand that was not going to happen on the real show and there wouldn't be a real show if Rory didn't seem accomplished with a hook. The choice was to either talk to Adele again and reinforce the idea that she was supposed to be teaching Rory how to crochet or go straight to Rory.

I decided to try the Rory option and caught up with her as she headed into the café, which gave me the perfect opening. I suggested we have a coffee together.

"I was going to get mine to go," she said, but seeing how all eyes in the place were on her, she changed her mind. She even called out a Dance Break as we waited for Bob to hand us our drinks.

As we went to a table, Rory made eye contact with several people at the tables. Someone stood up and mimicked her Dance Break routine, and she gave them a thumbs-up. I was still getting used to her behavior, which was so different from CeeCee's. CeeCee always seemed like a regular person who happened to be a well-known actor. She'd sign autographs if someone requested one or take a selfie with them, but she didn't court it.

Now that I had a chance to talk to Rory, I was suddenly at a loss for what to say. I mean, who was I to tell her how she had to act on what was supposedly her own show? I needed to say something to get a conversation going while I figured out how to segue into her crocheting. I looked back into the bookstore and saw Marianne and Janine walking up to the cashier stand, and I had an idea.

I pointed to the two women. "So, I guess the woman with Marianne is her new companion."

Rory seemed disinterested and was fiddling with her iced tea. I saw her looking at a creamy frozen drink someone was picking up at the bar. "I'd love one of those, but I can't do it."

I thought I knew why but asked her anyway. She gestured to the people at the tables. "I don't want someone taking a picture of me drinking it and then posting it on social media with a caption like 'Rory Graham pigs out.'"

Even though it seemed like she was a glutton for attention, good or bad, I guess even she had her limits.

We both saw Marianne heading to the café door. Janine was a few steps behind and caught up with her. The companion pointed to her watch, and Marianne reluctantly turned back.

"It must be weird to have someone around all the time like that. After all, the person is a stranger, and they're there in the middle of your life kind of telling you what to do, or not to do. I could see how it could make someone resentful." I turned to Rory. "But then, I guess you know all about that, since you said you had some kind of companion."

Rory seemed more interested once it was clear that I was talking about her. "Yes, they're really in your business," she said. "Mine would have given me a lecture for even thinking about one of those drinks."

"It doesn't sound like you were exactly friends," I said.

Rory let out a mirthless laugh. "Hardly. She took her job really seriously. Too seriously. But then, she'd worked as a sober companion before she worked for me." Rory checked my expression. "You don't know what that is, do you?" I shrugged, and Rory explained that her aide had helped people who were overcoming addictions. Rory let out a sigh and starting talking about how her companion had been bonkers about cell phones and that it had to do with something that had happened to a woman who'd gotten off pills but become addicted to her phone, and she'd somehow felt responsible. It was all a little confusing trying to keep track of who everyone was in the story Rory was telling.

The best I could understand, the companion had felt bad about something that had happened to her previous charge and had taken it out on Rory by acting like the cell phone police.

"On top of that, she was judgy," Rory said.

Her comment surprised me. "But I'd think being on reality shows about your life would make you immune to what other people thought."

Rory drank some of her tea and avoided looking at the drink at the next table. "I'm okay with them filming me looking like a fool if it brings in viewers, but there's always stuff you don't want to get out."

I'd been neglecting my coffee and finally took a sip. "I suppose you couldn't have kept whatever the stuff was from her."

"Yeah, when someone is around you all the time like that, they know where the bodies are buried."

Rory was getting restless and I realized time was running out, so I made an awkward segue to the crochet situation. "You're very lucky to have Adele as a teacher," I said. "She really makes it easy, doesn't she?"

I watched Rory's shoulders drop, and she took a sip of her drink. "Whatever. I just need to have the idea of it. The show wants me for my personality and Dance Breaks. I think Adele has a great idea there, being my crochet double. They can focus on her hands and make it look like they're mine."

Before I could respond, two women in sweats came up to the table and called out, "Dance Break." As Rory got up already gyrating, she looked back at me. "See what I mean?"

Oh, no, we were in real trouble.

Chapter Fourteen

The animal brigade was waiting for me when I got home. I had stopped for groceries and, with my arms full, couldn't shut the door fast enough to keep the cats from slipping out with the two dogs.

The house was dark and the outside floodlights hadn't been turned on, which indicated that Samuel must have gone off somewhere while it was still light. That meant they hadn't been fed and Blondie hadn't had her walk.

I flipped on the indoor and outdoor lights and went searching in the yard for the cats. Cosmo and Felix were already engaged in some game of chase. Mr. Kitty was less of a problem. He usually just did a walk around the perimeter of the yard and then would actually come in when I called him. Cat was the one I was concerned about. Even at her advanced age, she was still a huntress and very generous about bringing whatever as a gift.

Mr. Kitty was black and white and easy to see when the light hit him. Cat was another story altogether. Her purplish-gray color seemed to blend in with the surroundings. I found her in the corner of the yard staring at something in the darkness, poised to jump on it when it moved. She protested being interrupted.

Because I had rushed after Rory, I'd missed saying goodbye to the group. When I'd returned to the yarn department, everyone had been gone. I'd done my usual cleanup and before leaving had checked on the placards for the upcoming author event. Mr. Royal was going to put them in their frames. I was pleased by how they'd turned out. Instead of the usual author photo, Missy Z was totally shrouded in shadow so she appeared as a silhouette.

I felt bad that I hadn't gotten a chance to talk to Dinah. It must have been mental telepathy, because just then the landline began to ring, and when I looked at the tiny screen, I saw it was her number. I kicked the door shut as I got the cats inside and grabbed the phone.

"Am I glad to hear from you," I said, before telling her how I'd just been thinking about her. I was about to ask her what was up, but she interrupted.

"Tell me you're up for company. I have to get out of here, like now." She sounded frantic, which was out of character. All those years of handling unruly students had given her the ability to deal with almost anything.

"Sure. Come over now. I was going to make dinner—" I suddenly realized I was talking to dead air and that she'd hung up.

As I unpacked the groceries, I was considering what the hang-up meant and whether I should call back when I heard the dogs start barking in the yard. When I looked out the glass kitchen door, I saw Dinah coming across the stone patio.

I opened the door, and she and the dogs came in like a whirlwind.

The dogs ran through the kitchen, and Dinah plopped down at the built-in table in front of the windows that looked over the yard. "Peace at last."

"What's up?" I said, looking at my friend with concern. "What do you need, tea, coffee, or wine?"

"Anything," she said. "Maybe tea would be good. Or, no, make that wine."

I wasn't much of a drinker. My idea of a glass of wine was what other people would consider a tasting pour. But I had a bottle of red wine I had opened to cook with the other night and poured her a glass. She sipped while I finished putting away the groceries.

"And I thought the yoga classes in the house were a problem. How can such a lovely man as Commander have such an unpleasant daughter? She wasn't comfortable staying in the bedroom across from ours and decided that she'd move into my lady cave. She didn't ask anyone, just did it. When I came home, she was fussing with Commander because she'd found a chair in there that had belonged to her mother and was acting as if I'd somehow stolen it. I just couldn't deal with any of it."

"You can stay here until she goes home if you want," I said, but Dinah shook her head.

"I'm just looking for some temporary respite and

maybe a little fun, and then I'll go back and deal with Cassandra."

I promised to try to provide some fun and gave her a reassuring hug before I suggested we start off with an evening stroll to give Blondie her walk. I was glad to have Dinah along. When I walked Blondie in the dark, I was always on the lookout for coyotes. It wasn't an idle concern. We'd encountered one on a number of occasions. There was something scary about being followed by the slender dog-like creatures that were clearly on the prowl. Blondie was about the same size as them, though a little fuller, and I doubted they would attack her, but I couldn't be sure. Thankfully, all Dinah and I encountered that night was a night jogger wearing a headlamp. The walk seemed to soothe Dinah, and she was back to her usual self when we returned.

"This gives me a chance to catch up on what's going on with you," Dinah said as she took her seat at the kitchen table again. She offered to help with dinner, but I told her to relax and enjoy her wine.

I had been eating rather haphazard meals lately and, when I'd gone to the store, had gotten things to make a real dinner. I preheated the oven while I pressed fresh garlic into a triangle tip roast. Once it was cooking, I took out some green beans and tiny potatoes and cooked them in the microwave. I added butter and seasoning to both and turned to making a salad. I kept it simple with mixed baby lettuces, green onions, Persian cucumbers, avocado, and heirloom tomatoes. I drizzled olive oil and balsamic vinegar and tossed it.

"I don't want to think about Cassandra right now. Tell me what's going on with you. What about Marianne? Did you find out anything more about what happened?"

I reminded her of our Sherlock Holmes game the other day, and Dinah's expression dropped. "Yes," she sighed, "in my lady cave." She shook her head in annoyance a few times and began talking about her situation again until she stopped herself. "Please go on. I need the diversion."

I began to give her a rundown. "I found out how Connie was electrocuted," I said, and suddenly Dinah perked up as any thoughts of her situation seemed to vanish. She was fascinated when I told her about the radio and the sprinklers.

"It must have been a freak accident. I mean, who would think up something like that?" my friend asked.

"That's a good point," I said, and told her about Marianne usually walking at night. "So, if it wasn't an accident, Marianne could have been the target."

Dinah moved to pick up her wine glass but knocked it forward instead, and the red liquid spilled on her black shirt. "Here I am asking you to spill information, and I'm the one spilling my wine. Great, now I'll go home and smell of alcohol. I can just imagine what Cassandra will do with that."

I told her to go help herself to something in my closet while I took the dishes and silverware into the dining room. The timer went off, and I took the meat out of the oven. I was just slicing it when I thought I heard a soft knock at the door. When I went to check, the door was already open and Barry was coming in. He held up a bag.

"Doughnuts, the official food of cops." He said it in his normal Barry voice instead of the terse tone he used when he was in his detective mode. I was surprised by his casualness and that he'd obviously used his key to come in instead of calling first. I waved my hand, trying to signal him that something was wrong, but he seemed oblivious. "I found out something very interesting."

For a moment, I was stunned. Was he actually about to tell me something? But reality broke in and I realized I had to make him stop talking before Dinah reappeared. "We were just about to eat," I said, with a heavy emphasis on the *we*. He suddenly got it and glanced around apprehensively.

"Oh, a cozy dinner with Mason." He sounded uncomfortable and sniffed the air. "It smells good." He backed toward the door. "I didn't see his SUV. I thought the coast was clear."

I heard footsteps on the wood floor. "I hope you don't mind that I took this." Dinah stopped by the entrance hall when she saw me standing there. The overhead lights in the vaulted ceiling were turned very low and the area was barely illuminated. It took a moment for the two of them to see each other.

They both let out a surprised "oh," but with a different meaning. Barry's sounded relieved and Dinah's very curious.

Barry had moved the bag of doughnuts behind his back,

and by now Cosmo and Felix had joined us. The doughnuts might have been hidden from view but not from Cosmo's nose, and he went behind Barry and started jumping at the paper sack.

Barry was quick on his feet and announced that he'd stopped over to take care of his dog. He even showed off the key and explained he'd come by to brush Cosmo.

Dinah gave him a quizzical look. "It seems kind of late."

He mumbled something about being on his way home, and she dropped it.

I noticed him sniffing the air again. I couldn't blame him. It smelled delicious, if I did say so myself. What could I do but invite him to join us? He accepted without the slightest hesitation.

Dinah kept looking from Barry to me and then around the room. I saw her gaze rest on the switch plate that had been loose. Barry had tightened the screws the last time he'd been there. I knew she was playing the Sherlock Holmes game all by herself and seeing what she could deduce.

"How often do you come by to see Cosmo?" Dinah asked as she passed him the platter of meat.

"It all depends on when I have time," he said. "Crime never sleeps in LA."

I almost choked. Had he really just said that? It sounded like something off a book jacket. For a few minutes, no one said anything and the only noise was the scrape of the silverware against the plates and our chewing.

"It's admirable that you're so attached to Cosmo," Dinah

said. "You must be exhausted from tracking criminals all day, and yet you still have time to come by for him."

"I do the best I can," Barry said.

"Then I guess this must be an off night," she said. She paused and then let out her zinger. "Because you seem to have forgotten what you came for." She leaned toward him and gave him the death stare she used on her students when she'd caught them at something. "You said you were here to brush Cosmo."

Barry didn't miss a beat but pushed away from the table and said he'd do it now. I brought out dessert, my famous Chinese Jelly. That was what Samuel had named it the first time I made it. It wasn't Chinese and it certainly wasn't jelly. It was actually my rendition of something we'd had at a Japanese restaurant that had the texture of Jell-O. It was made with milk and half-and-half, a little sugar, gelatin, and some almond extract. I put some into ice cream dishes for the three of us. And then it became a standoff to see who was going to leave first. In the end, Dinah and Barry walked out together.

I hadn't found out what Barry was going to tell me, but I did find the sack of doughnuts.

Chapter Fifteen

Since the Hookers didn't have happy hour on Tuesday, once I took care of my morning tasks, I planned to take the rest of the day off. My first order of business was to place the signs for *The Hot Zone* event around the bookstore. More than once, I was stopped by a woman wanting to know if the book was in stock yet.

"Is the author really going to read some of it out loud?" one woman asked, punctuating her question with a nervous laugh.

As soon as I said she was, the woman wanted to know if she could reserve a seat. She was momentarily disappointed when I said it would be first come, first served, but then she recovered and asked how early she could get there.

I met with Mr. Royal about the author's demand for a private backstage area. We figured we could create an enclosure by moving around some bookcases.

We had a mindful meditation group meeting that morning, and I went to see how they were doing. The seven of them were sitting in a circle in the event area. They all had their eyes closed and seemed to be chanting something, so I left them alone.

Ethan, the director from the Craftee Channel, called wanting to know when they could come by and see the Hookers in action creating the Make-and-Take project. Even though the group hadn't made one of the bracelets at our gathering yet, I had no doubt they could manage it with ease. I was concerned about Rory and so put them off until the next week.

I checked on the order for the supplies we needed to make up the kits. As I was about to leave the store, Marianne called and invited me over. I'd never say no to a chance to get more information, and I had found that I really liked her. I picked up a red eye on the way out and headed to her place.

I loved working at the bookstore, but still there was a feeling of freedom as I drove away. Finding the private street was a nonissue now, and I continued on through the open gate when I got to the end of the cul-de-sac. A truck with gardening equipment was parked close to the opening to the grassy area. Two men in nondescript work clothes were walking back and forth onto the lawn. I wondered if they realized that the tarps they were walking over covered the spot where Connie had been found.

I pulled behind the truck and got out of my car. Another man in similar work gear was steering a riding mower around the large lawn. I looked at this as a bonus opportunity. I knew the gardeners had talked to the cops, but maybe they'd have something else to say to me.

I greeted the two men, and they stopped what they were doing and looked up.

"That's a lot of yard to take care of," I said, glancing around the property. "What are you working on?"

One of them pointed to a strip of dirt that ran along the back of the lawn, and I saw the flats of pansies nearby. "Last week we took out the dead plants. This week we put in flowers."

"It must get kind of boring. Too bad you don't have some music," I said in a nonchalant, friendly tone. Both men seemed to flinch.

"No, no music," one of them said emphatically. "We like it quiet." The man driving the riding mower drove past us and went through the open garage door and cut the motor. Trying to act as if my snooping was just me being friendly, I followed him in and asked him about the riding mower, like I was interested in getting one.

He looked at me, shrugged, and mentioned another brand he liked better. Meanwhile, I had a look around. There was metal shelving on the wall, and I noticed a number of old appliances. It wasn't a stretch to think the radio could have come from there.

Another man in work clothes came into the garage and barely seemed to notice me as he walked to a box on the wall. I had something similar at my house and recognized it as automatic sprinkler controls. I tried to get a look at what he was doing. "I have the same thing at my house, and I've never figured out to operate it," I blathered. "Mind if I watch?" Since he didn't object, I got closer to see what he was doing.

I hadn't exactly been truthful about not knowing how to operate the sprinkler controls, and as I watched him I saw that he was checking the times and length of watering.

"Was there some kind of problem?" I asked.

He seemed annoyed. "How did this happen? You don't run sprinklers for an hour." He muttered that it was good that they had turned off the system.

"You mean someone reset the sprinklers?" I asked. He looked at me, suddenly suspicious.

"Who are you?" he demanded.

Just then, Marianne stuck her head in the open door. "There you are. We heard someone drive up, but nobody came to the door." I wished the gardener a nice day and went outside and saw that Janine was with Marianne. Marianne took one glance at the area covered by the tarp, and I tried to read her expression. It was pointless because her face had the blank masklike look that seemed to come from the drugs.

"Why were you talking to the gardener?" Marianne asked as we walked to the house. It was hard to tell from her tone if it was just an idle question or something more.

I could hardly tell her the truth, so I made something up on the spot. "I saw they were planting pansies and I had a question about growing them." I glanced at her to see if she'd bought it, but I couldn't really tell.

We got to the door and went inside just as the old clock I'd seen in the living room struck the hour with a repetitive bong. Marianne stopped inside the entrance and glanced toward the living room and then in another direction. "We'll go into the den."

Janine lagged behind me as Marianne led the way to a large room at the back of the house. I remembered that when I'd come over before, there had seemed to be an issue about the room making her uncomfortable. When I saw the view, I understood why. It looked across the lawn to the guesthouse, though the spot where Connie had fallen wasn't visible.

The den had a southwestern feel with rusty red–colored pavers on the floor covered with some Native American–print rugs. There was a seating area with a couch and some chairs around a coffee table made out of a weather-beaten old door. The furniture was comfortable looking and appeared as if it had been there a long time. There were some modern touches, like the flat-screen TV that hung above the fireplace. I noted some video equipment and a stack of DVDs.

Janine was hanging in the doorway. "I don't want to interrupt your conversation," she said, taking a step back.

"Could you get us some sparking water?" Marianne said.

"Sure," Janine answered, quickly leaving the room.

Marianne and I sat down. She seemed tired and sank into the couch. Marianne swallowed a few times, and I could tell that her mouth was dry. "It was a rough morning. I felt exhausted and achy." She looked in the direction that Janine had gone. "And she wasn't much help."

Janine came in with a tray with two glasses and two bottles of sparkling water. She set them on the table and was already on her way to the door. "I'll be in my room if you need me."

"I certainly don't have to worry about her hovering too

much." Marianne poured some of the sparkling water in her glass and quickly drank some.

"It must be easier now that you have a permanent replacement for Connie," I said.

"I'd rather have no replacement, but sadly my brother has convinced me that I need someone to keep tabs on things."

"I suppose that Connie knew what you needed and now it's like starting out all over again. And since Connie was with you so much, you must have become somewhat friendly."

"Errol reminded me that I'm not supposed to talk about her. My lawyer's sure that her death is going to be ruled accidental and the cops will drop it, but for now he's supposed to be the only one doing any talking about what happened." She turned to me. "But I'm sure it's okay to talk to you. It's not like you're looking to turn me in or anything."

Her words struck me as strange, and I looked to see if it was another attempt at a joke, but her expression was impossible to read. "What's your lawyer afraid you'll say?" I asked.

"I don't know. I had a strange arrangement with Connie. My brother hired her, and I think she viewed him as her boss. She was unrelenting when it came to stuff he wanted her to do."

"Like what?" I asked.

"Like making sure I took all my meds." I could hear her tongue sticking to the roof of her mouth, making it hard for her to speak. She drank some more of the sparkling water and swallowed a few times to get rid of the cottony feeling. "I know they're supposed to help, but it makes it so hard to do anything." She put her head down in shame.

"She caught me trying to dump the pills in that plant." She pointed to a small olive tree growing in a planter.

"I suppose having someone around all the time meant she was in the middle of your business, too. I don't know how I'd feel about that," I said.

"It's the pits. I hate this. I have no privacy. I'm not a child. I couldn't believe it when Connie started commenting on what she'd overheard."

"Like what?" I asked, trying to sound off-handed.

"She overheard my brother talking to me about selling this place. She thought it might be a good idea. At times it almost seemed like she was trying to talk me into it."

"But you must have been upset about what happened to her," I said.

"Of course." She closed her eyes and let out a heavy sigh.

"Did you know much about her life away from you?" I asked. "Like what she did on her day off?"

"Not really. That was the point of a day off." Marianne managed a little smile. I remembered that she'd said that she used to be funny and that the drugs messed with her timing. She hadn't totally lost either attribute.

"How horrible that you were the one to find her," I said. I remembered my conversation with Mason. "It's lucky for you that you didn't get electrocuted or shocked yourself."

"By then the grass had dried out," she said. There was no reaction in her voice, but it was impossible to tell if that was her or merely the drugs.

"There you are," a man's voice said. We both started at

the interruption and turned to the doorway to the room as Errol Freeman came in, though I wondered how long he'd been there before he announced his presence. His gaze stopped on me and he seemed distressed. "You're here again?" Then he turned to his sister. "Where's the new woman—what's her name? Why isn't she in here with you?" He sounded impatient and annoyed.

"There was no reason for her to stay in here," Marianne said. "I'm not as incompetent as you seem to think. I can have a friend over without someone standing over my shoulder."

At last I understood why she'd invited me over. She looked upon me as a friend. That didn't sit well with him.

"What were you two talking about?" he said in a worried tone.

"I don't know, just stuff," Marianne said. "What are you here for?"

He appeared frustrated. "You have a new helper and I was just checking to make sure it was going okay. Where is she?"

"She went to her room." Marianne seemed displeased. "I think we should have her move into the guesthouse. There's nothing—"

"Enough," Errol said, interrupting. "I'll take it from here." He gave me a death stare, and I figured our visit was over.

Chapter Sixteen

On Wednesday, it was back to normal at Shedd & Royal. I got there early and stayed all day. Adele put on story time and was dressed as a female pirate complete with eye patch as she greeted the kids. Adele was very big on the idea that women could be anything. The supplies for the Make-and-Take kits were delivered, and I moved the boxes to the back room. By afternoon, I was already looking forward to our happy-hour gathering and seeing everyone.

Around four thirty, I grabbed my second red eye of the day and headed for the back table to get things ready for the Hookers. I hoped Marianne would show up. My exit had been rather abrupt after her brother's arrival, and I hadn't had a chance to encourage her to come today. I was still thinking about her as I removed a few stray skeins of yarn that had been left on the table and picked up a coffee cup someone had left. Each time I'd seen her, I'd gotten more of a sense of what her life was like. And a better idea of what her relationship with Connie had been. At first it had seemed as if Marianne had been in charge of Connie, but after the last visit, it seemed like the one in charge was really Errol. I felt for her. It was almost like she was a prisoner in her own home.

Everything was in order and I was straightening the chairs when Mrs. Shedd came over.

"Any progress with Rory Graham? It didn't seem very promising when I saw her in action the other day," my boss said, looking toward the spot Rory had occupied.

"I'll talk to the group," I said. "Maybe if they understand what's at stake, we can figure out a way to get through to Rory that there isn't going to be someone to step in for her on the show."

This seemed to put Mrs. Shedd's mind at ease, at least for the moment, and she went back across the bookstore to her office. She just missed passing CeeCee as our leader came back to the yarn department.

"How's it going with the prep for the taping?" she asked, putting down her large tote bag. I considered talking to her about Rory but decided to wait until everyone was there. "The Craftee people want to see the group making a bracelet."

"Then we absolutely have to have everyone make one tonight." She looked over the empty table. "Maybe Sheila can help Marianne. They seem to have a rapport."

CeeCee shushed herself as Marianne and Janine came toward us. There seemed to have been a shift in their relationship. Janine took the chair next to Marianne instead of wandering off into the bookstore.

By five, everyone was there but Rory, and CeeCee looked to me.

"No delays this time," I said, and spoke to the group. "I heard from the Craftee people, and they want to see us actually make a Gratitude Circle. I got them to push back until next week, but—"

"I get it," Rhoda said. "We need to be smooth and we haven't even made one yet."

"Exactly," CeeCee said.

Elise got up and handed out the same kits she'd handed out before. I kept looking at Marianne, wondering how I could ask Sheila to help her without letting on. I was pretty sure Marianne was aware of her crochet limitations, but I didn't want to make her feel uncomfortable. But then, maybe because she had helped Marianne before, Sheila sat down next to her unbidden and helped her unload the bag.

I glanced toward the front of the store, hoping to see Rory making a ripple of Dance Breaks as she made her way through, but it was all quiet. Adele was watching for her, too, and I noticed my coworker seemed a little tense. Thank heavens that Adele had changed out of the pirate outfit.

Dinah picked up on my worried look and offered me a reassuring smile.

I grabbed one of the kits and emptied the contents in front of me. "Okay, let's make a bracelet." The table went silent as we all gave our full attention to the project.

The focused silence lasted only a few minutes before it seemed as if everyone had an idea for a variation. "I think heavier cord would be more masculine," Eduardo said.

"But then you'd have to use big clunky beads," Rhoda said.

Elise wanted to add a lot more beads onto hers and change the name to the Count Your Blessings Bracelet, and then CeeCee stepped in.

"You're getting it all wrong. We all have to make the same bracelet—exactly the same bracelet. You need to follow the instructions exactly. They want to see what we're going to be offering. And remember, this Make-and-Take project is supposed to be easy enough for anyone who stops in."

The table fell silent again, and everyone made the same bracelet. Sheila helped Marianne, and she turned one out that looked quite good. Janine even made one. Everyone slipped theirs on and admired their achievement.

I looked at Rory's empty seat and shook my head with dismay before standing up and taking the floor.

"There's something else we need to discuss," I began. "It's great that we all made sample bracelets tonight, but there's another much bigger problem."

I focused on Adele at the end of the table. Instead of looking at me, she was staring down at something she was making out of lime-green yarn. I could see her hook moving along the piece. Was she avoiding looking at me because she knew what I was going to talk about?

"I don't know if all of you realize this, but Rory sold herself as a crochet expert to get the gig hosting *Creating With Crochet*. I think she thinks she can somehow fake it for the show. But I met the producer at an event."

"An event? What kind of event?" Rhoda said. "Who'd you go with?"

"It was one of those charity dinners," I said. "I went with Mason."

"How come you didn't say anything about it?" Elise asked. "You've been pretty mum about your social life. So you're with Mason now, and Barry's gone from the scene for good?"

I saw Dinah looking at me with a smile, and I rolled my eyes. "We're getting off the point I'm trying to make. It doesn't matter where I went or who I was with; the fact is, the producer recognized me from the bookstore, and he asked about Rory's yarn abilities. And then he told me that if she wasn't the wizard with a hook that she'd presented herself as, there would be a big mess and the taping here could get postponed or dropped altogether."

Adele's head shot up. "But can't they just film my hands if they have to and make it look like it's her? Just like she said, I could be her crochet double."

"No, Adele. I tried to tell you before. You're supposed to be helping Rory, not trying to arrange a spot for yourself on the show."

"I'm doing the best I can," Adele said, jiggling her head with annoyance so that the flower on her beanie wiggled. "She isn't the easiest student."

I gave Adele a hopeless expression. "Mrs. Shedd is almost in a panic over this. I know how much having the program tape here means to her. She's got dreams it will turn Shedd & Royal into an international destination, which I admit is a little far-fetched, but we all owe her. The Hookers wouldn't have a home if it weren't for her letting us meet here."

"And she supports our charity projects by providing the yarn," CeeCee said. "We do owe it to her to make sure this comes off. Rory is so typical of the new crop of celebrities. All they care about is getting attention, not how they get it. The idea that she would mispresent herself as a master crocheter is appalling. What can we do?"

Janine was ignoring the whole conversation while Marianne seemed to follow it closely. The rest of the group looked to me for some kind of answer.

"I tried to talk to her, but maybe if the group says something, she'll actually listen."

"I know what we should do," Rhoda said. "We surround her and tell her what's what."

"You mean like an intervention?" Sheila asked.

"Exactly," CeeCee said.

It seemed like we were all in agreement about what to do, but there was only one problem. We needed Rory to show up.

"I hope that wasn't a waste of energy," Dinah said when we were alone at the table. She held up her wrist to admire her newly made bracelet. "At least we finally all tried the Make-and-Take project." She started to help me gather up the snippets of cord and a few beads that had broken loose. "What if Rory thinks she learned enough already and doesn't show up until the taping?"

"I hope not. But never fear, our secret weapon is on the case."

Dinah looked at me with a quizzical expression, and I smiled. “I guess you didn’t see Adele rush off and grab her cell phone. I’m sure she’s calling Rory right now.”

I was going to suggest that Dinah and I get dinner, since I was free to leave, but I saw Commander come in the door then. His face lit up when he saw Dinah.

“I called a conference with him,” Dinah said. “We’re going out to dinner, just the two of us. I haven’t really said anything to him about the problem with Cassandra until now, and I’m not sure how he’s going to take it.”

I gave her a good-luck hug, and she left. I left shortly after, feeling at loose ends. The situation with Rory had me worried. And I had an uneasy feeling about Marianne after our visit. What if Detective Heather was right and Marianne was responsible for Connie’s death?

My house was dark when I got home, but the moon was bright enough to cast shadows across the flagstone patio as I walked across it to the kitchen door. I could see my waiting committee through the glass door. I let Felix and Cosmo run out as I went in. I was reaching for the light switch when I saw a red light flashing on my phone, indicating a message.

I hadn’t heard from Barry since he and Dinah had been at my place together. The message must be from him. I punched in the code to retrieve it, expecting to hear his voice. At first there was just silence, and I was going to hit the button to erase it, but then I began to hear breathing.

Loud creepy breathing that reminded me of Darth Vader. Operating on reflex, I hung up the phone with a shudder.

I stared at the cordless lying on the counter for a few minutes. It must have been just a disgruntled salesperson annoyed that no one had answered. What else could it have been?

Chapter Seventeen

Once I got over the creepiness of the Darth Vader breathing, I was annoyed that it wasn't a message from Barry. He'd been keeping in touch pretty regularly since he'd given me my undercover job, and now suddenly there was silence. He was supposed to be the one to make contact, but I punched in his cell number anyway.

"Greenberg," he said in his flat detective tone when he answered.

"It's me, Molly Pink," I said, saying my name very crisply. I heard something on the other end that sounded like a laugh.

"You've made your point. In case you hadn't noticed, I tried being more casual the other night and it backfired."

"I realized I hadn't heard from you—"

"About that," he said, interrupting. "What happened the other night made me rethink the plan. I'm not so sure it's a good idea."

"What? Just like that you cut me off from my undercover

job?" I said. I didn't mean to sound so emotional, but the words just fell out of my mouth.

"I can't really go into that now," he said, returning to his cop tone. Of course, I had no idea where he was, and who knew who was standing next to him. "We could take up this matter later," he said, still keeping his professional voice.

"Fine," I said, trying to sound cool about the whole situation.

"It's not what you think," he said just before clicking off.

I looked around then, surprised that I hadn't turned the lights on. But then, the moonlight coming in the two large windows had been enough to illuminate the phone. I could see the dogs running around when they came out of the shadows of the orange trees. It almost seemed a shame to flip on the floodlight and turn on the ones in the kitchen.

There was no note from Samuel, so I assumed the dogs hadn't been fed or Blondie given her walk. My younger son seemed to be gone more than usual, which I took to mean that he'd met someone new. I made sure the cats' bowl had plenty of dry food and gave them each a dab of chicken puree. I put dog food in each of the three bowls and made sure the water was filled to the top.

Cosmo and Felix were at the door when I opened it and rushed in, going straight to their bowls. I had to go across the house to get Blondie out of her chair to come and eat.

Dogs certainly didn't savor their food. The bowls were

empty in a flash. Cosmo and Felix retired to the living room for an after-dinner nap while I got the leash for Blondie. I had started the habit of walking her when I'd first adopted her. It seemed to be the only time she perked up. Cosmo and Felix didn't seem to mind being left out, though the two cats always followed us to the door as if they hoped to go with us.

There was something eerie about being able to see Blondie's shadow as we began our trek. We always took the same route, and she made the same sniff spots. Other than being on the lookout for coyotes, it was a good time to get lost in thought. My mind flitted from wondering about Rory and if she'd be able to get it together to thinking of Marianne in the house on the hill. I was so lost in thought I almost didn't notice something in the shadows of the trees skittering alongside us. The shadows ended and moonlight drenched the dog-sized creature. It was bony thin, and there was something sinister in its step.

Blondie was looking straight ahead as if she didn't know the coyote was there, or maybe it was wishful thinking. I'd forgotten the walking stick I usually carried when I was alone. I tried yelling at it to go home. Which was ridiculous anyway. If it had had some warm snuggly place with a bowl full of food, would it really have been out looking for dinner?

Would it attack Blondie even though they were a match in size? I didn't know and I didn't want to find out the hard way, so I picked Blondie up against her wishes and lugged her home. I looked back when we'd gone up the driveway and saw the coyote standing in the street. The light caught its eyes as it offered a last menacing stare.

Unfazed, Blondie plodded back across the house and climbed into her chair. I let out a breath of relief as I put away her leash.

Barry hadn't given any indication when *later* would be. But knowing that he was coming gave me a chance to prepare. I'd make some food to soften him up. And I'd offer him some information without a hassle. I wanted him to change his mind. I didn't want to give up my undercover job. It was too much fun.

I realized the food couldn't be too elaborate or he'd figure out what I was doing and it would seem too desperate. I was still regretting that I'd been so straightforward on the phone. I looked around the refrigerator and began pulling out the fixings for mushroom stroganoff. I boiled the pasta and cooked the sauce. I ate some before packing it up and putting it in the refrigerator so it would look like leftovers.

The hours began to tick by. I tried to occupy myself by crocheting another Gratitude Circle. I was trying to figure out what about it made you feel grateful. I finally got it—it was just about the name and the wearer's expectations—in other words, marketing. Couple a great name with a super-easy project and it seemed to have success written all over it.

I thought about Rory. If we could just get her to master the most basic skills, she'd be able to pull it off. It had gotten quite late by then, and I began to think that Barry wasn't going to come, but then the phone rang.

"It's Green—I mean Barry. I'm out front." I was already at the door and pulled it open before he clicked off.

He was standard late-night Barry. Suit and tie without a wrinkle but shadows under his eyes that showed his fatigue. I was probably too quick to offer him food, but I think saying it was just leftovers made it a little less obvious.

He followed me into the kitchen just as Felix and Cosmo showed up for their treat. I intended to be quiet and let him talk, but before I could stop myself, I blurted out that it wasn't fair for him to give me the job and then take it away without even saying anything.

"Wow, you're really wearing your heart on your sleeve about it, aren't you?" he said with a smile. "I told you it's not what you think," he said. "I was actually thinking more about you. You heard Dinah. She didn't buy that I was here for dog care. She had to think there was something else going on that you hadn't told her about. I realized I'd put you in a terrible position with your best friend. I was going to talk to you about it, but I didn't know quite what to say." He leaned against the counter, and his face broke into a half smile. "But it looks like I just did."

"Oh," I said, suddenly feeling like a jerk. I should have learned by now not to assume. It had almost permanently wrecked things with Mason when I'd assumed he was back with his ex-wife. "It's okay with Dinah. I can convince her that you were just here for Cosmo." I wondered if I should add the rest, that Dinah believed his trips for dog care were just an excuse to see me. I decided to leave that out. I was surprised at his reason for backing away, though. Barry usually had tunnel vision when it came to his work. But it seemed he'd put concern for me ahead of his desire for information.

"Well, if you're sure it isn't too uncomfortable for you to keep something from your best friend," Barry said, studying my face for a reaction.

"I don't like doing it, but she'd understand if she knew," I said.

I dished him up a plate of the noodles and creamy sauce with some chopped salad I'd just thrown together on the side, and he took it to the dining room. "You're not eating?" he said, seeing I was empty-handed.

"I already ate. Remember, I said it was just leftovers." We sat down facing each other.

"So then should we pick up where we left off?" he said.

"I kind of remember last time you said you had something to tell me, and then you saw Dinah," I said.

"Isn't it always ladies first?" he said.

I shrugged and agreed. "Well, I talked to the gardeners." Before I could continue, he looked up from his food with a surprised expression.

"Why talk to them? We already questioned them."

"Because I thought they might tell me something different," I said.

"So, did they?" he asked, almost as a dare.

"Not exactly, though they did seem pretty nervous when I asked them about music. I did find out that someone tampered with the sprinklers so they ran for a much longer time. But there's something you might not have noticed. The gardeners were all dressed in the same nondescript outfit. Anyone dressed similarly could have come onto the property, and if anyone noticed them, they would just think it was one of the gardeners."

"Okay, that could have happened," he said, but then his brow furrowed. "Why were you even talking to the gardeners? That sounds like investigating to me, which you weren't supposed to be doing."

I changed the subject by offering him seconds.

"There's still more left? You must have made an awful lot of it to have so much left over." He leveled his eyes at me, and I was sure he was measuring my response. Had he figured out what I had done?

I took his plate without a comment and got him a refill. "Well, I told you mine. Now it's your turn."

"Oh, right," he said. "It's related to something you told me."

"Really?" I said, perking up. "Something I told you was important?"

He looked at me with an understanding smile. "I get it. You're trying to remind me of your value." He seemed to be taking his time and started to load some of the creamy noodle dish on his fork.

"So what is it?" I asked.

He chuckled at my impatience and put down the fork. "Maybe this is a mistake and we should leave things as they are. You tell me, but I don't tell you." His tone didn't sound completely serious.

"No fair. You can't almost tell me and then not," I said. I saw him smile. "You're playing with me, aren't you?"

He half shrugged. "Maybe I am. Kind of payback for all the times you answered my questions with questions," he said with a wry smile. "No more games. Here it is. I paid attention when you said that Marianne might have been the intended victim. I found out that Errol Freeman has been talking to developers about taking that property, getting rid of the house, and dividing it up and building multimillion-dollar homes—"

"But Marianne told me she controls the house and land," I said, interrupting.

"Exactly," Barry said.

"She said that Errol was trying to get her to sell the place. He thinks she ought to go to some assisted-living place. His wife mentioned it, too. Marianne said that even Connie had suggested she ought to sell the place. But Marianne told me she wanted to stay there. I get it. And Errol didn't like her decision and decided to get her out of the picture. Then he set up the whole thing." I stopped to take a breath. "Then why aren't you arresting him?"

"Hang on, Sherlock," Barry said with a laugh. "That's all conjecture. There has to be real evidence—"

"Maybe I can find some," I said, jumping in. "Marianne talks to me. She thinks of me as a friend. Well, I really do like her." I was about to say more, but Barry's expression darkened.

"But be careful. There has to be a reason she's on all

those drugs. Who knows what behavior they're keeping in check. She could be dangerous."

I shook my head at the warning. "I don't think so—"

Barry interrupted before I could finish. "Just keep it to talk. No more investigating on your own, right?"

"Sure," I said with a smile.

"C'mon, Molly, I know that look. You're just telling me what I want to hear while you're probably already making other plans."

"No," I said innocently. "I get it, you're the boss on this."

Barry blew out his breath and shook his head. "Maybe I should really take you off the case." He smiled, and I realized he was playing with me again.

"You're not going to do that," I said. "You know that you need me."

I was going to add a breezy comment, but our gazes caught and then seemed locked. I felt my face start to flush, as if someone had turned up the thermostat. I heard Barry swallow hard. Then he abruptly pushed away from the table, muttering that he had to go. A moment later I heard the door shut. I never got a chance to offer him dessert.

Chapter Eighteen

"Adele," I called as my coworker rushed across the bookstore toward the kids' section. I was sure she heard me, but she didn't turn. I had to practically jog to catch up with her. Finally I grabbed her arm, and she came to a stop.

"I know you're trying to avoid me," I said.

She fidgeted with her costume of the day. She was dressed as some girl wizard, and I'd seen the sign that they were reading a chapter from *Veronica Lightning Bolt*.

"You never told me if you reached Rory and if you did what she said." Adele was trying to squirm from my grasp, but I held on to her arm. "It's not going to help anything if you avoid it."

"Okay, Pink, here's the scoop. I talked to her and she said she'd be back for tonight's happy hour."

"Did you tell her it's really important that she take it seriously?" I asked.

"Sort of," my coworker said.

"What exactly did you say?" With Adele, *sort of* could mean anything.

"That she was doing great with the crochet and I'd be there as her backup."

Adele tried to pull away again, this time successfully, and she disappeared into her domain. I would have followed her in, but I was suddenly surrounded by kids and their parents gathering at the entrance. Adele reappeared with her clipboard and greeted the assembled group. The kids got all excited when they saw her, and I heard some wows about her cape.

I wasn't about to interfere with any more questions. Difficult as she was, it somehow worked with the kids. They honestly seemed to love her. And she managed to bring a lot of business to the bookstore.

I made a *grrr* sound in frustration. What could I say to make Adele understand that she wasn't going to somehow end up in the spotlight doing the actual crochet work? It had actually gotten worse. This morning I'd heard from Ethan, the director, that not only did they want to see the group make the bracelets, but they'd like us to bring in some customers to see how it went with strangers, and that they planned to have Rory act as the host of it all.

I cringed just thinking about her calling for her crochet double, not realizing I had an audience.

"You look troubled. Maybe this will help," a voice said, startling me. I glanced up from my work in the information booth to see Mason standing there with a carrier holding two cups of coffee. "It seems like forever since I've seen you," he said.

He set the carrier down and took the lid off one of the paper cups and handed it to me. He knew I didn't like drinking through the lid because I always burned my mouth. He'd been tied up all week, and when he'd had time, I hadn't.

"I think this is just what I needed." I looked at him with a warm smile. "Both the red eye and seeing you."

"Ditto. I was on my way in to the office," he said, taking his coffee out of the holder and drinking it with the lid on. "I think we have to make some changes so we can spend more time together. We can't even depend on the weekend anymore."

It was true. Weekends were busy at the bookstore, and we were thinking about having events on Sunday afternoons now too. Mason took another sip of his coffee, and I saw him looking at his watch.

"What if we planned something for a couple of weekdays?" he said.

"Can you do that?" I asked, surprised.

"I never would have before, but my priorities are changing." He reached over the counter and touched my arm. "We could go someplace and get away from it all."

I couldn't believe what I was about to say. "That sounds wonderful. But . . ." I looked at him with a rueful smile. "I can't even think about it right now. Maybe after they tape *Creating With Crochet*, I can arrange something." I explained the current problem with Rory and her hook work.

He looked disappointed. "It seems like neither of us can get away from dealing with troublesome celebrities." He leaned over the counter and kissed me warmly. "There's more where that came from. We just have to find the time."

* * *

I spent the rest of the day nervously awaiting happy hour. How odd. It was supposed to be the time of the day I got a chance to relax, and here I was all jittery about it.

The saving grace was that Dinah and I had made plans for a girls' night afterward. I'd given Barry a heads-up so that he wouldn't show up unannounced. Besides, I didn't expect to have anything new to tell him anyway. And Mason had some hand-holding to do with a client, so I knew I wouldn't see him, either.

I was in the yarn department when the group began to arrive. Dinah got there first and said how much she was looking forward to our girls' night and that she had a lot to tell me about her conference with Commander. She seemed so energetic and upbeat, and it was like a tonic to see her. She always wore a long scarf wound around her neck. This one was white with sparkles that lit up her face.

CeeCee came up to us. "Any word if Rory will be joining us?"

She said the name with distaste, and I knew she didn't approve of the younger celebrity. I said I thought she was coming and then added the news of the added requirements of our Make-and-Take rehearsal.

CeeCee began to fret. "I wonder if the powers that be

told Rory what they expect of her." She put down her tote bag. "Dear, I hope we have enough kits made up, because we ought to do a repeat of last night." She discussed how she thought it would go for the actual show. "We'll probably be in the background making our own Gratitude Circles and then Rory will be helping the Make-and-Take people." She shuddered when she said it. "I can't imagine her managing that with her current skill level. Even her slip knot was a nightmare. Maybe when she hears the Craftee people are coming to watch us, she'll finally stop fooling around. She can't seem to get it in her head that she has to crochet like it's second nature." CeeCee went to the head of the table. "At least we can all make a bracelet together tonight."

When Elise arrived, CeeCee asked her if she had any kits left. Elise showed that she still had a bag full and put one at each person's seat. I appreciated that she'd provided them for the Hookers, but she did have an ulterior motive. We were already talking about selling bracelet kits in the yarn department after the show taped, and Elise wanted to be our supplier.

"So, we're going to try again," Rhoda said, pulling out her chair. "I hope Rory shows up this time."

Errol must have talked to Janine, because she seemed totally changed. She was hanging so close to Marianne now that she seemed like her shadow. She helped Marianne with the kit and took one for herself. I wondered if it had anything to do with her finding out we were going to be on a TV show. There was a good chance she was an aspiring actor working as a companion while she waited for her big break.

Marianne seemed withdrawn, and Janine nudged her. It took Marianne a moment to compute what the nudge meant, but then she nodded with recognition and offered a stiff greeting to the group and said how happy she was to be there.

We all watched when Rory made a stir coming through the bookstore. She stopped at least twice to do a Dance Break with a customer before she joined us. She was all smiles and seemed clueless that anyone was upset with her. Adele appeared just then, which made me think she must have been hiding out until Rory arrived.

"So, what's happening, everybody?" Rory said, seeing the kits on the table.

CeeCee looked at me. "Why don't you explain, dear. I'm sure you'll be better at it than me."

I knew what CeeCee was really saying—that I could manage to explain the upcoming rehearsal without casting aspersions. As I explained, I kept glancing at Rory, trying to read her expression. Did she already know about the rehearsal and was she worried about it? She seemed unconcerned, which had me worried.

"Let's not waste any time," Eduardo said, picking up his bag of supplies. Rory watched the rest of the group and didn't make a move. I gave Adele a look, and she pushed Rory's bag toward her.

"Why don't you stand up, Rory," CeeCee said. "Since you're going to be the host."

Rory reluctantly got up and looked around at the group.

"Hey, let's start off with a Dance Break." I watched as the whole group half closed their eyes and shook their heads with dismay.

No one joined in Rory's Dance Break, and the extent of her crocheting was holding a hook and walking around the table as the rest of us worked, adding what she called *color*. "That's what they want me for," she said when CeeCee gave her a sour look.

The bracelet making went fine with the old guard of the group, but Janine had to make Marianne's. Rory only managed to make a slip knot. I shuddered. Could it get any worse?

* * *

"It's time to put it all behind you," Dinah said as we walked out of the bookstore together. We'd already decided to start our girls' night by eating at a new place that had opened down the street. It was what now seemed to be called casual dining, which meant that you ordered at the counter. It was done to appear like a diner, and the food was all comfort items like meatloaf and macaroni and cheese. Dinah and I gave the woman at the counter our food order, and Dinah went to grab a table while I stood off to the side to wait for our dinner.

A moment later, Marianne and Janine came in. I was stuck behind a row of tall plants and they didn't see me. Janine walked Marianne to a table and got her situated and then came back to the counter. She placed their order, and when she stepped away to wait, she saw me.

"It looks like we both had the same idea," Janine said. She looked toward her charge. "Marianne wanted dinner out. I guess the person who had my job before me just did whatever Marianne wanted. Did you know her?"

I explained my dealings with Connie, which were minimal. "To be honest, none of us in the group knew what her relationship with Marianne was. Did they tell you what happened to her?"

Janine's face grew serious. "Errol Freeman is the one who handled hiring me. He made me an offer I couldn't refuse, though it'll be better when they let me move into the guesthouse. I heard it was a freak accident and she got electrocuted. But getting electrocuted is like getting struck by lightning. It never happens in the same spot twice, right?"

I didn't want to tell her that wasn't exactly true for lightning and certainly not true for a freak accident. Before I could say either, Janine stuck out her foot.

"I wear rubber-soled shoes anyway."

The counter person set some trays of food out, and we both looked to see if it was ours. When someone else stepped up to collect the food, we went back to talking.

"I suppose you know all about Marianne's problem." I said it as if I knew what the problem was, hoping Janine would feel comfortable talking about it.

She shrugged. "I didn't ask and they didn't tell me," she said. "My job is mostly to make sure she takes her meds. Then it's he said, she said. He wants me to be with her all the time. She wants me to give her some space."

I thought about what Rory had said about having a

companion. “I suppose you’re right in the middle of the affairs of whoever you’re working for,” I said.

“It’s kind of like you know stuff whether you want to or not. Like, with this one, I don’t really want to know why Errol Freeman’s wife seems so upset with Marianne.”

The counter man brought more trays of food. When I looked up to see if it was Dinah’s and my order, I noticed that Errol had come into the restaurant. He seemed to be watching his sister, and then he came over to Janine and fussed at her for leaving Marianne at the table alone and seemed concerned about the kind of place she’d taken his sister to.

“I’ll go sit with her until the food comes, get it packed to go, and then you can take her home,” he said. It was only then that he seemed to notice me and offered me a curt greeting.

When he was gone, Janine looked perturbed. “I don’t like working with someone looking over my shoulder.”

Our food came up next, and I took it to the table. I’d barely had time to tell Dinah what was going on before we saw Janine head to their table carrying a shopping bag. It didn’t look to me like Marianne was that anxious to leave.

Dinah and I dug into our food and ate it with abandon. It was one of those meals where we threw health concerns to the wind and feasted on fried chicken, mashed potatoes with a pool of melted butter on top, and creamed spinach. We were too full to eat the apple pie we’d ordered and got it packed to go. Dinah followed me to my house and helped me deal with the pet brigade.

"Where's Samuel?" she asked as I turned on the lights.

"He's been a no-show a lot lately. I think that means he has a new girlfriend."

Dinah glanced into the living room. "Look at all that space. And no snippy person finding fault with everything you do."

"So your conference with Commander didn't go well," I said as I dished out dog and cat food.

"He had no idea what was going on. Cassandra is always pleasant when he's around. He didn't even know about the yoga classes. I had to tell him that his daughter was trying to paint me as a villain after her mother's stuff." Dinah threw up her hands in distress. "One of the reasons he moved to my place is that I didn't want to live in the house he'd lived in with his wife, surrounded by all her things."

We took Blondie on her walk together, glad to move around after the heavy meal. We made it home with no coyote encounters this time.

When we got back, we starting talking about the group. "Janine is certainly different than Connie," Dinah said. "It's funny how little we know about Connie, but then I guess her job was to stay in the background." Dinah paused to see what room we were going to settle in. "What happened to that whole investigation of Connie's death? There was that one short news article and then nothing. Did the cops close the case?" my friend asked as I led her into the den. Mine was much smaller than Marianne's, but like hers, it had a view of the yard.

"They're still investigating, but I don't think they agree on what happened," I said.

We both sat on the couch facing the built-in wall unit. There was a spot for a TV, but it had been built for the old-fashioned kind and I'd had to perch the flat-screen outside the boxlike housing. Dinah and I had played the Sherlock Holmes game just once on this case, and that had been mostly about Marianne. We really hadn't talked about Connie's death at all. I showered her with the information I'd gathered.

"Wow," she said when I'd finished. "I'm surprised that you didn't tell me any of this before. We usually shoot ideas back and forth." She sounded almost hurt. "You sure seem to know a lot. Where are you getting your information? Mason?" Then she leaned closer. "Or was it Barry?"

I didn't say anything and tried not to react, but she picked up on a flicker in my expression.

"So Barry's giving you information? That seems odd, since he's usually trying to keep you out of stuff. He seemed pretty friendly the other night." She let it hang in the air, and I bit my lip.

Dinah knew me all too well and moved closer. "I know what you're doing. You're holding something back."

"I can't say anything," I said finally.

"Aha! So there is something going on. Something with Barry."

She saw me freeze.

"And it's a secret."

When I stayed mute, she said, "Okay, I get it that you can't talk, but I can guess." She was smiling, intrigued by the game and took a moment to think it over. "This is a crazy thought—but are you working with Barry?"

When I didn't say anything, she laughed.

"How about you blink if that's what it is."

I blinked a number of times, and her face lit up.

"That Barry," she said, shaking her head with a giggle. "He found the perfect way to keep spending time with you."

"That's not why he's doing it," I protested. "You can't let on that you know."

I got her to promise that she wouldn't say anything if the three of us were together again. Then I told her that Detective Heather had decided what had happened but that Barry didn't agree. Since Marianne had lawyered up, she wasn't talking. He knew that I was friendly with her and thought she might drop some information in my lap.

"I was just supposed to give him information and he'd put the pieces together, as he put it. But you know me," I said with a smile and a shrug. "I worked it out, so we're putting together the pieces, together."

"And Mason doesn't know about it?"

"Barry swore me to secrecy. I think his biggest concern is that Detective Heather not find out that he's looking for information that would prove her wrong. It's just business between us, anyway. Though it is kind of neat being on the same side with him."

We decided to have our pie while we watched TV. I let

Dinah play with the remote and flip through the channels looking for something interesting.

"Stop," I said when I saw Rory on the screen. Dinah put down the remote and we both stared at her image.

"She sure doesn't mind showing herself in a bad light," Dinah said as we watched Rory stumble into her kitchen with no makeup and rumpled clothes. We determined it was a repeat of the last reality show she'd been on—*Rory in Real Life*. She went to the counter and pulled out a loaf of bread and a jar of peanut butter. Another women came into the frame, and as Rory picked up a knife, presumably to make a sandwich, the woman grabbed the bread and peanut butter.

"Look at her," Dinah said, leaning closer to the screen. "That almost looks like—"

"It is," I said interrupting. "That's Connie Richards."

Chapter Nineteen

The bookstore was bustling when I came in Friday morning. Adele was doing a special story time and the kids had already started to arrive. The mothers were making their way to the café as I headed to the information kiosk. I saw a number of them look at the sign advertising Missy Z's upcoming book signing. Mrs. Shedd stopped me before I went into my so-called office.

"The Craftee people called a while ago. They said they'd be in this afternoon to see the Make-and-Take run-through. I assume you know what they're talking about."

"It wasn't supposed to be until next week," I said, trying to keep the panic out of my voice.

"The person I spoke with was very casual about it, as if they're just coming by to observe the Hookers in action." She began to pick up on my panic. "Am I to assume you're not ready?"

I had to set aside my own nerves to calm her. I fudged a little and said that my biggest concern was getting something together in the afternoon.

It seemed to appease the store owner, and she gave my shoulder a reassuring pat. "I'm sure you'll manage just fine. You always seem to come through."

My mind was already clicking on how I was going to do what she seemed to think was so easy. I'd call some of the Hookers. Rhoda was usually free in the afternoon. I hoped that CeeCee would be able to come. Sheila worked down the street, so she could probably take a break then. Adele would be there, and I was sure Dinah would come if she didn't have a class. I'd snag some customers from the bookstore to do the Make-and-Take. I was feeling reassured that we'd manage until I thought about Rory. I thought back to the last get-together and her nonexistent skill with a hook.

I knew Adele's event was for younger kids and Rory had brought hers before. No adults other than Adele were allowed in when she was hosting the kids, but I was able to peek in. I saw that Rory's two kids were sitting in the front, and I went to look for her. I found her sitting in a corner of the café holding court with some of the other mothers.

It was an effort to get her to step away from all the attention, but I finally managed to pull her aside. "I assume the people from the Craftee Channel contacted you about a rehearsal of the Make-and-Take," I said.

"Someone called this morning," she said, seeming unconcerned. "I said I'd be there."

I was stunned that she seemed to think that all that was needed was her presence.

"You do understand they want to see the bracelet

making in action. They must be expecting you to take part in it." I looked at her to see her reaction.

"Don't worry, it'll be fine." She glanced at the table and made it clear she wanted to rejoin her admirers.

I suddenly remembered the previous night and seeing her old reality show. "Before you go," I said. "Dinah and I were flipping through channels last night, and suddenly there you were on the screen."

Rory seemed pleased as I went on about how brave she was to be on camera in the morning without any makeup. But then her expression changed as she seemed to think of something. I heard her mutter something like, "Oh, no, I had no idea they were still playing repeats."

"Why didn't you mention that Connie Richards worked as your companion?" I said, and she seemed to shrink back.

"Would you believe that I forgot?" she asked.

"No," I said.

"Just please forget that you saw that and don't tell anyone about it." She abruptly started to pull away. "I never thought I would say this, but I hope nobody is watching me on those old shows." Before I could react, she'd already gone back to her adoring fans.

* * *

The Hookers came through, and only Eduardo couldn't make it. Marianne and Janine arrived early. Marianne seemed worried, but I told her all that was required of her was that she work on one of the bracelets.

Elise had brought the kits for the Gratitude Circles, and

she acted as their custodian until we had some actual Make-and-Takers. When Dinah came to the table, I wanted badly to tell her about Rory's odd reaction when I'd mentioned seeing Connie in the reality show, but there was no time. CeeCee arrived, seeming a little more put together than usual. She might have been playing the part of a participant in this, but she knew she was a celebrity and likely to draw more attention than the rest of us. Sheila and Rhoda came in together and sat down. Adele cruised into the yarn department looking like a crochet display. She was wearing a black sweater decorated with crocheted flowers in all different colors and designs.

Adele started to take her usual seat at one end of the table, but I reminded her that Rory needed to sit there. Adele snagged the seat next to it. I checked my watch and looked at the empty seat nervously.

"I'm here," Rory said, finally coming into the yarn department. "You can't start without me," she said gaily. She glanced around the area. "So the Craftee people aren't here yet?" She took the seat I'd set aside for her and folded her hands on the table. "Now what?"

I suggested that I get some customers to take part in the Make-and-Take. I trolled the bookstore and couldn't get any takers. My last resort was bookstore employees. Mrs. Shedd was glad to step in at the checkout counter so I could pull in our usual cashier, Rayaad, and one of our new hires, Jordan.

When they were seated at the table, Elise handed them each one of the kits.

"But I don't know how to crochet," Rayaad said, looking at the small plastic bag of supplies as if it contained something dangerous.

"Me, either," Jordan said. He was half away from the table as if he wanted to make a run for it.

"That's the point of the Make-and-Take. We teach you how to make it," CeeCee said. Then we all waited for the Craftee people to show up to go into action.

We were all keyed up when the small group from the show finally arrived. Michael Kostner took the lead and introduced everyone. Ethan, the director, wanted to get an idea of "the optics," as he put it, of the interactions between our group and those taking part in the Make-and-Take. Arnie, the writer, wanted to see what dialogue he would need to write. Felicity, the set designer, was back, though she gave no reason why. There were also some nameless production assistants who seemed to merely be part of the entourage.

"Why don't you just go ahead and start. Act like we aren't here. It'll be good practice for the actual taping," Michael said. He looked over the arrangement of people around the table and nodded with approval. "I like having a celebrity as the anchor at either end of the table."

"But I'm the host. Doesn't that mean I'm more important?" Rory said, standing up.

"Absolutely right," Michael said. "We want to see you working with the novices who've come to make the bracelets. That's why we hired you. The public loves seeing celebrities with special talents." He turned to CeeCee and bowed his head slightly. "Unfortunately, our budget didn't allow for an Academy Award nominee."

CeeCee gave him a magnanimous smile, but Rory's face clouded over. "Hey, I'm not some kind of bargain-basement stand-in."

Michael realized he'd made a mistake. "Of course not, Rory, you are perfect as the host. You're young, fun, and you're an expert at crochet." Then, mentioning they had limited time, he turned the floor over to me.

I explained the Make-and-Take concept to all of them. "Our volunteers don't know how to crochet, but with the help of the group, they will learn enough to make the Gratitude Circle, which, by the way, is a great accessory for men or women. They will leave with a finished product."

He asked who the Make-and-Takers were as he looked over the group around the table. His gaze stopped on Marianne and Janine. There was flicker of concern in his eye, and I was afraid he was reacting to Marianne's stiff movements. I quickly pointed out Rayaad and Jordan as our Make-and-Takers.

"Good that you've got a guy," he said. "Let's have Rory work with him." He got Adele to move and put Jordan next to her. He placed Rayaad next to CeeCee. He smiled and looked at the rest of us. "No offense to the rest of you, but celebrities are channel stoppers."

Wasn't that the truth. I looked at Dinah, and I knew she was thinking about the previous night at my house. "We'll get shots of the rest of you making the bracelets," he said, continuing to attempt to smooth things over.

He stepped back and waved his hand like a conductor. "Okay, just go ahead like we're not here."

Everyone at the table suddenly became animated, and I got a knot in my stomach, sure that Rory was going to be outed. CeeCee had Rayaad take out her supplies, and she demonstrated how to make a slip knot. Our poor cashier looked like she wanted to be anywhere but there. She reluctantly followed CeeCee's directions. Rhoda took out the length of cord and used her hook to make a slip knot. She saw that Marianne was struggling and helped her manage one as well. I was standing back with the observers and was afraid to look in Rory's direction. There was nothing I could do to save her now.

While she struggled to make a slip knot, the one in my stomach tightened. Michael had made it pretty clear that if Rory wasn't as she'd sold herself, they'd have to put everything on hold until they found someone to take her place. And then who knew what might happen? Would they still want to do the first show at the bookstore, and if so, when?

I was afraid to look, and yet I couldn't look away. I saw Rory swallow hard as Jordan looked to her for direction. Then she smiled. "Of course, what else, Dance Break," she said, standing up and beginning to gyrate.

She got everyone at the table to join her. I couldn't read Michael's reaction. Finally Rory called out the final "hi yo" and sat down. She looked at the table and glanced up smiling as she held up the length of chain stitches. Jordan had something similar in front of him. "And that's the way it's done," Rory said, holding it up triumphantly.

"Don't forget the next row," Rhoda said from across the table.

"That's right," Rory said cheerily. "With slip knots."

"You mean slip stitches," Rhoda said, holding up her work and demonstrating.

"I get it," Jordan said, and matched what Rhoda had just done. All eyes were on him, and I saw Adele grab Rory's piece and replace it with hers.

"That was fast," Jordan said, looking over at Rory's work. "I didn't get a chance to see you do it."

"Now you attach the ends," Rhoda coached.

"We do it with a slip knot," Rory said, holding up the strand of stitches.

"Not a knot, a slip stitch," Dinah said under her breath, and Rory quickly corrected herself and feigned dropping her work in progress. Adele bent to retrieve it and appeared to hand it back to her, but she'd done a switcheroo again. The ends were not only joined now, but the beads had been added.

Jordan examined it and figured out on his own how to finish it off. "That's easy-peasy." He threaded the beads on the end strands and added a knot after each bead before snipping the excess cord. He slipped it on his wrist and wound it around several times before holding his arm up to admire it.

"Rory, you did yours so fast I didn't get a chance to see you do it," Michael said. "But of course, when we're taping, we'll have a camera trained on you so nobody will miss a move of your hook."

She smiled and tried to hide it, but I saw her swallow with a *glunk*.

"Well, that's a wrap," the producer said. "I think we all have an idea of what this Make-and-Take thing is going to look like." He turned to Rory. "Good move about the Dance Break. We need something to liven things up." He turned to go and waved for his group to follow.

I stuck next to Michael as I walked them out. "I hope you're satisfied with everything," I said, trying to sound bright.

"So far, so good," Michael said with a smile. "How's Mason?"

"Busy," I said.

Then he got serious. "Two things," he began. "Remember the recipe I told you about? Be sure it's made with our sponsor's flour, and we'll write some copy for Rory to say when she tastes the—" He looked to me for an answer.

"Coffee cake," I said, filling in the blank.

"Sounds good," he said, giving me a thumbs-up. "Another of our sponsors is a yarn company, and they're going to want Rory to do promotion for them. I've worked with her before, and I know her tricks. We don't want to look like fools." He looked me in the eye until I nodded with understanding. She was going to have to be able to hold her own with a hook.

It was time for the group to have that talk with Rory.

* * *

"That was a close call, but somehow it seems to have gone okay," Dinah said when I got back to the table.

"It's hardly settled," I said, before telling her about the latest problem the producer had dropped in my lap. "I thought if the group did an intervention, maybe she'd get it together." I looked around at the empty table. "But that's not going to happen now."

"As soon as the production group left, everyone scattered," Dinah said.

I mentioned that I'd seen a hand-off with Marianne. Her brother had been waiting at the front of the store and Janine had left on her own.

"It seemed like Rory disappeared into thin air. When I looked up, she was just gone."

"I didn't pass her when I walked back here," I said. "She probably hid out somewhere and took off when the coast was clear."

"What's wrong with her? If she'd just stop goofing around, she could learn how to get past a slip knot and actually crochet."

Dinah pushed away from the table and suggested we get drinks in the café. I was all in from all the tension of the last hour and agreed readily. I almost considered getting a black eye, which had two shots of espresso, instead of a red eye, which had one.

When we had our drinks, we found a table near the window. I mentioned seeing Rory in there earlier. "It was really weird. I told her about seeing her on the reality show and mentioned Connie. She more or less told me to forget what I'd seen and not tell anybody about it. Then she said something really strange. She said she hoped no one was watching the old shows."

Dinah took a sip of her café au lait, which left a

steamed-milk mustache. She sensed it and wiped it away with a chuckle. "The obvious reason is that she doesn't want anyone to know she has a connection to Connie. It is strange how she mentioned having a food companion and then conveniently didn't mention who it was. Particularly when we were talking about Connie and referred to her by name."

"Maybe it's because she's dead," I said.

"With Rory's desire for publicity, I'd think she'd be more likely to use it as a way to get her name around. Something like 'The woman who acted as my food companion died in a freak accident.'"

I thought for a moment. "Do you remember what else Rory said about companions? She said they were in the middle of your business and that they, and I quote, 'know where the bodies are buried.'"

We tried to remember how Rory had acted when Connie had come with Marianne but realized that Rory had joined us the night Marianne and Connie hadn't come to happy hour, which was also the night after Connie died, so they never crossed paths.

"I wonder what food companion means?" Dinah said.

"From the way Rory talked about how her food companion would have reacted to her desire for one of Bob's rich frothy drinks, I'm guessing it was to keep her on a diet," I answered.

Seeing that we'd reached a dead end on Rory, I changed the subject and asked Dinah how it was going with Cassandra and Commander.

"I think he finally understands the problem," she said. "Commander is a practical man. To him, a chair is just something to sit on, and it doesn't matter who sat on it before." She looked at me. "Thank heavens I never took the diamond earrings."

"He tried to give you his late wife's earrings?" I couldn't help but make a face.

"He meant well," Dinah said defensively. "Though I admit, it did bother me at the time. It doesn't matter. Cassandra has them now."

"Did you give them to her?" I asked, and Dinah laughed.

"No way. That would have been like pouring water on a grease fire. I made sure he gave them to her."

"So then all's well now?" I asked.

Dinah let out a sigh. "Nope. She still has possession of my lady cave, and I have to go home and see all her yoga people lying around."

When we finished our drinks, we parted company and I went to the information cubicle. There was a white paper sack sitting on the counter with my name on it in red marker. Something about the color of the writing made me uneasy, particularly since the ink had run and it almost looked like it was dripping.

I took a breath and opened the bag. When I saw what was inside, I shuddered. It was an old cube-shaped white radio connected to an extension cord. Written on top in red marker were the words *Back Off.*

Chapter Twenty

I asked around the bookstore to see if anyone knew who had left the package. Nobody had a clue. All the focus seemed to have been on our rehearsal. I thought back to the weird phone message of menacing-sounding breathing and now wondered if it was connected to my gift. It was not the first time something like this had happened. It always meant the same thing. I was stepping on somebody's toes. I wondered if I should be worried and whether I should share what had happened with Barry.

My impulse was to keep it to myself. He would overreact, and that would be the end of my undercover job. I was anxious to tell him about Rory's connection to Connie Richards.

There was no happy-hour gathering, since we'd had the impromptu rehearsal earlier in the day. It didn't mean that I left the bookstore any earlier, though. When things slowed down that evening, I spent the extra time making arrangements for the book signing the following evening. When I finally left, the chairs were all set up in the event area and I'd placed a table at the front with a mock-up of *The Hot Zone.* There was a big sign next to the table promoting the event.

There had been arranging to do because of the author's insistence on remaining anonymous. Mr. Royal and I had worked together to make an enclosure out of bookcases adjacent to the event area. We'd left a small opening and hung a sign that said PRIVATE. The plan was that the author would arrive there on her own, which I imagined meant she would come in the bookstore like anybody else and then slip in behind the bookcases, where she'd don her disguise. All the mystery just added to the excitement.

I came home to a dark house again and no note from Samuel about animal care. Ah, young love. It was so easy to let everything else in your life slip into the background. It sure wasn't that way for me anymore. Much as Mason and I wanted to spend time together, we couldn't ignore our responsibilities. Had we become that dull? What had happened to throwing caution to the wind and taking off on a surprise trip?

I took care of the animals and made myself a hasty dinner of leftovers. Barry's visits were always impromptu, and I wondered if I'd hear from him that night.

The phone rang around ten o'clock, and I figured it was him. "Have I got stuff to tell you," I said without waiting for his greeting when I picked up the phone.

"Then you knew it was me?" Dinah said.

I laughed and told her I'd thought it was Barry calling.

"It sounds to me like you're pretty anxious to see him," she said. No matter what I said to the contrary, she seemed convinced that Barry and I still had a connection. Maybe she was sort of right. But I think he and I both knew it was best left alone because it would never work out.

The news all came from her side. "I told you things weren't settled. I think the diamond earrings just whet Cassandra's appetite for what else there was. She went through the house when no one was home and collected all the things she connected with her mother. I told Commander to let her have them, but the thing is, they're part of his past, too. I thought you might have some insight, since you must have gone through something like this after Charlie died."

"With me, it was some bottles of beer." There had been some bottles of Charlie's favorite hefeweizen brew that I'd kept for the longest time. When I'd started seeing Barry, I'd almost cut off his hand when he tried to take one. "I got over it and finally tossed the beer. You know my sons had some problems with me dating." I groaned at the word. "It's probably better to say having relationships. Though it seems it was mostly Peter and mostly about who I was seeing. Neither of them has a problem with Mason. But then, they don't seem that sentimental about things either."

I asked her if she wanted to come over and get away from it all for a while, but she declined. Dinah wasn't one to run away from things. When it came to her students, she dealt with them head on about their behavior, and those that survived and didn't drop out of her class finished the semester as real college freshmen. I knew she'd figure out a way with Cassandra.

After I hung up, I cleaned up the kitchen and was about

to turn out the light when the phone rang again. This time I merely answered with a hello.

"It's Detective Greenberg," he said, but there was a lightness in his tone that made it clear he was giving the formal greeting to tease me.

"Am I to assume you're at my front door?" I asked.

"I wasn't sure you'd be home, since it's Friday night."

"You of all people should understand that Friday night is not the beginning of a weekend off for everyone."

I heard him laugh. "Married to your job, huh?"

There was silence after that. It had been part of the problem between us that his cases and clues had always come first. It wasn't quite the same with my work, even now. Nobody was calling me in the middle of dinner telling me I'd just been assigned to a murder. I didn't respond to what he said but invited him in instead.

He was still coming up the walkway when I opened the door. So, he really had thought I might not be home. One thing was different about him this time. He'd pulled his tie loose.

"After all this, I hope you have something to tell me," he said. "Despite that the radio wasn't exactly tuned to a station and that the sound was turned off, the powers that be seem to be settling on that it was a freak accident because the gardeners wanted entertainment while they worked. Heather is still hanging on to the idea that Marianne Freeman somehow masterminded it to get rid of her caretaker."

"What about you?" I asked, and he smiled, hopelessly rocking his head.

"You're into the questions already? I'm interested in finding out the truth, which is why I'm here."

"Wow, you sound like one of those determined underdog detectives on TV," I said.

"So, are you going to help me be a hero?"

He seemed different this visit. There was no pretense of his cop face and keeping everything professional. I liked this unplugged version of him.

"Shall we talk over tea?" I chuckled this time, catching myself answering his question with one of my own.

"What kind?" There was a gleam in his eye as he kept the question game going.

"Earl Grey or Constant Comment?"

"What do you think?" The gleam was still there.

I threw up my hands. "You win. All the questions aren't getting us anywhere. I suggest Earl Grey. Is that okay?"

He let out a real laugh. "You can't help yourself, can you?"

"No more than you can," I said. "See, no question that time."

Cosmo and Felix had joined us and were unrelenting in trying to get Barry's attention and a treat. He finally offered them both and then went into the living room with the dogs close at his heels. They surrounded him when he sat down on one of the couches. I watched Barry lean back and close his eyes with what seemed like some kind of relief.

The citrusy fragrance of the tea wafted up as I brought in the tray. He took one of the mugs and set it on the coffee table. I went to the other couch and set down mine.

Of course, I'd added some food to the tray without even

asking. At this time of night, it was a given that he was hungry. "It's just a cream cheese, tomato, and cucumber sandwich."

I'd barely gotten the words out before he was already working on the sandwich. It was really a little more than that. I'd sprinkled some Trader Joe's Everything but the Bagel seasoning on top that had all sorts of seeds and spices. It took the sandwich from bland to delicious as far as I was concerned.

The sandwich was gone in a couple of bites. He finished it off with a slug of the tea. "We ought to get down to business. What have you got for me?"

"I suppose the biggest news is about Rory Graham."

Barry suddenly sat up straight. "How is she involved?"

"Connie Richards worked as a food companion for her."

"A food companion? What's that?" he asked.

"Rory didn't explain what it meant, exactly, but I'm guessing it was to keep her on a diet. But there's more." I explained how Dinah and I had found out who the food companion was. "Rory never let on that she had any connection with Connie when the Hookers were talking about her death. When I mentioned the TV show, she abruptly ended the conversation and told me not to mention it to anyone. And there's even more besides that. When Rory was talking about having a companion, she said something about them being in the middle of your business and, as she put it, 'knowing where the bodies are buried.'"

"I'm impressed."

"Really?" I asked, surprised at his comment.

"You're doing exactly what I'd hoped for." He paused and drank some of the tea. "Everything you said is useful, but not enough. Could you find out more?"

"I can't believe you actually said that. I'm so used to you telling me to stay out of everything, and here you're telling me to get in the middle of it." If there had been any chance I was going to tell him about the radio in the bag, it was over now. "I'm on it," I said.

He drained his mug and set it down. "Unless there's anything else," he said, standing.

"That's all I can think of for now," I said, getting up and walking him to the door.

He had his hand on the handle. "Jeffrey has suddenly become the concerned dog owner. My son is concerned that he hasn't seen Cosmo in a while. He might want to come over on the weekend. We have a key and all, but I wouldn't want to interfere with any plans you have."

"Don't worry, any plans I have wouldn't be taking place here," I said.

It was hard to tell in the shadowy light of the entrance hall, but it looked like Barry's expression dimmed.

"Well, thanks for the tea and food."

I thought he was going to leave then, but he turned back and looked at me, and I sensed he was trying to figure how to say good-bye. His final choice was a complete surprise as he reached out his hand to shake mine.

Chapter Twenty-One

Any plans for some weekend fun with Mason got trimmed down to brunch on Saturday. He picked me up and we went to a restaurant in Agoura Hills that looked out on the mountains. It wasn't that far away from Tarzana, but it felt like a different place. We sat outside with a view of a tree-lined creek that ran below the patio. The wind rustled the trees above us and the shadows of the leaves seemed to dance over our table.

"Alone, at last," Mason teased. "I don't suppose you could play hooky for the rest of the day and night."

"I wish, but the author event is my responsibility." I thought about what I'd just said and laughed. "I'm afraid I've become a very dull girl."

"Never," he said, reaching across the table to put his hand on mine. "You are one adventure after another. I would never ever think of you as dull."

"This book signing sure isn't going to be dull. Maybe you want to come and hear the mysterious Missy Z read from her book. It's supposed to be so hot the words sizzle off the page." The server came just then and handed us menus.

"I think I know everything I need to in that department," Mason said with a chuckle before looking over the menu, which was the size of a book. We stuck to the beginning that had breakfast items.

I ordered pumpkin pancakes and he ordered eggs Florentine with the plan that we'd share.

"So tell me what else is going on," he said. "I heard it looks like what happened to your Hooker's helper might have been a freak accident caused by something with the gardeners." It was a statement, but it came out sounding like a question.

"That's what I heard, too," I said. "But I'm not buying it. The gardeners insisted they didn't put the radio out there, and the sound was turned off."

Mason seemed surprised. "Really? How did you find that out?"

I couldn't tell him about Barry, but since I'd been to Marianne's house a few times now, it was easy to pass it off as something I'd heard there. I didn't like leaving Mason out of the loop, but it would only cause problems.

There was nothing stopping me from talking about Rory, though. I told him the same thing I'd told Barry about the TV show and seeing Connie in the background. I added the bit about what Rory had said about how people working for her had access to information she might not want to get out. "Any idea what she could be hiding?"

Mason rolled his eyes. "Probably so much, or for that

matter maybe so little. You can't believe what stupid stuff they don't want the public to know."

"You seem to know all about her. Did she do something naughty and end up as one of your clients?" I asked.

"No, I've never had the pleasure," he said. "Is she doing any better with the crochet?"

I told him about the rehearsal at the bookstore. "The worst is that she doesn't seem to care. She thinks she can cover anything with her silly Dance Breaks. But it's going to catch up with her." I mentioned my chat with the producer and what he'd said. "By the way, he said to say hello."

The food came, and we were occupied with cutting things up and moving them onto other plates. Then we just ate and talked about the food and the view. Mason suggested we take a walk after breakfast, but I had to get back.

"I'm telling you, I have become a dull girl."

He laughed and said there was always tomorrow.

Mason seemed unusually thoughtful on the way back, and I asked what he was thinking about. "I had this thought that the incident with the radio and the wet grass seemed somehow familiar, and I was trying to figure out why. It just came to me," he said, his tone changing to excitement. "It was in a TV movie. It was called something like *The Grass Is Always* something."

I typed THE GRASS IS into the search box of the movie and television database I'd pulled up on my phone, and a drop-down menu listed several titles that were similar.

"Could it be *The Grass Is Always Greener*?" I asked, and he nodded enthusiastically.

"That's absolutely it."

I clicked on it, and a screen appeared with the synopsis. I began to read it out loud. "'TV movie that follows the investigation of a wealthy heiress who dies in freak incident when a boombox electrifies the lawn.'" I scrolled down to look at the cast. "I can't believe it," I exclaimed. "Rory Graham played the heiress," I said. "What would I do without you?"

"I like the way that sounds." He reached over and touched my shoulder affectionately.

* * *

He dropped me off at home, and I hurried to get myself together to go to the bookstore. I'd save the information about where the killer might have gotten the idea of how to set up the murder scene until I heard from Barry again, but in the meantime I wanted to share it with Dinah. Since she lived just off Ventura Boulevard near the bookstore, I made a quick stop there after I parked the Greenmobile in the parking lot that served Shedd & Royal and the other shops on the block.

Cassandra answered the door and eyed me suspiciously. It was my first chance to see her up close. She had the same lean build as her father, but that's where the resemblance stopped. Commander's face naturally settled into a pleasant expression, but hers seemed unhappy. Dinah came to the door and told the younger woman that it was okay and Cassandra moved away, but not without giving me a last hard stare.

Dinah closed her eyes with consternation and then

invited me in. I naturally gravitated toward her lady cave, but she grabbed my hand and took me through the kitchen to a small eating area that looked out on the backyard. "It's the closest thing to private these days," Dinah said, offering me a seat.

I turned down the offer of coffee or tea and told her I could stay only a short time.

Her eyes lit up. "You have to get ready for tonight. I'll be there." She stopped to listen for a moment, as there was the sound of a sliding glass door closing. She looked at the wall that separated where we were from the lady cave. "She has a whole pile of things she gathered from the house. It's almost all stuff that Commander brought when he moved in. Now he's upset that she's claiming it."

"How long is she supposed to stay?" I asked.

"For more than another week. She would have left sooner, but then there'd be problems with her plane ticket. I'd be happy to give her the change fee," Dinah said.

"Or you could look at it as some time to use your Dinah magic to straighten her out." Dinah didn't get it at first, and then I reminded her of all the freshmen she'd brought around.

"That's an interesting way to look at it," my friend said. "But I don't think you stopped here to discuss Cassandra. What's up?"

I told her that Mason had come up with something interesting. Dinah's eyes lit up, and she wanted details of our time together. She was disappointed that it had only been brunch.

"It's what happened on the car ride back," I said, and then I told her about *The Grass Is Always Greener*. "Rory played the heiress who died. She could have gotten the idea from the script."

Dinah didn't seem to share my enthusiasm. "As your Dr. Watson, I have to point something out. Millions of people watched that TV movie, too. Not only when it was on, but since. They probably came out with a DVD."

"You're right. It's hardly a smoking gun."

* * *

I would have liked to hang out longer with Dinah, but I had to get to the bookstore. When I arrived, Mrs. Shedd was helping at the cashier stand and came over to me. We were usually busy on Saturday, but there was an extra buzz of customers, and my boss seemed a little frantic. "Molly, I'm glad you're here. We've been getting calls all morning. And people have been coming in, too. It's always the same—they want to reserve a book and a seat for tonight. The ones on the phone are paying in advance with credit cards."

She let out a nervous laugh. "We haven't had so much excitement for a long time. I guess it's true that sex sells. Joshua and I talked it over just now. We think we should have all the attendees purchase their book before the event. We've already put in an order for an emergency shipment that will come this afternoon. We don't want to turn away any customers."

"Of course not," I said.

She went on to their office, and I went to check out the event area. There were scraps of construction paper with names written on them sitting on some of the chairs. The signing table still had a small placard touting the event, but the mock-up was gone.

Mr. Royal came up next to me, and I asked him about the book cover. "It disappeared. Somebody must have taken it. I was going to replace it with a real copy from the books that came in." He seemed bemused by all the frenzy. "We're going to need more chairs."

He helped me push the chairs closer together, and then I made a hasty call to a rental place. They said we'd have the seats within the hour.

The rest of the day went by in a flurry of unfolding chairs and unpacking books. We even took the chairs from around the table in the yarn department, since the Hookers didn't have happy-hour gatherings on the weekend. By six o'clock, everything was ready. Even though the actual event had been planned for eight, people began coming in early. I stayed near the enclosure I'd created out of the bookcases and watched as they came in. We'd put up signs all over to tell the crowd they had to purchase their books first, and Mrs. Shedd was hanging near the front entrance telling people as they came in.

The crowd was almost entirely women, and most of them came in pairs or groups. I was surprised to see Marianne arrive with Janine. Seeing her from a distance, I had this sense of someone locked behind a curtain. I had gotten so caught up in finding out Rory's connection to Connie Richards, I'd forgotten I'd thought Marianne might have been the intended victim.

I thought back to what Barry had said about Errol. He certainly had a motive for wanting his sister out of the way. Then he could do what he wanted with the property, since it seemed likely it would all go to him. And he wouldn't have the burden of looking after Marianne. The way it was, it all fell on him. He had to step in during the companions' time off, hire them, and deal with any problems that arose. He had to have felt resentful. His wife Kelly didn't seem very happy about the current arrangement either. I remembered what Janine had said about problems between Errol and his wife. And there was no doubt that he knew about Marianne's nightly walks.

"What are you thinking about?" Dinah said. She'd already put her jacket on two chairs to save them and had come up to the front to join me. I tried to gesture toward Marianne without giving it away and told Dinah what had been going through my mind.

"You're right," Dinah said. "Marianne could have been the intended victim. Her brother was very upset with her the night she came to happy hour without a companion. And his wife seemed annoyed that she'd had to step in for her husband. Life would certainly be simpler for them with Marianne out of the picture."

"And they'd be a whole lot richer. Can you imagine what that property is worth?" I looked at my friend. "But none of that is a smoking gun either. Now if I had some proof to hand over to Barry, it would be a different story."

Rhoda came in just then and waved. Dinah went to join her and show her the seats she'd saved. I almost missed seeing Adele slip into the last row. She wasn't wearing a stitch of crochet and, instead of her usual bright colors, was all in gray. For once she didn't seem to want to stand out.

I made sure the lights were lowered just before eight o'clock. The seats were all full and people were still coming. I had been continually checking the enclosure to see if our author had arrived. So far, she hadn't. Instinctively, I kept my eye on people coming in the bookstore, though there was no way I'd recognize her.

All the seats were filled and there were people standing in the back. I had my fingers crossed she wouldn't be a no-show. Mrs. Shedd had come back into the event area and gave me a worried look, and I knew she was thinking the same thing.

People were rustling in their seats, and I could feel their impatience. Then I heard a loud *psst* coming from the opening to the bookcase enclosure.

I followed the sound and found myself facing someone about my height, shrouded in a black veil that reached all the way to the floor. A hand came out from an opening in the netting and grabbed mine.

"Missy Z," a feminine voice said, shaking my hand. Her hand was slightly sweaty and her voice had a slight tremble, which made me think she was nervous. "I guess this is it," she said.

I went back out and picked up the small microphone and did my introduction, but all eyes were on the table next to me and the spot where the author would sit. Since she was going to be reading and had requested that the lights be low, I'd set up a book lamp that made a small pool of light to illuminate her reading material.

There was a vibe of anticipation as the lady in black came out and some applause as she took the seat behind the table. And then I stepped away and let her take over.

She spent the first few minutes talking about writing the book. The idea had come from an overheard conversation, and she'd been lucky enough to have a job that gave her time to write. When she opened the book, it sounded like the audience all sucked in their breath at once.

They were all hushed as she began to read. "'Dana looked out the small plane's window at the blue water below. She was anxious for the flight to be over and looked forward to being safely on the ground and on her way to the resort. She knew it wasn't fair to blame all men for the way Josh had dumped her, but for now she wanted no part of the other half of the species. She looked over at the other passenger. She knew his name was Alexander something or other. There was something stiff and proper about his crisp khaki pants and button-down shirt.

"'He'd tried to make conversation, but she'd rebuffed him. Everything about him was a turn-off, particularly that he was a man. She looked out the front window of the plane, hoping for a sight of the coast, but instead all she saw were towering dark clouds as the plane began to pitch . . .'"

My mind started to drift back to my job, and I vaguely heard something about a plane crash and the two passengers being left on a small island. I looked over the crowd and counted heads. It was going to be a chore to get them to keep moving through the line while Missy Z signed their books. I'd have to stand next to her and make sure no one started a conversation with her that would hold things up. How to be firm, but not rude?

I'd tuned back in, as I sensed by the tone of her voice that she was getting to the end of her reading. "'"The only way we're going to survive is if we stick together," Alexander said. He'd managed to make an enclosure out of driftwood and palm fronds. She was soaked to the skin from the unrelenting rain, and the thought of being someplace dry won out. Dana accepted his invitation and went inside.'"

"Where's the hot stuff?" someone from the audience called out.

Missy Z seemed to look at the crowd. "You'll have to buy the book for that," she said with a laugh.

I shifted over to her as the crowd got out of their seats. Mr. Royal helped arrange the line, and I heard him telling them how to page their books. It made it quicker to move people through if they had their copies already open to the signing page.

Missy Z had her pen ready, and I began to let people through while keeping an eye on them to make sure they didn't dawdle. Because of the low light, I couldn't see who was who until they had handed her their book. She was gracious and accepted compliments as she scribbled her name. I had to step in only a few times when someone started telling the author their life story.

Rhoda came through with a nervous giggle. She and Dinah had decided to share a copy. She said Dinah had left already and had asked her to say good-bye to me. Marianne was right behind, clutching her copy. I realized it must have taken a lot of determination for her to do anything because of the cloud of medication. She set down her book, and Missy Z gave her hand a squeeze before she wrote something. Then the next person moved up.

The line seemed to go on forever. I went to see where it ended and noticed Adele edging along the side with a copy of the book in her hand. When she got almost next to me, she turned to the next person in line and said she was a bookstore employee, as if that gave her a special privilege. The woman shrugged and Adele moved into position to be next.

"There you are. I knew you were up to something when I saw the drab clothes. It's my duty to keep an eye on things," a voice called out. My head shot up, and I saw that Lenore Humphries, aka Mother Humphries, had come into the event area and was staring directly at Adele. "Wait until I tell Eric you're hanging out with people who write smutty books."

Missy Z must have thought the outburst was aimed at her and stood up and moved away from the table defensively, not realizing that Adele had somehow stepped on the veil. The dark covering pulled free, and the whole world got a view of her purple T-shirt with a dancing cat on the front before she darted back into the enclosure.

I gave Adele a dirty look and left her to deal with the crowd while I grabbed the veil and followed the author.

The woman Adele had butted in front of had grabbed

my coworker's arm. "You said you were a bookstore employee. Your better fix this."

I looked back as Adele dithered between making a run for it and being the center of attention. Apparently running won. "Gotta go, folks. I'm sure Molly will fix everything," Adele said as she took off.

Missy Z was cowering in the corner, trying to hide her face, but I could see enough of it to realize that the so-called publicity person was really the author. I held up the veil, which had been ripped in the accident, and we had a short conference on how to proceed. I managed with the help of a stapler to repair her shroud for the time being, and she reemerged from the enclosure. The line of people still waiting gave her some excited applause.

When the last person got their book signed, it was past closing time. Missy Z went back into the enclosure and seemed at a loss for what to do. "I can't go out like this, and if I take off the veil, the people outside will know it's me." She looked down at the purple cat T-shirt and grumbled at herself for wearing something so noticeable.

I told her to stay put for the moment and I'd work it out. I found Mrs. Shedd and Mr. Royal at the front of the bookstore. They both seemed elated about the success of the event and also worn out from dealing with it. They were relieved when I suggested they could leave and that I would lock up.

When I'd made sure the place was empty, I told the author she could come out.

"You've seen my face, so there's no point trying to keep

this on," she said, tossing the veil off to the side. "Memo to me, always bring a spare." When I'd met the so-called publicity person, I hadn't paid that much attention to her, but now that I knew I was speaking to the one and only Missy Z, I looked her over more carefully. She was a plain-looking woman who, frankly, would have gotten lost in a crowd. She told me she'd just walked in with the others and then detoured to the enclosed area, where she'd put on the veil. "I had expected to exit the same way."

I suggested she just give it a little more time to make sure everyone had cleared the area outside and then we could leave together.

"How about a drink while you wait?" I led her to the café and opened the door. She was going to follow me in and then noted all the windows, realizing someone could see in. I sent her back to the yarn department, since it was in the back and had no windows, before going behind the counter and making us coffee.

I snagged some leftover cookie bars and brought everything back to the yarn department. She had idly picked up a crochet hook and some of the cotton yarn left on the table and began to make a chain.

"You crochet?" I said, surprised, and she nodded.

"It's a nice hobby," she said.

"Is the name you gave me before your real one?"

She nodded with a regretful expression.

"So then you're Frances Allen?"

"I'm afraid I didn't think that through. It's lucky I'm not trying to write spy novels."

She thanked me as she took one of the coffees and a cookie bar. I realized I hadn't asked her how she took it and was relieved she drank it black like me. I congratulated her on the crowd she'd drawn.

"It must be exciting to be such a big success."

"I'm still getting used to it," she said. "To think, not so long ago this was a dream." She had connected the chain into a circle, and I could tell she was making a flower.

"You said something about writing at night," I said. The coffee and cookie bar were giving me a much-needed lift.

"It was really all thanks to the job I had. It came with a guesthouse, a salary, and time to write." What she said struck a bell, and then I remembered something odd that she'd done during the signing.

"You didn't happen to work as some kind of companion?" I asked. She seemed surprised and nodded. Then she seemed a little worried.

"I hope it wasn't that obvious from what I said. I tried to be vague."

"Did you work for Marianne Freeman?" I said, and the color drained from Missy Z's face.

"How'd you know?" She seemed dumbfounded.

"I saw that you squeezed her hand when you signed her book. I didn't see you do it to anyone else."

"It was an automatic reaction when I saw her. I'm going to have to think before I do stuff." She'd begun working on the petals of the flower.

"I suppose you heard about what happened to her recent companion?" I asked, and she shuddered.

"I walked that same way all the time," she said. "I haven't been able to get it straight. Was it an accident?"

I wasn't sure how much to say, and really what I wanted was to get her talking. "I think it's still undetermined," I said finally.

She asked me if I'd ever seen the property, and when I said yes, she shuddered again. "I always parked my car right in front of the entrance to the lawn where it happened. It was the shortest way to get to the guesthouse." She thought for a moment. "It's lucky it wasn't Marianne. She always ended her day with a nightly walk around the whole lawn."

She wondered how I knew Marianne, and I mentioned that she had joined the Hookers.

"I'm the one who taught her the basics of crochet. It never occurred to me to bring her to a group. I wish I had thought of it."

"It sounds like you really cared about her." I thought of Connie and Janine's indifference to their charge.

"We were both new to it. I'd never been a companion before and she'd never had one." She mentioned that her previous job had been teaching preschool. "Now you understand why I don't want to go public with my identity." She rolled her eyes. "You never know the future, and I might need to go back to it."

I steered the conversation back to Marianne. "Maybe I can ask you. Do you know why she's on such heavy medication?'

"I was told that she was suffering from anxiety and depression. She'd had some bad life events and had fallen apart." She finished the last petal and fastened it off. I handed her some scissors to cut the yarn. "It used to break my heart to see her trying to find her way through that drug fog. I can't say I blame her for not wanting to take them. I hated being the warden, but her brother made it clear that she couldn't function at all without them. I sometimes wondered if it was something else. Something physical maybe, but I suppose she just snapped."

I asked why she'd stopped working for Marianne, and she sighed. "I felt bad about leaving her. I'd worked for her for over a year, and it was like I was living her life the whole time. I was grateful to be able to finish my book, but I was burned out and needed to have my own life again. My boyfriend suggested I move in with him, and I had some money saved up. I needed to have more freedom, too, while I finished up the arrangements for *The Hot Zone*. When you self-publish, there's a lot to do."

"Did you know Connie Richards?" I asked.

"Sure. I trained her. Well, really she didn't need any real training. She'd had a couple of jobs as a companion before," Frances said. I asked what kind of person Connie had been, and she shrugged. "I don't think she planned to make a career of being a companion. She said something to me once about wanting to save up her money and then travel." She'd already begun making another chain of stitches.

I suddenly felt sad for Connie. The author's comments were the first that made me think of the dead woman as a whole person with dreams and aspirations, all of which had ended.

I asked about Errol, and she sighed. "I didn't know what

to make of him, to be honest. I never could figure if he was a concerned sibling or if he was trying to control her. They both had trust funds, but she has control of that house and property.

"I'm eternally grateful for the chance that job gave me. It's too bad I couldn't just tell Marianne to her face. If there's anything I could ever do for her."

She looked around at the darkened bookstore and out one of the large windows that faced Ventura Boulevard. "Do you think the coast is finally clear?"

I offered to go outside and check. There was nothing like a mystery to fire up people's curiosity, and when I went outside, there were still a few people hanging around the parking lot, talking. I heard a few wisps of their conversations and got that they were waiting for her to come out. I pretended to be getting something from my car, and as soon as they saw me, I was swarmed by them.

"Is she coming out? You must know her real identity."

"She left a long time ago," I said. "Some mysteries are best left unsolved," I said. It wasn't really an answer, but it seemed to satisfy them, and they finally got into their cars.

I went back inside and got Frances. I wondered what her fans would have thought if they had seen the steamy romance sensation get into a Smart car.

It had been quite an evening.

Chapter Twenty-Two

After what I'd heard from Marianne's former companion, I really wanted to talk to Marianne again and preferably alone. But it was going to have to wait. When I got to the bookstore the next morning, I was faced with the cleanup from the night before. I was glad that Sunday mornings were usually quiet, with most of the activity in the café.

Adele came in as I was folding up chairs. She seemed in a daze as she stopped in the middle of the bookstore, as if she didn't know where to go. She gave the kids' department a dismissive shrug and headed back to the yarn department, probably for some therapeutic crochet time. I could only imagine what she'd gone home to.

Mr. Royal came to help me, and we moved the bookcases back into their original arrangement. He always seemed so youthful and enthusiastic about life. He said that he and Mrs. Shedd were off to brunch and that they'd be back in a couple of hours.

We'd sold out of *The Hot Zone*, and there were just

empty boxes to flatten. I put away the microphone and book light before setting up the table we'd used for the signing as a display table of beach reads.

I grabbed a red eye and went to the information booth. I'd barely sat down when I sensed someone standing in front of the enclosure and looked up. Barry? I checked around to see if there was anyone within earshot before I responded.

"Isn't it kind of chancy for you to come here?" I said. "Heather could pop out of the café or something." Though when I noticed his clothing, he was clearly off duty. The well-worn jeans and pocket T-shirt under a flannel shirt soft from countless washings were not work clothes.

Barry smiled. "I'm not here about that." He moved a little to the side, and I saw Jeffrey resting his elbows on a table, reading something. Barry leaned a little closer and lowered his tall frame toward me. "Why? Do you know something?"

"Maybe I do," I said. I couldn't help myself and said it in a teasing way.

He saw that no one was around. "You could probably tell me now."

"It's not like it's a sound bite," I said. "It will take some explaining, and I might have more later." Just then, Jeffrey joined us, and Barry straightened.

"Jeffrey needs a book for school," Barry said, before Jeffrey got upset with his father for speaking for him. I saw Barry close his eyes and shake his head from side to side in frustration. It had been a major adjustment when Jeffrey had first come to stay with him. He had been pretty clueless about being a single father and was still struggling with the balancing act of stepping up to take care of him and stepping back to let the boy test his wings.

I had cared about Jeffrey when Barry and I were together, and I still did. The feeling seemed to be mutual, though because of the breakup it had become awkward, and I only saw him in passing if I was home when he came over to see Cosmo.

Jeffrey rolled his eyes at his father. "It's a book on set design," he said, explaining that he had a part in the upcoming school play and was going to be working backstage. "I want to know how everything works," he said, sounding very manly. This time it was Barry who rolled his eyes.

On a hunch, as I led them to the section of books, I asked if they'd seen a movie called *The Grass Is Always Greener*. Jeffrey said no and Barry gave me a puzzled expression. I left them to check out the selection of books and returned to my work. A little while later, they passed the information booth on their way out. Barry held up a book and mouthed a *thank you* as he and Jeffrey went to the front to pay.

* * *

When Joshua Royal and Pamela Shedd returned from their brunch, I told them I was taking lunch and had a few things to take care of, so I might be gone a little while. They were fine with that. After Barry and Jeffrey left, I'd called Marianne. I'd come up with a ruse to get her to invite me over. I'd offered to give her some personal help with making one of the bracelets so it would be smoother when the show finally taped.

Marianne seemed aware that her crochet skills were a little shaky, and she accepted my offer without hesitation.

By now, the drive to Marianne's house had become routine, and I had no trouble knowing where to turn off Wells Drive. The gate across the private road was open, and I wondered if it was ever closed. There were several cars parked at the top, and I parked behind a Toyota. The area where Connie had died was uncovered this time, and I saw that the grass had been dug up and it looked like they were putting in a stone walkway.

Marianne must have been listening for my car, because she had the door open as I came up the short front walkway.

She seemed more in a fog than usual, and her movements were stiff as she led the way down the hall with Janine walking behind her. I flinched when the clock in the living room began to sound the hour. Marianne noticed my reaction. "Sorry, it's not even accurate." I checked my watch and saw that she was right. It was already ten minutes past the hour.

We ended up in the den, and both of us sat on the couch. I put my tote bag on the coffee table and looked out the window across the lawn to the guesthouse. If the public only knew that this was where Missy Z had written her sizzling book.

"You don't have to stay," Marianne said to Janine. "I don't need two companions." There was a moment of silence, and Marianne glanced from Janine to me. "That was supposed to be a joke." She shook her head regretfully. "I have no sense of timing anymore." Then she groaned and leaned back against the couch. "And no energy either. It feels like weight lifting to pick up a crochet hook." She repeated her request to Janine. "I'll call you when Molly leaves."

Janine was gone like a shot. Apparently, they'd let her move into the guesthouse, because I watched her walk across the lawn and disappear into the small stucco building with a red tiled roof. Marianne offered me some sparkling water and then went to get it. It seemed important to her to play hostess, so I didn't offer to help.

There was no tray this time or glasses of ice the way Janine had served it. Marianne carried in two bottles and set them down on the coffee table.

She opened hers and took a drink as soon as she sat down. It only seemed to give her momentary relief; a moment later it seemed like her mouth was dry again.

I opened mine and took a sip, mostly to be polite. "I thought we could make bracelets together." I brought out two of the kits that Elise had made and offered her one.

She leaned forward and tried to pick hers up, but it slipped from her fingers. I was caught between wanting to help her and at the same time not wanting to make it seem like she was helpless. In the end, I let her work at it until she succeeded in picking up the bag and pulling it open.

I was still a novice compared to most of the Hookers, but this pattern was so simple I could do it without thinking. I got Marianne making the chain stitches and helped her keep track so we ended up with the right amount. She had given me an easy opening by bringing up how different things used to be for her.

Now that I knew what her problem was, I felt sympathetic. "Maybe it'll get better. How long has it been like this?" I asked. She didn't seem to understand what I was talking about, so I added, "How long has your timing been off?"

She stopped making chain stitches and seemed to be calculating in her head. "My brother is always telling me not to talk about it, not even to my 'companion du jour,' but keeping it in forever is hell." She set down the hook as if it was too exhausting to hold it. "I've seen the way the Hookers look at me, and worse, talk to me. They always speak slowly and deliberately, but also extra loud. I just hate it." She looked directly at me. "You don't know how much I like your company. You're the first person who has come over who wasn't paid to spend time with me. Well, except my brother and his wife."

She stopped again to collect her thoughts. "You asked me a question, and I just went off on a tangent without answering. What was it again?"

"I wondered how long it's been like this for you."

"Of course, that was your question, and I was figuring it out before I thought of something else. It's been a little over a year and a half since my life crashed and burned. My life used to be so different. I had a great job in advertising and promotion, and then the company I'd been working for merged with another company and overnight my position disappeared. At the same time, my boyfriend announced he'd met someone else and they were getting married. This after telling me for ten years that he never wanted to be tied down." She reached for the sparkling water and took a long sip. "I can't remember the feeling I had when all that happened anymore, but I remember not wanting to think about it, and at the same time not being able to not think about it. I tried running away to Point Reyes Station. I loved it there, and I thought the long walks along the water and hikes among the trees would help. But I felt worse when I came back. I was so tired I couldn't move and at the same time was having panic attacks. My brother is the one who got me to his doctor, and they loaded me up with drugs." She looked like she was about to cry. "I thought it was just temporary and I could stop taking all this stuff, but they keep insisting I take all the pills."

"What happens if you don't take them?" I asked. She had to drink more sparking water before she could answer.

"It's only happened one time. I kind of went crazy and felt like suddenly all my feelings were turned back on at once. Laughing and crying at the same time. Then anxious and depressed. But at least I felt alive." She took another drink from the bottle. "I haven't said that much in the longest time. The only companion who was any good was the first one I had. She seemed to care. But then I guess it was really just a job. I never heard from her again after she quit."

Marianne looked so forlorn, I almost told her about Missy Z and the hand squeeze. She went to pick up her crochet work. "Here I am going on and on, and you came to help me with crochet."

I excused myself to use the bathroom, and she directed me to a powder room off the hall. I used the facilities and then leaned against the sink for a moment to let everything she'd said sink in before going back to join her. I was half-way down the hall when I heard voices and stopped to listen.

"What are you doing having her over again? I hope you haven't said anything about anything. That's why we have the lawyer—to keep a lid on everything." I recognized Errol's voice, and he sounded almost panicky.

"I need to have company. I feel like a princess stuck in a castle."

"You're the one who insists on keeping the *castle*. You know we're all for you selling this place."

"And have me move someplace where they lock the doors and decide when and what I'm going to eat. I believe I'll get better." She paused, and I imagined her drinking some sparkling water. "I really don't need a companion. I thought when Connie died that would be it and I'd manage on my own."

"No, you need someone here. If something happens to Janine, I'll just find somebody else." His comment made me shiver. "Where'd your company go?"

"Bathroom break," Marianne said.

"It seems like a long time." He said something about going to look for me.

I instantly reacted, and I made a lot of noise clearing my

throat and making loud footsteps to announce my arrival, and he stopped midsentence.

"I'm sorry, Marianne, I didn't realize how late it had gotten. I'll have to give you a rain check on the crochet help." I crossed the room to gather up my things, feeling his eyes on my back. As I grabbed my tote bag, the handle snagged on a stack of DVDs sitting on the table. They clattered to the floor, and I bent to pick them up. I began to replace them and swallowed hard when I saw the title of the one that hadn't fallen. I thought of what Dinah had said when she did her Dr. Watson thing. Rory might have been in it, but millions of people had watched *The Grass Is Always Greener*, including, apparently, Marianne.

Chapter Twenty-Three

"I think everybody must have come last night," Mr. Royal said, looking around as the late afternoon sun threw shadows across the floor of the empty bookstore. "Pamela and I can more than handle things. You went above and beyond your duty last night. Why don't you take the rest of the day off?" He nodded toward Mason, who was standing in the front of the store.

I'd run into Mason when I'd come back from Marianne's. He was off doing errands and had stopped by to see if we could at least get a drink together. Mr. Royal's offer was even better.

"We can leave," I said, coming up to Mason and giving him a hug. He grinned at my show of affection and hugged me back.

"We're just like a regular couple going to the grocery store and the cleaners together on a Sunday afternoon," he said. No suit today; instead, he was wearing his usual casual wear of jeans and a Hawaiian shirt. The afternoon air was warm, no jacket required.

"I got an idea where we could go for a weekday trip," I said when I got into his SUV. I told him about Point Reyes Station and how I'd happened to think of it. "Though it didn't seem to work out that well for Marianne. Maybe I should find somewhere else," I said.

"That doesn't mean it would work out badly for us," he said. He said he'd look into finding a nice bed-and-breakfast and was full steam ahead on making plans, but I reminded him that until things were settled with the show taping, I couldn't make any plans.

When Mason heard that I'd skipped lunch because I'd gone to Marianne's, he insisted we get food first. We got to the waffle place just before they closed and sat outside in the courtyard overlooking a pond filled with koi fish.

I told him all about the book signing and the surprising connection to Marianne. "It was the first time I'd heard anything much about Connie Richards."

"Don't you have enough on your plate with the show taping and the difficulty with Rory and her crocheting? It's not as if Connie Richards was a close friend. Why are you so interested?"

I certainly couldn't even hint that it had anything to do with Barry. And helping him wasn't even my main motivation anymore. I just wanted to know what really happened. Though I wasn't sure what I would do if it turned out Marianne had been behind Connie's death. "You know me," I said, "Always wanting to see how the pieces of the puzzle fit."

After the food, we did errands. He had dry cleaning to

pick up, a hardware store stop to make, and we both needed groceries. "Where to next?" I said. "I was thinking about tonight. Maybe we could do something fun."

Mason suddenly looked uncomfortable. "I have a family thing. In fact, I have to buy a gift. I can drop you off first, if you want."

"No problem," I said, and suggested we go to Luxe. We went back to almost where we'd started, since the lifestyle store and the bookstore shared the same parking lot. I didn't ask for any details about his family thing, and he didn't offer any. It was best for everyone to keep us all separate.

Sheila came up to us as soon as we walked in. I let my fellow Hooker take over with Mason, and I went to wander around. When he was finished, he found me looking at the tea selection.

Sheila put up the CLOSED sign as we walked out the door. "Sunshine, you're the best," Mason said, slipping his arm in mine. "Thanks for the understanding. I will make it up to you." I saw that he was carrying a gift-wrapped package. "I bought one of those beautiful blankets Sheila made." I gave him a spontaneous kiss on the cheek. "What's that for?" he asked, clearly liking it.

"Thanks for giving her the business," I said. It was getting dark as we walked back to the parking lot, and I went to grab my groceries and move them to my car.

"Your phone's ringing," he said as I reached for one of the paper bags filled with food. He laughed when I seemed surprised before noticing the vibrating on my wrist and the music coming from my purse.

It was Dinah, and she sounded unusually discombobulated. I couldn't even get in that I was close by her house.

"I thought the yoga classes were bad enough," she said. "I'm actually talking to you in my yard. Cassandra invited over a bunch of relatives from her mother's side. They all just got here, and you can imagine how they viewed me. I have to get out of here."

"Come to my place," I said, finally getting a word in. She issued a lot of thank yous and hung up.

"Maybe things are working out for the best. It sounds like Dinah needs you," Mason said. When I seemed surprised that he knew what she had said, he pointed at the phone still in my hand. "I could hear both sides of the conversation. Who's Cassandra?"

"Commander's daughter," I said, and Mason began to nod with understanding. I filled him in on the rest of it as he helped me transfer the bags of groceries to my car.

"It sounds worse than my situation," he said. "At least Thursday likes you," he said, referring to one of his daughters.

It was true we got along fine. She had even stayed with me at one point because of problems with her mother.

"I'm sure you'll make it all better for Dinah." He set the last bag in the Greenmobile and took me in his arms. I snuggled close, and he said we'd have to work out that trip up north. Then we had a long, lingering kiss in the dark parking lot.

* * *

Dinah was parked in front of my house when I pulled into the driveway. She got out of her car and walked up to me. "I couldn't stay there," she said as we carried in my packages. "There was nowhere to go to escape them. I have work to do." She held up an envelope full of papers. "I don't think she even told Commander she'd invited them over."

As we walked across the yard in the dark, she continued telling me how the guests had looked at her when Cassandra said who she was. We got to the door, and I struggled with my key and dropped it. As I leaned down to get it, I saw there was something else on the doormat. And then I screamed.

Dinah stopped midsentence and joined me in looking at the mat. And then she screamed. Even in the darkness, I could make out the small animal that was clearly dead. I managed to get the door open without the dogs running out and flipped the switch for the floodlights on the back of the house. I really wanted to go inside and pretend it wasn't there, but I knew that wasn't an option. I forced myself to look again now that the light illuminated the spot. It was a rat caught in one of those wooden traps.

"What are we going to do?" Dinah said with a squeal.

"We have to get it out of here," I said. Picking it up was out of the question, and then both Dinah and I thought of the same thing at the same time.

"The pinchy winchy," we both said. It was a long claw arm left from when my boys were younger. It was great for snagging socks that had fallen between the wall and the washer and also anything I didn't want to get close to.

I went inside and returned brandishing the pinchy winchy and a red shoebox I was going to put the deceased in. I set the shoe box on a chair and then, with Dinah behind me for moral support, opened the claw and tried to grab the trap. I managed to lift the trap off the ground, but before I could move it, it broke free from the pinchy winchy. Several more tries ended up the same.

"What are we going to do?" Dinah asked from behind me.

"There's plan B," I said, putting the tool down. I had been hoping to avoid this, but it seemed there was no other option. I went inside and put on gloves and took the broom and dust pan outside. There was no way to do it without getting much more up close and personal than I cared to. As I crouched down and prepared to sweep the trap up, I noticed something strange about the animal. I took a chance and poked it with my gloved finger. Dinah saw what I was doing and squealed.

"It's not real," I said. She came closer and looked at it in the light. "It's just a toy, though a little too lifelike for my taste. I've seen them at IKEA." We both laughed at our hysteria.

But the relief lasted only until we got a look at the underside of the trap. *You could walk into a trap next* was written in blood-red marker.

Chapter Twenty-Four

The good news was that Dinah forgot all about Cassandra and her party for the relatives. The bad news was that the trap with the toy rat and threatening message was now sitting in the shoe box on the umbrella table. Even though we couldn't see it, we couldn't forget it was there.

We tried to distract ourselves by putting away the groceries and making some food, but as soon as we sat down in the dining room with the omelets and salad, we started to talk about it.

"Just a guess, but could your gift be connected to Connie Richards's death?" Dinah asked.

"If the pieces fit, it must be it," I said. "Connie walked into a trap, and somebody is saying there could be one in my future," I said, trying to be light about it.

"Then I think it's time for the Sherlock Holmes game," Dinah said. "Dr. Watson at your service." She gave me a salute.

"You're right. Maybe we can get to the bottom of the whole thing." The food was sitting on my plate untouched, as the gift had destroyed my appetite. "I don't know how to begin, and I'm not sure what you know or don't know."

"Then the obvious is to begin at the beginning," Dinah said. "We know that Connie Richards died, we know how she died, but we don't know why she died."

"Or if she was the intended victim," I added.

We might have started at the beginning, but that didn't mean we continued in any sort of order. I'm sure the real Sherlock Holmes would have covered his face in horror.

"What about we just skip to the threats," I said. "We can go back to the rest of it later."

"Threats, as in more than the gift you just got?" Dinah seemed surprised. "Dr. Watson needs all the fact if she's going to help, Sherlock."

"I'm not sure one incident was a threat, and I didn't get a chance to tell you about the other one." I looked at the food on my plate and tried to will myself to eat something, with no success.

"Then give me the details now." There seemed to be no problem with Dinah's appetite, and she finished off the last of her omelet. I guessed that was a clue to how bad things were at her house—finding a fake rat in a trap at my back door was a step up on her day-to-day.

"There was a phone call with really heavy breathing, but it could have been a disgruntled telemarketer, annoyed that I didn't answer their call."

"Then it was a phone message, not a call?" Dinah asked. "I hope you saved it."

"Hey, you're talking to Sherlock Holmes here. Do you

really think there's a chance I would have erased it?" I might have been giving myself too much credit. It was more like an accident that I still had the message. I had just hung up the phone without punching in anything, which left the message on the machine as if it was unheard.

"Anything else?" she asked. I told her about the radio and the cord at the bookstore.

"That seems pretty specific," my friend said. "It would be hard to call that anything but a threat. Maybe we should move on to who knew you were investigating. That might give us a hint as to who's been leaving you surprises."

"I'm afraid that includes a big group. Remember what Rhoda said right after it happened? I don't recall her exact words or even who was present, but she said something about me looking into Connie's death and that I was some sort of independent investigator."

I made some coffee for us, and we went into the living room. Dinah sat on the couch and looked around at the large, airy room. "Ah, it's so peaceful here, I may never leave." I knew she was joking, but I said she was welcome to stay forever if she wanted to.

"Dr. Watson back on duty," she said, doing her mock salute again. "Does Barry know about the phone call and radio?"

"No," I said with a guilty shake of my head. "If he knew I was getting threats, he'd pull the plug on my helping him."

"How about withholding information? Are you telling him everything you know?"

I leaned back against the couch. "Dr. Watson, you

caught me. I haven't not told him anything yet, except maybe about the phone call and radio, but after this afternoon I was considering not telling him something else."

"But you will tell me, right?" Dinah said.

"Of course," I said, and proceeded to tell her about what I'd found out from Missy Z. I kept my promise and didn't divulge her real identity, but Dinah didn't seem that interested anyway. "At least now I know why Marianne is on the heavy drugs and that it hasn't been for that long a time."

I told Dinah about Marianne's job situation and the breakup. "It's too bad she got worse after she came back from a trip up north. But then I guess everything that happened just caught up with her." I digressed and told her about the town and that it had sounded so nice that Mason and I were planning a trip up there.

"There was some other startling news. Guess who has a copy of the *The Grass Is Always Greener*?"

"Marianne?" she said, surprised, and I nodded.

We were interrupted by my doorbell and then insistent knocking. The dogs went crazy at the sound and charged to the door with me right behind. I checked the peephole and saw Commander on the front porch. He was fidgeting from side to side and seemed upset. I opened the door.

"I need to see Dinah," he said, barely giving me a chance to invite him in. He went right into the living room. "Why did you leave without a word?" he said to her.

"There was nothing to say. I was an outsider in my own home," Dinah said as she stood up and faced him.

It seemed like a good time to retire to my crochet room.

I told Commander there was coffee in the kitchen and to help himself. I went into the small bedroom with Cosmo and Felix at my feet. When we were all inside, I shut the door. I suddenly completely understood the concept of being an outsider in one's own house.

I heard the phone ringing in the other room. Commander and Dinah were still talking when I came out. I didn't hear words, just the tone, and it sounded like they were discussing rather than fighting.

I clicked on the cordless and said hello.

"It's Detective Greenberg," Barry said, in his teasing tone again. "I see cars out front. Are you having a party?" he asked.

"Hardly. Are you here for the information drop?"

"It depends. Who's there?" When I told him it was Dinah and Commander, he started to beg off. "If Dinah sees me coming over again, she's going to know something's up."

I considered if I should tell him that she'd already figured it out, but Barry being Barry, no matter how much I insisted she wouldn't tell anyone, it would be the end of our nighttime meetings and I'd be off the case. "They're in the midst of some serious negotiations," I said. "I doubt they'd even notice you come in. If you don't mind talking in the room with all my yarn." I heard him chuckle and then agree.

There was a pocket door that led from the hall to the entrance way. I was able to answer the door without Dinah and Commander even noticing. Barry followed me back to the former bedroom with the dogs at his feet. I sent him on in and got him some treats to give the dogs. I took a quick glance into the living room as I slipped into the kitchen. Commander and Dinah were huddled in conversation, and they didn't even look up. While I was there gathering the treats, I grabbed some snacks and a couple of bottles of sparking water and then slipped past the doorway to the entrance hall and living room beyond.

"I brought treats," I said as I began to unload my pockets. Barry took the dog treats and handed them out. He laughed when I handed him his snacks and sparkling water.

"Aren't you the hostess with the mostest?" he said, accepting my offering.

The room was like a mini den, with a comfortable chair and a love seat that folded out into a bed. I had turned the bookcases into yarn receptacles, and there was a plastic bin that held my works in progress. I had thinned out the yarn supply recently, and it looked like a regular room again instead of a yarn warehouse. The dogs were already on the love seat, and I suggested Barry join them while I took the chair.

He looked around for a place to put down the bottle and bag of snacks. I kept a folding table in there and handed it to him. He unfolded it with one hand, and we put both of our bottles on it.

"So?" he said. "What have you got to tell me?"

"Have you ever heard of a movie called *The Grass Is Always Greener*?"

"Oh, no, you're doing the question thing again. Anyway, you asked me about it before." He gave me a disparaging look. "Why does it matter if I've heard of it or not?" he asked, then added, "See, I can play that game, too."

"I wasn't trying to give you a hard time. We're supposed to be on the same side, right?"

He choked out a yes.

"It's just a figure of speech. When you're about to talk about something, you ask if the person has ever heard of it first."

Barry seemed surprised when what I said didn't end with a question. "Okay, I apologize for assuming you were doing what you usually do when you talk to me. No, I've never heard of the movie. Were you going to offer a movie review, or does it have something to do with the case?" He saw my eyes flare at his question. "Hey, it's okay for me to ask questions. It's my business," he said.

He noticed one of the small blankets I'd made and picked it up, unfolding it. It was basically a big granny square with blocks in shades of rust and burnt orange with rows of black separating them. "Very nice," he said, holding it out. He glanced around the room at the rack of scarves and a stack of works in progress. I was not one of those straight-through-to-the-finish people. I'd work on something for a while, then set it aside and move on to something else. I'd never really given Barry anything I'd made.

"Take it, it's yours," I said. He seemed hesitant but then accepted it.

"Really? You're sure?" I nodded, and he folded it up and put it next to him. "It will be nice to have some color at my place," he said. "Now back to why I'm here. You were going to tell me about a movie."

"First of all, it does have to do with the case," I said.

Then I told him about the boombox setup and the sprinklers coming on. His expression went from smirk to keen interest.

"Guess who was in the movie?" I said, and Barry began to shake his head again.

"Just tell me."

"Okay, it was Rory Graham. She played the heiress who got electrocuted."

I realized my information giving had been rather disorderly, and I reminded him of the connection between Connie Richards and Rory.

"Right," he said, nodding. I added that Rory had intimated that Connie might have information on her that she didn't care to have made public.

"Is there anything else?" he asked.

I bit my lip, wondering about bringing up what I'd learned about Marianne. I was concerned that if I said anything about her, he might decide that Detective Heather was right and Marianne was responsible for Connie's death. I decided to keep it to myself until I was sure what it meant. Besides, she'd never talk to him directly. It would all be through her lawyer. And then there was the matter of the fake rat in the trap sitting in the box on the table in the backyard. I wasn't about to tell him about that either.

"No, it's ten-four for now." I smiled and he rolled his eyes.

He finished off the bottle of sparkling water and crumpled the snack bag before getting up. "It's been a pleasure as usual," he said with a smirky smile. "Thanks for the blanket." He looked at the door. "Do you want to see if the coast is clear?"

I opened the door and slipped down the hall. The couch was empty except for the sleeping cats. Commander and Dinah must have worked things out. I called to Barry that there was no one to hide from anymore, and he came out of the room. He went through the pocket door to the entrance hall.

He stopped for a moment and glanced back toward the living room. "There's never a dull moment around here," he said. Then he left. No handshake this time.

When I was finally alone, I thought back over the warnings. The radio had clearly been a threat, and the same seemed true of the toy in the trap. I wondered about the phone call.

The breathing was so creepy, I hesitated to listen to it again while I was alone, but finally I got up the nerve to do it. A mechanical voice stated the date and time, and then the breathing began. I wanted to shut it off after the first couple of moments, but I forced myself to stay on for the whole minute or so of it. It was like having Darth Vader breathing in my ear, and I pulled the phone away toward the end, preparing to hang up, but I heard something at the very end and sensed there was some noise in the background. I hit replay and it began again. This time I ignored the breathing sound and concentrated on the noise in the background. I had to play it again to be sure. There was no doubt this time, and suddenly I knew where the call had come from.

Chapter Twenty-Five

Now that I knew for sure that the breathing hadn't been an angry telemarketer, I didn't know what my next move was, and in the meantime, life had to go on.

The lull in business at the bookstore was over by Monday. The romance readers met in the afternoon. They always got dressed up for their meeting, and Bob brought in tea and finger sandwiches. No surprise, this month they were discussing Missy Z's book. I overheard a number of them talking about who they thought she really was, from a poor Russian princess to someone who had been on one of the *Real Housewives* shows. I'm afraid they would have been very disappointed to know that she was a rather plain former preschool teacher.

Dinah and I played phone tag during the day, and I still had no idea how things had worked out with Commander. I hoped she'd come to happy hour and fill me in. We were getting closer to the taping of *Creating With Crochet*, and I replaced the signs around the bookstore advertising Missy Z's appearance with notices about the Make-and-Take.

I was still worried about Rory's crochet skills, and time

was running out. I pulled CeeCee aside when she came in and told her what the producer had said about having a camera on Rory's hands during the taping.

"Oh, dear," CeeCee said, rolling her eyes. "What a mess. She's all flash with no substance. Honestly, can you picture her playing Lady Macbeth? She'd probably add a Dance Break in the middle of the play."

She took out the small afghan she was working on. It was the same pattern as the one I'd given to Barry. And the same one Elise was using for the afghans she was sticking in her open houses, hoping to at least sell the afghans even if she couldn't move the property. It was a perfect kind of project to work on to relax. It was repetitive but, because of the change of colors, not boring.

"I think we're going to have to go through with the plan to confront her and make her understand she isn't going to be able to fake her way through this. The idea of her being the host of a crochet show is an absolute slap to the craft." CeeCee caught herself and laughed. "Oh, dear, I'm beginning to sound like Adele."

"Are you talking about Rory?" Rhoda asked, joining us. "She still doesn't seem to be taking it very seriously."

I added my agreement about talking to her and wondered if I should add that I thought of her as a suspect in Connie's murder. But other than the time Marianne had come to happy hour with her sister-in-law, there hadn't been much conversation about what had happened to Connie. I think they all felt uncomfortable talking about it once Marianne started bringing her new companion.

Elise came in excited, and Rhoda asked her if she'd sold a house. "No, but the afghans are selling as fast as I can make them." She sat down and pulled out the one she was working on, and her hook started to fly.

Sheila and Eduardo came in together, talking about the world of retail. Mostly it seemed to be about dealing with customers.

I kept looking to the front for Dinah. Marianne came across the store with Janine in tow. Marianne greeted everyone and took a seat. When she saw everyone was working on their projects, she pulled out the wobbly scarf.

Adele came out of the kids' department, looked at the seat on the end, and seemed unsure about taking it. I noticed a copy of *The Hot Zone* sticking out of her tote bag, and everyone else did, too. Questions started flying about the book signing and the book. Was it as hot as everyone said?

I was surprised when Marianne spoke up. "I really liked it."

She suddenly had the whole table's attention, not so much for what she'd said but because she'd spoken at all. I knew how much she liked being part of the group. I really hoped she was as she seemed.

She spoke slowly and deliberately, and they all listened patiently, nodding to show they were listening. She seemed frustrated after a few moments. She kept swallowing and putting her lips together, and I realized she didn't have any sparkling water. I suggested Janine get her some.

CeeCee brought up the idea of confronting Rory when and if she showed up. "Maybe if we all band together and say something to her, she'll get it."

"You mean like an intervention?" Eduardo asked. When CeeCee nodded, he sat back. "I see the sense in it, but I think I'll let you handle it."

Dinah rushed in as we were talking about how to handle the lecture. I looked at my friend with a big question in my eyes, and she mouthed, "Later."

"It might have been an exercise in futility," Rhoda said, pointing out that Rory's chair was still empty and there was no sign of her.

Suddenly Adele got in the middle of it and started defending Rory. I'd wondered why she'd been so quiet before, and then I'd seen she was reading *The Hot Zone* under the table. I'd given her a dirty look, and she had shut the book and put it away. After Mother Humphries's outburst at the book event, I guessed she couldn't read it at home.

Finally, Rory came into Shedd & Royal like a gust of wind. She buzzed around the people in line to pay for their purchases, doing her Dance Break thing. She seemed to have added on to it and was now holding up her arms and knocking hips with our patrons. She stopped to sign a few autographs and take some selfies. I saw her point toward us, and she did a last jiggle of her hips and came across the bookstore seeming in good spirits.

When she got to the table, she saw that everyone was looking at her with a serious expression. "What's going on? You're all staring at me like I'm naked or something."

Janine arrived with the sparkling water and opened the bottle with a whoosh. Marianne quickly took a large swallow and then turned her attention back to Rory.

"We're her to help you," CeeCee said. "You don't seem to be taking crochet seriously at all. Can you even make a length of chain stitches?" our leader asked.

"Who tied your underwear in a knot?" Rory said. "I'm the host of the show. They're not really expecting me to work with yarn." She saw we were all still staring at her, and she picked up a hook and some yarn. She made a slip knot and, with Adele's coaching, made a couple of chain stitches. One stitch was ridiculously big and the next one so tight she couldn't pull the yarn through it. She slapped it on the table. "There, are you satisfied?"

We all said no in unison, which surprised her.

I stepped in and reminded her of what Michael had said. "They're planning to have a close-up on your hands during the Make-and-Take."

Rory looked at Adele and started to say something about a crochet double, but I shook my head. "He's not going to fall for it." And I told her why it wouldn't work.

Now that she was cornered, she put her head in her hands. "I thought I had it all under control," she muttered. Then she broke down and began to cry. "You have no idea what I'm up against. I can't explain, but everything is falling on me. I pushed to get the hosting job and said whatever I had to."

"None of that is going to mean anything if you can't crochet. They'll fire you and then you'll let everyone down, your kids and all of us," Rhoda said. Adele started to protest, saying she could crochet something and hand it to Rory like she did in the rehearsal.

"That's not going to work," I said, reminding her that they were going to have a close-up of her hands.

"I can't lose this job," Rory wailed. "I can't let it happen. "What do I do?"

"It's easy. Stop fooling around and learn how to crochet," CeeCee said.

"I would if I could. I've tried, but I always mess up." She picked up the hook and then shifted it to her other hand before trying to do another chain. As I watched her struggle, I suddenly knew what was wrong.

"You're left-handed, aren't you?" I said. She gave me an odd look and nodded. I turned to the others. "We've been teaching her how to crochet with her right hand. No wonder she can't manage it."

We all focused on Adele, who was looking down, pretending to be engrossed in her crochet. She felt our eyes on her and finally raised her head. "I get it. You all think it's my fault." She started to get a defiant look and I was expecting a barrage of excuses, but then her expression changed to what I could only think of as guilty. "I guess I should have noticed it, but she never said anything."

"The important question is, can anyone teach her how to crochet with her left hand?" CeeCee said to the group.

"I can do it," Adele said, not wanting to give up her position as crochet companion. "I saw a book that should help." She rushed off to get it.

The rest of us looked at each other with the same thought. Would Rory and Adele come through in time?

Chapter Twenty-Six

"Not so fast," I said to Dinah as she pushed away from the table.

The Hookers were all scattering as the hour ended, and Adele had taken Rory into the kids' department for a private crochet lesson using the information in the left-handed crafts book.

"You and Commander disappeared last night. You can't leave without telling me what happened," I said, pausing before I began my usual straightening up.

"Sorry, I didn't mean to leave without saying good-bye, but when I saw the door to your yarn room closed, I figured something was up. Then I looked out front and saw Barry's Tahoe," she said with a meaningful smile. "I can't help but be your Dr. Watson even when we're not playing Sherlock Holmes."

"His Tahoe?" I repeated. "Of course." I shook my head before continuing. "Some Sherlock Holmes I am. It didn't even register that he wasn't wearing a suit."

"Then it was a social call?" There was a twinkle in Dinah's eye.

"The clothes and SUV might have made it seem that way, but Barry is never not working, and it was all about trying to get information from me."

"Whatever you say," my friend teased. "Did you tell him about our find at the door?"

"No." I stopped as I thought of my discovery about the phone call. "Oh, and I listened to the phone call again, and I heard something."

Dinah put down her work and turned all her attention to me. "Tell me."

"I'll let you judge for yourself." I used my cell to call my landline and handed Dinah the phone as I got the message to play. Her eyes bugged out as she heard the breathing and she pulled the phone away from her ear, but I told her to keep listening.

Finally, she looked at me. "I do hear something else, but what is it?"

"It's a clock chiming the hour," I said. "You didn't hear the date and time stamp at the beginning, but it was actually already past the hour."

"And," Dinah said, encouraging me to go on.

"There's an old clock at Marianne's that chimes like that and is ten minutes slow."

"Wow." Dinah sat back, incredulous. "Marianne is the one behind the threats?"

"Not necessarily. All it means is that the call came from

her house. I don't want it to be her, but I am beginning to think there might be more sides to her than I realized. It could have been her brother Errol. I know he goes there a lot. But it also could have been his wife, Kelly."

"Why would they be trying to scare you off?"

"I thought about that. Suppose Marianne was the intended victim. Errol or his wife could have set up the accident. They knew that Marianne always went for a walk at night. Errol certainly didn't seem happy that I was spending time with Marianne, and he said something like that she shouldn't talk to me. He could have been worried I'd figure out that Connie was just collateral damage."

I went on to explain the reasons why Errol or his wife might have wanted Marianne out of the way: "Errol wants her to sell the property. It was their family home. I don't know what their arrangement is, but Marianne seems to be in control of it. All that would change if she died. When Kelly came to the Hookers meeting with Marianne that time, it was pretty obvious that she was resentful that her husband had to drop everything to take care of his sister. That would all change if Marianne was dead."

"Have you told any of that to Barry?" Dinah asked.

"We kind of discussed it, but he said he needed evidence to do anything," I said.

"Well, Sherlock, do you have any plans?" Dinah asked.

"If Errol or Kelly tried to kill Marianne once, don't you think they would try again?"

"You're right."

"That's why we have to do something. I need to find out who made that call. Then I'd gladly tell Barry about it and let him take over."

"Dr. Watson has an idea. Talk to Janine. She might not have been there when the call was made, but at least she would know if Errol was at the house. Maybe that would be enough for Barry."

"Good thinking, but it'll be a two-man operation. Somebody has to distract Marianne."

Dinah laughed and raised her hand. "I love being your sidekick."

* * *

We decided not to wait and to go ahead with the plan to talk to Janine right away. I was concerned that Marianne might object to us inviting ourselves over, but I had a secret weapon. I said we'd bring cake.

"I hope it's chocolate," she said. "It would be nice to have some company in the evening." I made sure that Janine would be there to share in the treat.

Dinah and I went right to Bea's Bakery to pick up a cake. The shop had been in Tarzana forever, and there was always a line.

"So, then you didn't work things out with Commander?" I asked as we waited for our number to be called.

"Poor guy, he was so confused. He'd thought it was just about Cassandra's mother's things and that it was solved. I explained that when she brought over his late wife's family, she was trying to push me out of the picture."

Our number was called, and we picked out a chocolate cake with chocolate frosting and then headed to the door.

"What are you going to do?" I asked.

"Treat her like one of my students and tell it like it is. I suppose it won't be exactly how I deal with my students. I never try to make friends with them."

We took Dinah's car and worked out the details of our plan as we drove. I had to direct her to the private street that went up the hill to Marianne's. She pulled her Toyota to a stop near the spot where it had all happened.

It was Dinah's first time at the house, and she was wowed by the size of the property. Before we got to the front door, I pointed out where Connie had died. "She was coming back from her day off and probably didn't know what hit her," I said.

"I wonder how Janine feels about walking back to the guesthouse," Dinah said.

"I bet she makes sure the grass is dry," I said.

We walked to the door, and before I could ring the bell, Marianne opened it. I was glad to see that Janine was standing behind her. We all went inside, and Marianne took us into the den. The fireplace was going this time, and it seemed very inviting. I didn't sit but instead held up the cake box and spoke to Janine. "Why don't we serve this and make some coffee?"

Janine looked to Marianne for an okay, and then the two of us went into the kitchen. I knew my time alone with her was limited, so I got right down to it. To break the ice, I asked her how she liked the job.

She let out a sigh. “It’s kind of dull,” she said. “She stays home most of the time, and it’s pretty quiet around here.” She went to put the coffee on.

“I suppose you have to handle any company that comes over,” I said. I glanced around the kitchen, trying to figure out where we were in the house. A doorway led to what I supposed was a service porch and then outside, probably near the garage. The counters were covered with old-style yellow tiles trimmed with black, and there were a lot of windows. There were no curtains on them, making it easy to look out at the darkness—and probably to look in just as well.

“You’re the only company she’s had since I’ve been working for her,” she said with a shrug. “She was so excited that you were coming over.”

She waited while I put the cake on the counter and then opened the box. I picked up a long knife out of the wood block and held it as we continued to talk.

“What about her brother and sister-in-law?” I asked.

“I don’t think he counts as company, but he comes over every evening. I think it’s to check on me. But I don’t think he trusts Marianne either. He told me that no matter what she says about me being free to go back to the guesthouse, I should stay in the house with her.”

“Does he come at the same time?” I asked. I was still holding the knife out and hadn’t made a move to start cutting the cake, hoping to have as much time to talk as possible.

“It’s always around seven o’clock.” She glanced up at the

wall clock and got a puzzled look. "I'm surprised he isn't here by now." She'd no sooner said that when I heard a rustling noise. I looked toward the source just as Errol burst into the room from the service porch with an entourage behind him, and we both froze.

"She's got a knife," Errol yelled as he stepped aside, and I saw the two uniforms with Barry and Detective Heather right behind, all with their guns drawn. Barry's eye went directly to me. His expression stayed grim cop, but there was a flare of surprise in his eyes.

"Drop the knife," Detective Heather yelled.

"I was just going to cut the cake," I protested. Detective Heather moved her arm so that her gun was a little closer, and I realized she probably wouldn't mind shooting me, since she probably still blamed me for things not working out between her and Barry. Before I could let go of the knife, Barry stepped forward and took it away.

"She's the intruder you called us about?" Barry said.

"I'm an invited guest," I protested. "You can ask Marianne. She's in the living room."

Detective Heather, looking like a cop in a TV show with her heels, stylish suit, and perfectly coiffured champagne-blonde hair, hustled Janine and me into the living room with the uniforms and Barry close behind. Marianne and Dinah were sitting on the couch. Dinah and Marianne looked stunned as the group filled the room.

"What's going on?" Marianne said, standing up.

"I saw a woman in the kitchen with a knife, threatening your companion, and I called the cops," Errol said.

"I'll tell you what's really going on," I said, looking at Errol. "Is this another attempt to scare me off? I know you were the one who left me the message with the Darth Vader breathing."

"I don't know what you're talking about," Errol said. He turned to the cops. "She must be crazy."

Undaunted, I continued. "You can hear the clock chiming the hour in the background, only the clock is ten minutes slow, so it was actually ten minutes after the hour, according to the time stamp on the message. And the other little gifts came from you, too."

"That's ridiculous. Why would I do something like that?"

I put my hand on my hip and stared at him. "If it wasn't you, let's hear you breathe," I said. "Then I'll get the voicemail to play on my cell phone and they can all be the judge." He had begun to look a little nervous. "You were worried because I was getting too close." Out of the corner of my eye, I saw Barry closing his eyes in consternation.

"Whatever he did, my brother was just trying to protect me," Marianne chimed in.

"Aha, I knew it was you," Detective Heather said with a cocky stance.

"Don't say anything else. Let me call the lawyer," Errol said.

Marianne regarded her brother with shock. "Oh my God, Errol, you think I set up the accident that killed Connie Richards? Why would I do that?" Then she let out a breath. "I get it. You think I did it because I don't like having to have a companion."

"It's not her fault," Errol began. "With her mental state and all the meds she takes, I'm sure she didn't know what she was doing."

"Errol, really?" Marianne said. "Did you really think it through? I'm too out of it to know what I'm doing, but I'm sharp enough to figure out how to set up that bizarre accident? As if there's any way I'd know how to electrify the grass." She turned her attention to the assembled police. "If my brother did anything weird, it was just because he was trying to take care of me. He's been doing the best he could since I had my breakdown."

Errol appeared panicked. "I've got nothing else to say."

One of the uniforms spoke up. "I'm not clear. Was there an intruder? Are we going to arrest anybody?"

"Really? We brought cake," I said. "What intruders bring treats?" Marianne confirmed we were guests, and they all finally stood down. Detective Heather seemed uncomfortable that she had shown her hand when she made the comment about Marianne being the culprit. Janine's face seemed locked in a stunned expression. I patted her hand and said, "You probably won't be thinking this job is dull anymore."

The uniforms left first, and then Heather and Barry got ready to leave. As they were walking to the door, Barry turned back and zeroed in on me. It seemed like he mouthed the word *later.*

Errol made a hasty exit without a word as soon as the cops had left. The purpose of our visit had fizzled, and I didn't have to do any sleuthing now. Errol's reaction had made it clear he was the breather and gift giver. The question was, had he really done it to protect his sister, or was he worried about himself? Too bad I hadn't gotten to ask him about his meetings with the developers. Marianne made it clear our visit was over as she got up and herded Dinah and me to the door. It had stuck in my mind that Marianne had made a point of seeming not to know how to electrify the grass, as she put it, and yet I'd found a copy of *The Grass Is Always Greener* sitting on the coffee table as if it had been recently watched.

As we were about to go out the door, I brought up the movie.

"Oh, that," she said, not missing a beat. "After I saw that Rory Graham had joined the crochet group, I was curious to see the movie again."

"Then you must have seen how they used a boombox and the sprinklers to electrify the grass," I said.

"Really? That was in there?" She seemed surprised. "I only watched it for a few minutes before I turned it off. I found it pretty boring."

Her answer made sense but made me uneasy anyway.

* * *

Dinah dropped me off at my car and went to face the music at her house. I was pretty sure it was going to be the same for me. I pulled into the driveway and went across the flagstone patio to the kitchen door. The street in front of my house was empty, but for how long? I considered turning out all the lights and not answering the phone.

It turned out not to be an option. I didn't even have time to let Cosmo and Felix out in the yard when I heard a loud knock at my front door.

I didn't really have to look through the peephole to know who was there, but I did anyway. Barry was pacing across the small front porch and seemed pretty agitated.

I took a deep breath and pulled open the door. He shook his head and gave me a disparaging look as he asked if he could come in.

"Do I have a choice?" I said, trying to lighten the moment.

"No," he said curtly, but still waited for me to open the door wider before he came in.

The dogs must have heard him, because the gray terrier mix and the black mutt roared through the kitchen and into the entrance hall. They started jumping at his pant leg with excited yips.

He looked down at them, and I could see he was trying to maintain his fierce expression, but they cut right through it and he gave each of their heads a pat. However, when he looked up at me to announce he was going to give them a treat, his lips were compressed in frustration.

I stepped aside, and he went to the kitchen with the dogs in tow. I followed along.

"Sorry you missed out on the cake, but I have some butter cookies and tea."

"You don't really think you're going to buy me off with that?" he said.

"How about if I throw in a grilled cheese sandwich?"

He was shaking his head as he gave the dogs their treats. "It's not the food item that's the problem," he said in a terse voice.

"C'mon, I know you're hungry. So am I. I'm going to make the sandwiches anyway, and then you can yell at me."

"I'm not waiting for the food to do that," he said. "How could you?" He seemed almost too exasperated to talk. While he stood there, I pulled out bread, cheese, butter, and a tomato and began to assemble the sandwiches. I dropped some butter in a frying pan. "What was that business about a threatening phone call and some other gifts? You were supposed to tell me everything."

"I thought the phone message was just a disgruntled telemarketer, at first, anyway. It was only when I listened to it later that I heard the clock and realized it was slow just like theirs is."

"So you decided to take things in your own hands," he said.

"I was going to tell you all about it once I was sure who had made the call."

He shook his head with frustration. "That's Molly logic, not police procedure. It was supposed to be me doing the investigating and you just providing some information."

The sandwiches were browning in the frying pan, and the cheese was beginning to ooze over the side of the bread. The smell was making my mouth water and I figured the same was true for Barry, but he was doing a good job of hiding it.

"What about the *gifts*, as you called them, which I'm guessing were really threats?"

"Well, somebody left an old radio and an extension cord at the bookstore and implied I might get a nasty surprise if I didn't back off, and then there was this." I slid the sandwiches onto plates and then took him out into the yard. The shoe box was still sitting on the umbrella table. I pointed to it and he gave me a suspicious look.

"Is there some kind of booby trap in there?"

I shook my head, and he flipped open the lid and looked inside. In the semidarkness, I don't think he could tell if it was a real dead animal or not, until his detective skills kicked in and he realized there was no smell. He asked for details on where I'd found it. I pointed to the mat in front of the door.

"How did it get from there to here?" he asked.

"By way of the pinchy winchy and a dust pan and broom," I said. He started to smile and caught himself.

We went back inside and took our food into the living room and sat on different couches. Barry ate his sandwich in silence and then muttered a thank you before he put his plate on the coffee table. "You have no idea how upset Heather was about that comment of yours to Errol—about you getting too close." He sat back on the couch. "She thought we should arrest you for interfering with an investigation. If she knew I'd been using you as a source . . ." He groaned.

I wanted to do something to change the mood. "I'm sorry," I said, and started rambling. "I didn't know that Errol was going to be there, that is, until Janine said he came over at that time every night." I stopped to think about it. "But then she said it was to check on her, so there's no telling if he was doing that the night Connie died too. Though Errol was with his sister that night. Mason and I saw them at a restaurant." Barry was listening but not reacting. I decided to try giving him my latest tidbit to see if it would smooth things over.

"I do have something you might find useful." He sat up and turned to face me.

"Something else you've been withholding?" he said.

"Not really. I just found it out." I told him about seeing the DVD of *The Grass Is Always Greener* at Marianne's. "I asked her about it tonight, and she said she watched it because Rory Graham was in it. She claimed not to know about the boombox and the sprinklers and said she only watched the movie for a few minutes because it was boring." I let it sink in and then continued. "She could have said that to cover up that she knew about—"

"The murder setup," he said, finishing my sentence. "I don't need your assistance in figuring that out. I'm a detective, remember?" He said it almost in a joking way, and I thought we were good.

"None of it really matters now. Despite what Heather thinks, there's no real evidence to point to anyone else, so even with the issue of the gardeners denying they had anything to do with the radio, it seems like Connie Richards' death is going to be ruled an accident. And then that will be it." He looked at me intently. "Not that it matters to you. You're off the case." He got up to leave, and I walked him to the door.

"Says who?" I muttered to myself.

"I heard that," he said as he left.

Chapter Twenty-Seven

"You better make it a black eye," I said to Bob the next morning.

The barista gave me an appraising look. "Tough night, huh?"

I just nodded as an answer and took my coffee with two shots of espresso into Shedd & Royal.

Two men were coming in the door carrying a chair and some large folded pieces just as Mrs. Shedd caught up with me.

"The people from the Craftee Channel are getting things ready for the shoot." She smiled at her casual use of the show business term. "We're having them put the things in the back room for now."

I went to check the storage room to see what she was talking about. The door was propped open, and I looked inside. Mr. Royal was busy moving things around. I saw that he'd pushed the box of defective yarn I needed to send back next to a cardboard box marked LOST AND FOUND. The colorful cutouts of the Easter Bunny and Santa Claus were leaning against the wall. Strings of old-fashioned big Christmas lights hung on a straight-backed chair.

"Those are all things for the show," he said, pointing out some boxes and a chair with Rory's name on it.

"It looks like you have it under control," I said to Mr. Royal. I excused myself and was on my way to the yarn department when I heard my name.

Marianne and Janine were coming toward me. It was impossible to read Marianne's mood, and after last night I wasn't sure what to expect. I greeted them both and then waited to see what Marianne had to say.

"I'm sorry for the way my brother acted and for what he did," she began. Her timing was always a little off, but this time she seemed more awkward than usual. "He feels he has to protect me, even from myself." She swallowed a few times, and I was sure her mouth was dry. "But I'm still confused. Why were you investigating what happened to Connie? It was obviously a terrible accident."

I was relieved to see Dinah had joined us, and she answered for me. "Molly has a natural talent for solving mysteries. You must not have heard what Rhoda said that time when your sister-in-law came—that Molly's our local independent investigator. She was just trying to help."

"Oh," Marianne said. "Now I understand. I suppose Kelly must have told my brother about you and that's why he did what he did." Her expression didn't change, but she let out her breath and I sensed she was more relaxed. "I hope we can have a do-over of last night. This time we'll bring the cake."

Dinah and I both agreed.

"What's going on?" Janine asked, looking past me. She'd been hanging off to the side and must have felt it was okay to enter the conversation. I turned to see what she was talking about and realized I hadn't noticed that some of the Craftee people were in the yarn department, practically right behind me. I recognized the arty-looking set designer, the director, and the producer.

"They're here about the taping," I said. "I better go." Dinah took the cue and walked the pair away.

"Sorry to interrupt," Michael said. "We were trying to figure out which cubby we need." He gave the row of cubbies another glance. "I think the decision to take the middle one is correct." He punctuated his comment with a decided nod. "We're going to need it emptied out. Our yarn sponsor wants it filled with their brand."

My job was just to empty it. The set designer would place the sponsor's yarn in it and a banner over it. I assured him I'd take care of it and stood there while they looked around the area again. I was relieved when they left without making any more demands.

Mrs. Shedd must have been hanging nearby, because as soon as the three television types headed to the front, she found me. "Is everything all right?" she asked nervously.

I explained the cubby situation and assured her I'd handle it.

"What about the other problem?" She was staring as Adele and Rory went into the kids' department.

"Maybe we should do a little spy work," I said.

The two of us slipped up to the spot where the regular

carpet in the bookstore changed into cows jumping over moons and peeked. Adele and Rory were seated at one of the low tables and were too intent on what they were doing to notice us. I nudged Mrs. Shedd and gave her a thumbs-up as I saw Rory had a hook in her hand and was crocheting. She'd completed only a few inches of whatever she was working on, but even from a distance I could see it looked good. My boss gave me a happy hug. I tried to give Adele the credit, but Mrs. Shedd smiled at me.

"I know it was you. You always come through."

* * *

I had the cubby emptied and the yarn boxed and stored in the back room by the time I was ready to leave. There was no happy hour on Tuesdays, so Mason and I had planned on dinner together. I thought it was sweet the way he insisted on picking me up at the bookstore.

"It always makes me feel good to see you," he said when I joined him at the front. He leaned toward me and gave me a hello kiss and helped me on with my jacket.

"Ditto," I said. I felt like I could let out my breath when I was with Mason. It was just comfortable to be with him.

"Anything much happen today?" he asked, and I chuckled and said I'd tell him at dinner.

We decided to go to an Italian restaurant down the street. It had been in Tarzana for years and was an old standby of ours. The waiter knew us and offered us the table we liked by the window.

We didn't need to look at the menus to order. Mason

ordered chicken marsala, and I asked for spaghetti with oil, garlic, and vegetables. We would share a Caesar salad.

When the server left the table, Mason leaned on his hands. "Okay, now tell me everything."

"I suppose I should start with the phone call," I said. When I got to the part about the radio and toy in the trap, Mason started to look hurt.

"Why didn't you say anything?" he asked. "I could have helped."

"I'm sorry," I said, genuinely surprised. "I thought you were so busy thinking about your work, and I didn't want to bother you."

"It's never a bother. Some of our best times have been when I got involved in your sleuthing. I like that you're always after the truth," he said. "Did you find out who was behind the threats?"

"I figured out the call at least had come from Marianne's, and it wasn't much of a stretch to think the other two things were connected." Then I cut to the chase and told him how it had all ended up. "Her brother claimed he thought I was an intruder with a knife, and he called the cops. I was holding a knife to cut the cake I brought," I hastily added.

Mason was starting to grin. "It sounds like a typical Molly moment. Then what happened?"

"I kind of lost it and started accusing Errol of making the phone call, and I alluded to the rest of it. He tried to deny it, but I rolled out my proof. Then Marianne stepped in and said he was just trying to protect her. She was shocked when she realized her brother thought she had killed Connie Richards."

"And I suppose she denied it," Mason said.

"Sort of. She pointed out his faulty thinking, but she never actually denied it."

"What did the cops do?" Mason asked.

"They seemed to buy it."

"And you think she didn't do it?" Mason asked.

"I think her brother is a more likely candidate, but it doesn't really matter. I heard Connie's death is going to be ruled an accident and that will be the end of it."

"Maybe it really *was* an accident. Weird things do happen. I heard about someone who died using their cell phone in the bathtub." He looked at me intently when he finished. "Are you going to drop it?" he asked, and I shrugged noncommittedly as an answer.

Our food came, and he tried to get my mind on happier things. "I'm looking into arrangements for a trip up north. We just need to work out when." He pulled out a handful of pages. "My assistant found these online about the place. I thought you might want to have a look."

As an afterthought, he asked what cops had shown up at Marianne's. When I mentioned Barry was one of them, he said, "That must have been awkward."

"More than you know," I said, and dug into my spaghetti. Since my undercover job with Barry was over, I probably could have told Mason about it. But my rule about such things was that if something was going to upset someone, it was better to leave them in the dark. I knew

Mason did the same. He hadn't said a word about his family event the other day.

"I guess my timing's off," Mason said. "It probably doesn't matter anymore, but after all the talk about a movie you never saw, I got hold of *The Grass Is Always Greener*. I thought we could bring home some cannolis and watch it together.

"Your timing is fine. I'd still like to see the movie," I said.

"And then maybe a dip in the whirlpool and, if you like, a sleepover."

We left my car in the parking lot and took a box of the dessert pastries with us. Mason made us cappuccinos to go with the cannolis, and we sat on his couch. I asked to see the DVD box, but he explained he didn't have the actual DVD but had gotten it through a TV service of his.

We finished the cannolis and cappuccinos but not the movie. It was boring, just as Marianne had said, and Rory's performance would have been fine if it was supposed to be a comedy. Finally, Mason just fast-forwarded to the scene that had brought this all up. Of course, the setting was different from Marianne's, but the idea was the same. In the movie, a boombox was left sitting on the grass in a spot where Rory as the heiress did yoga at dawn. The sprinklers came on when she was doing downward-facing dog. I was glad they didn't show her getting sizzled. There was just a close-up on the boombox, a lot of crackling noises, and when they cut back to Rory, she was doing corpse pose.

"So what did you think?" Mason asked, after he fast-forwarded it to the end so I could see how it all turned out.

"I suppose somebody could have gotten the idea from it,"

I said. Then I realized that, with all our fast-forwarding, I'd missed something. "Did they show how someone set it up?" I asked. Mason started going backward in the movie until there was a shot of the lawn with the boombox. Mason went back farther and then pressed play. A number of gardeners were working on the property, and then one of them separated from the rest of them. He took something out of a sack he was using to collect leaves. It became obvious it was the boombox, and there was a close-up on the white extension cord the man was carrying. While the other gardeners finished up and took their equipment to their truck, the man made some adjustment to the boombox and placed it on the ground. His final move was to plug the extension cord into an outlet in the garage. He opened the automated sprinkler box and changed the watering time to coincide with the heroine's yoga time.

When he came outside, the other gardeners were gone, and he pulled off his hat and glanced up at an open window and said, "*Au revoir, mon chéri.*"

I watched mesmerized and then had Mason play that part again. "That's the important part. How it was done," I said. It had reinforced something I'd told Barry. I threw my arms around him. "You did help me!"

"I like where this is going," he said, hugging me back. "Let's forget about everything and take that dip in the whirlpool."

The night air was chilly, but the swirling warm water was wonderful, and since there was no chance Barry was going to show up at my house looking for information, I accepted Mason's offer of a sleepover.

Chapter Twenty-Eight

All things considered, it was probably best that I let the whole thing with Connie Richards go. Even if I found out something startling, what would I do with it? Would Barry even pick up my call?

I didn't have time to think about it, anyway. We were three days away from the taping, and it was all I thought about. We had two more mini Make-and-Takes during our happy-hour gatherings. Rory refused to take part in them, saying that over-rehearsing would take away her spontaneity. She did, however, get on her soapbox about what it was like being left-handed in a right-handed world. "I'm going to be there for my lefties," she said as the rest of us helped some drop-in people make bracelets. Then she announced that Adele was going to demonstrate how to make the bracelets for both right- and left-handed people.

Even CeeCee seemed impressed at the change in Rory, though she did promise she'd be keeping the Dance Breaks in. Adele had shown us some samples of Rory's work on the sly, since after everything we'd all still been a little leery.

The swatches and bracelets had looked fine, and we'd all let out a huge sigh of relief.

Rhoda brought in samples of the coffee cake recipe we were going to feature. She'd made sure to make them with the sponsor's brand of flour. She was a little miffed that the production company was insisting on providing the cakes for the show. She was, however, going to get credit, and they were going to be called Rhoda's Cake for a Break.

Once Marianne got past that rough spot with me, she seemed committed to the group. She had decided on her own that her job would be to hand out the kits to the Make-and-Takers and let the teaching and demos be done by the rest of the group. There seemed to be a constant battle between Marianne and Janine. Marianne would try to get her to go off to the side; then the companion would get a phone call I assumed was from Errol and she'd be back shadowing Marianne. Mrs. Shedd and Mr. Royal watched from the sidelines and seemed happy with the way things were going.

"Well, tomorrow's the day," I said to Dinah. After the second sample Make-and-Take, we'd gone to the café for a pick-me-up.

The first thing I did was ask how her situation at home was going. She put her head in her arms and then sat up again.

"That bad?" I said, and she nodded.

"You can't make friends with someone who doesn't want to make friends with you. Commander walked in on one of her yoga classes, and he finally understands why I was upset. I don't know what's going to happen." She let out a sigh. "I'd rather talk about something else." She stirred her drink. "Have you heard anything from Barry?" my friend asked, and I let out a laugh.

"And I'm not going to hear anything. Let's see, he has so many reasons to be upset. I didn't tell him about the phone call, the radio, or the toy rat. And then I said the whole bit about Errol being the breather because I was getting too close, making it painfully obvious that I was doing exactly what he'd told me not to, investigating on my own. I can't say I blame him. I'd do the same thing if I wasn't me. It was fun while it lasted."

"You're just going to drop it." Dinah watched as Marianne and Janine went past the café door and out the front door of the bookstore.

"For now, yes. I am not even letting myself think about how strange it was that Rory wanted to keep it on the QT that Connie worked for her. I'm sure the entertainment shows would have run something showing her mourning for her former companion. Couple that with the weird thing that happened to Connie, and those shows would really have eaten it up. Knowing that Rory is always looking for media coverage, it seems like it would have provided the perfect chance to grab the spotlight and promote the crochet show."

"You sound pretty worked up for someone who isn't investigating," Dinah said.

"Maybe I don't want to know if Rory is involved

anyway. Mrs. Shedd would have a heart attack if the host of the show got arrested and everything got put on hold."

"Good point," Dinah said.

* * *

The day of the taping, I understood how Dinah felt about Cassandra taking over her house and making her feel like an outsider. The yarn department was no longer my domain. The crew had come in before the bookstore was open and rearranged the table and chairs. Lights with screens to reflect them had been added. Rory's chair had her name on it, and it had been placed in CeeCee's usual spot and our leader had been moved to the other end.

The empty cubby was now full of the sponsor's yarn with a big banner draped across it. One of Rhoda's Cakes for a Break had been placed in the center of the table. A woman I'd never seen before was doing weird stuff to the cake. She'd sprayed something on it and brushed something on the edges so they glistened. A sign had been placed next to it that said Do Not Eat.

The Make-and-Take kits were all in a basket next to Rory's seat. Extra chairs had been added around hers. The only one getting makeup and wardrobe was Rory, and a dressing area had been fashioned out of bookcases in the same way we'd made the backstage area for Missy Z.

The director had picked out some Make-and Takers and had them waiting in the music and video department. The plan was that they would film straight through for an hour and then edit it down and add some inserts and come up with a half-hour show.

I met Rory at the front door and escorted her to the dressing area. I expected her to act like one of the Hookers, but she had totally morphed into being the star of the show. She looked askance at the area as she went to get in the chair.

"You call this a green room?" she said disdainfully.

Rory seemed nervous as she sat in the chair and the makeup woman began to work on her hair and face. I was going to excuse myself, but Rory grabbed my arm and begged me to stay. I didn't think for a minute that it had anything to do with me personally. She just wanted a body there, and I got a hint of what it must be like to be a companion.

Rory began talking to the makeup woman. I was only half listening, but she seemed to know her and rambled on about how you kept meeting the same people. I saw her looking toward the opening in the improvised backstage area as she spoke. She seemed to be looking at someone. But who? It seemed like everyone in the world was going by. Marianne was there with Janine. Errol and his wife were there as well. CeeCee passed by, talking to the producer and the director. The set director went past carrying a basket of yarn.

"We're done," Rory announced a few minutes later, snapping her fingers in front of my face to get my attention. I uttered a surprised *huh,* since my mind had been elsewhere. She pushed past me and went out into the bookstore. I blindly followed her and then stopped at the opening, still deep in thought. All these pieces were floating around in my mind. Something Rory had said and something I'd heard from someone else clicked together as if drawn by magnets.

I pulled out my smartphone and typed something in. As I read over the information that came up, I chided myself for not thinking of it before. I did a quick search and clicked on a link. I felt a shiver as I read an article, and it got worse as I studied the photo that accompanied it. A white phone charging cord decorated with a painted red flower was attached to what seemed to be an extension cord coiled like a snake. The design of the red flower looked like a crocheted one, and it triggered a memory.

"Wow, nobody would have figured it out," I said out loud. I had to tell Barry. I clicked on his number but was disappointed when I got his voicemail. I simply said, "I know who did it," and clicked off.

"Pink, what are you doing back there?" Adele said. Her voice snapped me back to reality, and I shoved my phone in my pocket and went out to join the fray. I was going to check on the yarn department, which was now being referred to as the set, when Mrs. Shedd stopped me.

"Good, you're here," she said, and pushed a box on me. "This needs to go to the back room."

She seemed all aflutter, so I quickly agreed and went back toward the front of the store. The back room was located near Mrs. Shedd and Mr. Royal's office at the back of an alcove that had greeting cards and writing supplies. It got a lot quieter as I got away from all the activity.

I opened the door and was reaching to turn on the light when suddenly I felt an arm come from behind me and grab me as the box fell out of my grasp. I was pulled into the darkness and then the door slammed shut.

"Just a hint for the future: you should really keep your voice down when you're talking to yourself," a man's voice said. I thought this was some kind of joke and tried to pull free, but his grasp held tight, and I felt something sharp against my back.

He mumbled something about having to improvise and turned on the light. I tried to turn my head to see my captor, but I already knew who it was. He pushed me onto the straight-backed chair and kicked around the boxes on the floor. He released his grasp on me, but the sharp point that I was sure was a knife stayed against my back.

I felt him lean down and grab something, and then he pushed the end of a skein of yarn in my hand and demanded I hold it. When I hesitated, the sharp point pushed through my shirt, and I knew my skin was next, so I grabbed the end of it. He began to wind the yarn over my upper arms and around the chair. When he got to my elbows, he dropped the knife and used both hands to finish wrapping me to the chair and tied it off.

I made the mistake of moving my legs, and he grabbed more yarn and bound each of my legs to one of the chair's. Finally he stood and came around in front of me.

All the charm in Michael Kostner's face was gone. "Now we can talk," he said in a grim tone. "What is it that you figured out?"

"Nothing really," I said. I would have put my hands up in capitulation if I could have moved them.

"I heard you and your friends talking about your independent investigating the other day. And then a few minutes ago, you did that Eureka thing before you called somebody and left a message and said you knew who did it." He stroked the fashionable stubble on his chin and gave me a menacing stare. He held up the knife. "How about you tell me about it." When I hesitated, he waved the knife in front of my face. "Talk," he commanded.

"Okay," I said, trying to swallow back my nerves. "It didn't occur to me until I heard Rory talking about meeting the same people again, and it came back to me that you had said something about working with her before. When I checked the crew from *The Grass Is Always Greener*, I saw you were listed as an assistant producer. That's where you got the idea, didn't you? All you had to do was dress like the gardeners and blend in with them to set things up. I thought that Marianne might have been the intended victim, but then I remembered something Connie said the first time you came to the bookstore." In my mind's eye, I was seeing Connie looking at the red crocheted flower and the square with the torn strand of yarn. "I misunderstood what she said at the time and didn't realize it had anything to do with you when she said, 'Now I get it.'" I glanced at his face, surprised at how hard his eyes looked.

"Mason said you were a client of his. He said you didn't do anything—but you did, didn't you?"

"It was over and done with. Case closed," he said in an angry voice. "I couldn't take a chance that Connie would tell her story to someone."

I was pretty sure I knew what he was referring to. The article I'd found was about the accidental death of Michael's wife. She'd been electrocuted when her cell phone fell into the bathtub. The phone had been plugged in, and the charging cord had appeared frayed. The accompanying photo had shown the charger with a red flower painted on the plug. The case was closed because it could have been suicide or an accident, and that had been the end of it.

"Connie worked for you, or should I say your wife." There had been a side note to the article about his wife's death that had mentioned she was a recovering opioid addict. "She was a sober companion, wasn't she?"

Rory had said that Connie had worked as a sober companion before working for her. She'd also mentioned that something bad had happened with a cell phone and that she seemed to be upset about it.

He nodded grimly. "I wanted a divorce, and she was going to clean me out. And she had a nice insurance policy." He mumbled something to himself about the problem not being original, but the solution was. "My wife was addicted to her cell phone. She practically had a panic attack if it wasn't with her and charged all the time. She was crazy about her charger too. She had to have a name-brand one and was upset with me because I used knock-off cords, which she insisted were inferior. She'd painted a flower in red nail polish on her plug so there would never be any confusion between hers and mine.

"She had to have the phone on the ledge next to her when she soaked in the tub. She plugged her charger into an extension cord that was plugged in outside the bathroom." I saw his eyes go skyward. "She insisted that made it safe." He stopped for a moment to collect himself.

"It was almost too easy. I took one of my no-name cords and painted a flower on it. She was right about the cords being inferior. It was easy to make nicks in the plastic with a razor so that when she used the cord, it would fray. It was no problem switching cords when she was sleeping. Then I waited until she was soaking in the tub. I walked in on her and, as I was talking to her, gave the phone a shove, and it fell in the water. I left without looking back. It was Connie's day off, and she's the one who found my wife when she returned." He was quiet for a moment, and I thought he might be having some regrets. But then he started grumbling about Connie again and how much she'd liked his wife and how upset she had been when she died.

"Here's the problem," he said. "She walked into my office as I was working on the charger cord. She didn't know what she was seeing, and I thought that she'd forgotten all about it, but the way she acted that night at the bookstore made me a little nervous.

"I called her cell phone later and apologized for not recognizing her. I said I hadn't realized who she was until after I'd left the bookstore. It didn't take long before she blurted out that she'd always felt there was something off about the charger cord that had been found with my wife but could never put her finger on it, but somehow seeing me, the yarn flower, and some other yarn had triggered something, and suddenly she'd remembered seeing a cord with a flower in my office. She said she knew then that I'd switched them. The cops still have the phone cord, and all she'd have had to do is tell them that my wife's cord was the name brand and they could see that the one they have isn't. I'm sure they'd reopen the case with me as a suspect.

"If nothing else, my position with the Craftee Channel would be screwed. Our viewers are mostly women. Do you know how it would look if one of their executives was in the middle of an investigation of the death of his wife?"

He went back to talking about Connie and seemed to want to talk about how he had set it up, as if he was proud of his cleverness. "I was already worried about Connie before I talked to her, so I went to the house. I left my car on the street and then walked onto the property. In the dark, they didn't see me, but I saw Connie walk across the lawn to the guesthouse. Then I got the idea to adapt what we'd done in *The Grass Is Always Greener*. I live in the area, and I know that gardeners come the day before trash pickup. I waited until the real ones were ready to leave, and then I set up the radio with a frayed extension cord and reset the sprinklers so they would leave a big puddle. I also knew that Connie always took Tuesdays off and her habit was to come back in the evening. Since it was still technically her time off, I knew she would go directly to the guesthouse and to get there would have to cross the waterlogged lawn, which would be electrified."

He looked at his watch and suddenly seemed impatient. "I'm afraid I have no playbook this time, and it's not my style to do anything too direct or with blood." I knew I was in trouble when he began to rummage around the storage room. I considered yelling, but considering where we were and with all the noise going on in the rest of the store, I knew no one would hear me.

I tried to keep an eye on what he was doing. He grabbed the big-bulbed Christmas lights and plugged them in, but they didn't come on. Then he flipped the switch above the plug, and suddenly the colorful bulbs lit up.

"I'll just have to adapt what I already know," he said under his breath as he flipped the switch to off. I watched as he used the knife to cut at the cord on the lights, and then he wound them around my shoulders. "It'll be sizzle, sizzle, flash and you're frizzled," he said gaily. This time he did look at me, and I felt my stomach clench in panic.

He pulled a water bottle out of his pocket and doused me with it. Meanwhile, I'd been looking around for something to help me escape. I looked at the boxes of yarn on the floor and the pastel Easter Bunny leaning against the wall. The water was soaking into the yarn and made it smell slightly gamy.

He'd unplugged the holiday lights before he strung them on me, but now he got ready to plug them back in, making sure the switch was turned off first.

"*Au revoir, mon chéri.*" He bent to plug in the lights, not realizing the cord was too short and they had pulled partly off of me and part of the cord was on his feet. His momentary distraction gave me time to make my move. When he got over the shock of seeing where the lights had landed, he looked up and gasped to see me standing in front of him as the rest of the colorful lights with the frayed cord fell on him. "I hope you don't have sweaty feet," I said, eyeing the light switch.

Just then the door flew open and Barry came in.

Chapter Twenty-Nine

I couldn't ruin things for Mrs. Shedd by disrupting the shoot, so I kept things quiet and got Barry not to flood the place with cops. Instead, Barry, Michael, and I had a cozy little conversation in the back room. Most of the talking was done by Barry and me. All Michael said was that he wasn't saying anything without his lawyer.

Actually, Michael did speak a little, just enough to ask how I'd escaped my bonds. "It's rather ironic," I said. "The yarn that made Connie think of that extension cord was defective. It frayed when you pulled at it. The water you dumped on me made it even weaker, and all I had to do was push out with my arms and legs and it came apart. That's it over there," I said, pointing to a box of yarn that said RETURN on the side. I pointed out the box of yarn next to it. "Now, if you'd chosen that yarn, it would have been another story." *And a disaster for me.* Those boxes contained the yarn I'd taken out of the cubby, and those strands were like iron.

Barry did his best to keep his cop face, but he still rolled his eyes. "As soon as I heard your message, I figured you would probably get yourself in trouble."

"Hey, maybe I did, but I got myself out of it too," I said, and we both looked at the state my clothes were in. Not only had the yarn broken and left pieces stuck all over me, but the dye had come off when it got wet. My khaki pants were smeared with blotches of purples and reds.

Michael might not have wanted to talk, but there was nothing to stop me from sharing what he'd told me. Barry wrote it down without a word.

Finally, I helped Barry take Michael out the emergency exit. I waited to see if Barry would say anything or even look back, but he was in full cop mode and Detective Heather was standing by the curb.

I didn't have time to think about it. I had to get back to work. Nobody batted an eye when I showed up in the hodgepodge of clothes I'd gotten from the lost-and-found box coupled with a pair of faded jeans I'd left there.

Everyone was in place and they were about to start shooting. With so many people milling around, no one seemed to notice that Michael was missing, though I'd already called the station and told them that he had been called away.

I didn't join the Hookers at the table. It was partly because of the outfit. Did I really want to be seen on TV wearing a T-shirt with a picture of a dachshund wearing a blonde wig? How had somebody left that at the bookstore, anyway? The other reason was that I seemed to be more of an arranger than a participant. I joined Mrs. Shedd and Mr. Royal to watch.

Rory did fine and came through in the crochet department. She helped the Make-and-Takers, threw in two Dance Breaks, and got in her pitch for left-handers.

The only time she seemed nervous was when she had to try Rhoda's Cake for a Break and do a pitch for the flour.

Afterward, she explained, and I understood why she hadn't wanted anyone to see the old reality show. It also explained why she hadn't tried to get publicity by connecting herself with Connie's death. Rory had gone gluten free, and it had been Connie's job to keep her from having even a taste of anything made with wheat flour. On the show, Rory had denounced gluten as practically being the devil's food, though she had since dropped the whole thing. She had been worried the current sponsor would find out about her past stance and that would get her fired.

Rory also confided that Connie had known she had split from her husband while they were appearing as a supposedly happy couple on the reality show. So that was the secret information she'd been worried about getting out.

Mason was the one to give me the news that Michael was being charged with first-degree murder for Connie's death and attempted murder for trying to do me in with the Christmas lights. As it turned out, it probably wouldn't have worked, but it was Michael's intention that counted. And his wife's case was being reopened. Michael had called Mason's firm looking for a lawyer as soon as he'd gotten his one call at the police station, but no one would take his case.

The Craftee Channel dropped him immediately, just as he had feared.

The Craftee Channel felt completely differently about the bookstore, however. They were impressed with what troopers we were, considering the circumstances, and decided to make Shedd & Royal the permanent set for the series.

Mrs. Shedd and Mr. Royal were overjoyed. Not only would they be paid for the use of the bookstore as a location, but Shedd & Royal would be a star for sure.

Adele didn't become the sidekick as she'd hoped. The new producer looked at all of the Hookers as being in that position. They did give her a credit as Crochet Consultant. She had a good time rubbing it in her mother-in-law's face.

Rhoda's cake was a big hit, and she was invited to be on one of the channel's cooking shows.

Elise made up kits for the bracelets, and they were sold on the channel's website and in the bookstore. She succeeded in getting the set designer to place one of her Color Square blankets on the back of Rory's chair, and then she added "featured on *Creating With Crochet*" to the ones she was selling at the open houses.

I found something in the pages Mason had given me about our planned trip that changed Marianne's life. When we had our do-over gathering, I showed the piece to her that mentioned that there were known to be ticks in Point Reyes Station that carried Lyme disease. I reminded her how much worse she'd been when she had come back from her trip.

She got tested and came in the bookstore several days after she got the results. Errol was with her, and she gave me a big hug.

"I never thought I would be hopeful after testing positive for a disease. I do have Lyme disease, but it's treatable with antibiotics. They're already weaning me off all the mental meds. Since I'm doing it gradually, there's no crazy seesaw of emotions."

I could see the difference in her already. There was a sparkle in her eyes and her face looked more animated. "The best news is no more companions. And Errol can stay home with Kelly and the kids instead of having to take care of me. And I'll be able to tell a joke again. I feel like I got my life back, and I owe it to you." She hugged me again and said that Errol had shown her a proposal for developing the property and she was thinking about it. Then she nudged her brother. "Errol has something to say."

He seemed uncomfortable, but after a couple more nudges, he finally spoke. "I'm sorry for what I did—the phone call and the other stuff. I was trying to protect my sister. That's all I was ever trying to do—to take care of her. It's lucky she's better, because I wasn't very good at it. I wish now that I had thought to help her get a second opinion when she fell apart."

Marianne gave him another nudge and told him to tell me the rest of it. He had a sheepish expression as he looked at me. "I'm sorry about calling the cops. When I saw you with the knife standing over Janine, I thought my sister had gotten you to help her get rid of another companion." Marianne nudged him again and said she still couldn't believe he'd thought she'd killed Connie.

"It all worked out in the end," I said, but inside I was thinking that Errol wasn't the jerk I'd thought. More like a doofus.

* * *

Dinah and I celebrated the success of the shoot and the solution to Connie's murder with a girls' night at my place. Things were a little better at her house. Cassandra's visit was almost over, but Dinah had overheard her on the phone telling someone she was thinking of moving back to town.

My son Samuel finally came home with his new girlfriend in tow. She was a musician as well, and they were planning to do some gigs together. Though, I was a little concerned when she brought a dog with her and then left without remembering to take it with her.

* * *

The night after the taping, Mason called and asked if I'd come over. "Sunshine, there's something we need to talk about."

The words and his serious tone made my stomach do flip-flops as I drove over. He had the front door open before I'd even gotten all the way up the walk.

Spike seemed to be aware of his master's mood, and the toy fox terrier barely yipped when I came in the door.

Mason gave me a welcome embrace and took me back to the den. I kept waiting for him to talk about whatever was on his mind, but instead he insisted on making us cappuccinos, maybe as a stalling tactic.

He put the frothy drinks on the coffee table, but he didn't join me on the couch.

"What is it?" I said. "The suspense is killing me." For the first time, he noticed the worried look on my face.

"I'm sorry. It's nothing terrible." He reached down and gave my arm a reassuring squeeze. "I've been thinking about this for a while, but the thing with Michael was the final straw. I didn't think he was responsible for his wife's death, but even if I had, my job would have been to do whatever I could to get him off. And then the thing with Connie Richards and almost you."

He looked down at the ground. "Is that who I want to be?" He answered with a sad shake of his head. "The answer is no. It's time to make some changes. I'm not giving everything up at once, but I want to devote some time to pro bono work, maybe working with the Innocence Project." He gave it a moment to sink in before he continued. "It'll mean changes in my life." He was looking at me directly now. "How do you feel about that?"

"I completely agree," I said. "The whole thing with Michael was so upsetting. What a relief that you see it too."

Mason suddenly looked as if a weight had been lifted off of him, and he sat down next to me and cuddled close. "It doesn't mean we won't still have fun or take that trip to Point Reyes Station."

"We're bringing insect repellent," I said with a smile and leaned in closer.

* * *

By Monday, the bookstore was back to normal, at least until the next taping. When five o'clock rolled around, the Hookers gathered for happy hour. It was just the core group for a change. There were no Make-and-Take projects to worry about or hovering over Rory to see if she could crochet. We had all pulled out our own projects and were happily crocheting and talking about our lives the way old friends do. I thought how lucky I was to have them.

* * *

When I got home from the bookstore that night, it was raining. A definite oddity for April in Southern California, where the rainy season seemed to end in February. The flagstone patio was just getting wet and had a dusty smell of rain as I walked across it. I could see the greeting committee waiting by the door. With the upcoming tapings, there was always lots to do, and I seemed to come home later every night.

Cosmo and Felix ran outside, not caring if they got wet. I managed to keep Mr. Kitty and Cat inside. I was glad to find a note from Samuel that he'd been home and taken care of all their needs. Though I did still get Blondie out of her chair and bring her across the house. She joined the other two outside.

I was looking forward to having dinner, watching a

romantic comedy, and forgetting about everything. When the dogs were back inside, paws wiped, and treats given, I put the movie on and heated up some leftover soup.

I was surprised when the phone rang and more surprised at who it was.

"It's Barry," he said. "Can I come in?"

I hadn't seen him since the whole thing with Michael. Any dog care had been taken care of when I wasn't home. He hadn't given a reason for his visit, but I said okay and went to the front door. I was surprised to see him come running up the stone walkway, but then it *was* raining.

Droplets glistened in his short dark hair and on his suit with no wrinkles, but this time his tie was pulled loose.

I stepped aside and he came in.

We stopped in the entrance hall, and I waited to see the purpose of his visit. He didn't say anything for a minute, and I finally looked at him and said, "Well . . . ," and gestured with my hand, hoping to get the ball rolling.

"You're probably wondering why I'm here," he said, and I nodded enthusiastically. "I know I said you were off the case, but I have to admit, you bring things to the table that I don't."

"Yeah, like maybe nabbing the killer," I said.

"And you almost got yourself fried in the process," he said. I saw his shoulders drop, and he started looking frustrated. "But there would have to be parameters. No more keeping stuff from me, and absolutely no investigating on your own."

"Really?" I said. "You actually do want my help?"

"I wouldn't call it help as much as giving me your take on things."

"You'd have to tell me stuff, too. None of this one-way street business."

"You're going to be difficult, aren't you?" he said.

"What do you think?"

"And here we go," he said with a smile.

"C'mon, you wouldn't want it any other way."

"Is that what you think?" He shook his head in disbelief. Then he seemed to give in and blew out his breath. "I guess we'll have to work it out as we go along," he said. "When I get a case I think you can help on, I'll be in touch." He turned to leave.

"I was just going to have some soup," I said. "Want to stay?" As if there were a chance he'd say no.

CeeCee's Gratitude Circle

Easy to make

Supplies:

15 ft. 20-pound cord
2 9mm beads
Small piece of thin wire to thread the beads
Size D/3 (3.25mm) hook
Stitches used: chain (ch), slip stitch (sl st)
Directions:
Leaving a 6-inch tail, ch until approx. 35 inches long. Turn work, sl st into second ch from hook, sl st across. Join with sl st to make a circle. Fasten off, leaving 6-inch tail.

Tie the two tails together in a double knot. Slide one bead on each tail; knot several times, making sure knot is big enough to hold bead on. Trim tail near knots.

To wear, wind around wrist several times.

Elise's Color Square

Easy to make
Size: approx. 47 × 47 inches

Supplies:

4 skeins Lion Brand Homespun in 4 complementary colors
1 skein Red Heart Super Saver, black
Size K/10½ (6.50mm) hook
Large-eyed needle
Stitches used: chain (ch), double crochet (dc), slip stitch (sl st), half double crochet (hdc)
With color A of Homespun, ch 3 and join to form a ring with sl st.
Round 1: Ch 3, work 2 dc in ring, (ch 2, work 3 dc in ring) 3 times, ch 2, sl st to top of first ch 3.
Round 2: Sl st over dcs to ch 2 corner space, ch 3 (counts as first dc), work (2 dc, ch 2, 3 dc) in same corner ch 2 space, {ch 1, work (3 dc, ch 2, 3 dc) in next ch 2 corner space} 3 times, ch 1, sl st to top of first ch 3.
Round 3: Sl st over dcs to ch 2 corner space, ch 3 (counts as first dc), work (2 dc, ch 2, 3 dc) in same corner ch 2 space, {ch 1, *work 3 dc in next ch 1 space, ch 1*, work (3 dc, ch2, 3dc) in next ch 2 corner space} 3 times, ch 1, work 3 dc in next ch 1 space, ch 1, sl st to top of first ch 3.

Round 4: Repeat round 3, repeating * to * as many times as necessary to get to corners.

Repeat round 4 two times, and on the last round at the sl st, attach the black yarn (6 rounds of color A).

Repeat round 4 with black yarn, and at sl st change to color B of Homespun.

Repeat round 4 for 6 rounds. On sl st of last round, change to black yarn (6 rounds of color B).

Repeat round 4 with black yarn, and at sl st change to color C of Homespun.

Repeat round 4 for 5 rounds. On sl st of last round, change to black yarn (5 rounds of color C).

Repeat round 4 with black yarn, and at sl st change to color A of Homespun.

Repeat round 4 for 3 rounds. On sl st of last round, change to black yarn (3 rounds of color A).

Repeat round 4 with black yarn, and at sl st change to color D of Homespun.

Repeat round 4 for 4 rounds. At last round, sl st and ch 1. Sc evenly around, making 3 sc in each corner, and at sl st to first sc, change to black yarn.

Edging:

Round 1: Sc around, making 3 sc in each corner. Attach to last sc with sl st.

Round 2: Ch 2. Hdc around, making 3 hdc in each corner. Attach to last hdc with sl st.

Round 3: Ch 1. Sc around, making 3 sc in each corner. Attach to last sc with sl st. Fasten off.

Weave in all ends.

Molly's Chinese Jelly

2 cups milk
½ cup half-and-half
3 tablespoons sugar
1 envelope unflavored gelatin
1 teaspoon almond extract

Sprinkle gelatin on half-and-half to soften and let sit while heating milk and sugar to almost boiling. Add hot milk and sugar mixture to half-and-half and softened gelatin. Stir until gelatin is completely dissolved. Add almond extract and stir. Pour into bowl and chill until set. Approx. 5 servings.

Rhoda's Cake for a Break

Cake:

2 cups unbleached flour
½ teaspoon salt
2 teaspoons baking powder
¾ cup sugar
½ cup butter, cut into cubes
1 egg
1 cup milk
1 teaspoon vanilla

Topping:

4 tablespoons unbleached flour
10 tablespoons brown sugar
1 teaspoon cinnamon
4 tablespoons butter, cut into cubes

For cake: Sift flour, salt, baking powder, and sugar. Cut in butter with a pastry blender. Break the egg in a measuring cup and beat. Add milk to egg to make 1 cup. Beat egg and add to dry ingredients with the vanilla. Mix to form a soft dough. Pour into a greased 9 × 13–inch pan.

For topping: Combine the flour, brown sugar, and

cinnamon. Cut in the butter with a pastry blender until the mixture is crumbly.

Sprinkle topping on and bake at 350 degrees for approx. 25 minutes.